THE VALLEY OF DRY BONES

THE VALLEY OF DRY BONES

Arthur Henry Gooden

GUNSMOKE

First published in the UK by Harrap

This hardback edition 2010
by BBC Audiobooks Ltd
by arrangement with
Golden West Literary Agency

ISBN 978 1 408 46302 4

British Library Cataloguing in Publication Data available.

Printed and bound in Great Britain by
CPI Antony Rowe, Chippenham and Eastbourne

To

my good friend

The Reverend John Atwill, **D.D.**

who unknowingly gave me

the idea for this book

CONTENTS

Chapter

1

A VOICE IN THE DESERT

HE MOVED through the endless monotony of parched rabbit bush and greasewood with the slow, dogged perseverance of a resolute man who draws grimly upon the last remnants of strength and courage. Now and again he paused and carefully scrutinized the sunbaked scene. He made these frequent examinations unhurriedly, and there was no hint of panic in him as his calculating gaze deliberately absorbed his surroundings. He had the look of a man who coolly strove to recall once familiar scenes, which indeed was the purpose in Ross Chaine's mind. Not that fifteen years could much alter the harsh face of this country, but he knew that landmarks, man-made, had a way of disappearing.

His enfolding look drew in closer and came to rest upon a big greasewood that fierce desert winds had partially uprooted and tilted against a neighboring bush. Their entwined branches formed a thickly matted arch that now made a dense screen against the high noonday sun.

Ross hesitated, enticed by the promise there, then pushed slowly toward the friendly shade.

He sprawled full length on his back, grateful for a brief respite from the fierce assault of the sun, and for perhaps the space of five minutes lay without movement.

He wanted to think this thing out calmly. *Water*. He must have water — and very soon.

From where he lay, face upturned, he could see tiny black specks floating against the backdrop of the hot sky. He knew the meaning of those specks. Buzzards — gathering to feast on his dead horse. Somewhere near the horse would be a man — a dead man.

A wry grimace distorted his swollen lips. No time now to speculate about the stranger who had waited back there in the chaparral for a shot at him. Another and vastly more interesting problem was awaiting the use of his wits.

He lifted painfully to an upright position and sat there, cool calculation again in his bloodshot eyes. Somewhere within a circle of five miles should be the old stage station of Skeleton Wells, and the Wells meant water — meant his life.

He picked up the faint glimmer of Guadalupe's snow-capped peak and with careful deliberation drew a line across the sweltering landscape to the sharply defined saw-toothed ridge of the nearer, low-lying Chuckwalla Range. He drew another line from the slender spire of Chuckwalla Peak, and that line hit the lone upthrust of red rock that he knew was Skeleton Butte.

Ross got slowly to his feet. His eyes had taken on the dogged look of a man who keeps on, no matter the odds. He had no intention of dying if anything could be done about it. Another hour would bring him to water.

The thought revived hope within him, fed fresh strength into lagging muscles. He pressed on, was suddenly aware of low-growing trees that took shape as he drew closer to the red butte. *Skeleton Wells*. But the cluster of buildings that once marked the old stage station no longer met the eye. Only that clump of cottonwood trees. Something had happened . . . raiding

Apaches ... it didn't really matter ... the wells would still be there — *the water*.

Those green trees with their promise of cool water pulled him into a shambling run. Almost instantly he fell back to his slow, patient stride. No time now to be mastered by hysterical impulse ... Another twenty minutes ... he could hold out that long.

A split-rail fence showed in the high, overgrown brush. It had been sturdily built by competent hands and only a few of the rails were down. The signs told of long years of disuse.

Ross crawled through a break and stood for a moment, anxious eyes searching beyond the cottonwoods. He caught sight of a trough, its wooden sides caved in. The watering trough, more than twenty feet long, in the old days always brimming with water. The big wooden tank was gone, and the windmill that had lifted the water from the well. Ross guessed that the high brush concealed their charred wreckage.

He made no further effort to hold feverish impatience in check, went plunging through the harsh undergrowth. It was plain that the big well was out of commission, but he was recalling a smaller dug well worked with windlass and bucket. A picture of that well came to him as he stumbled across what was once the stage-station corral. It had stood close to the kitchen door.

Ross remembered how the cook would come out and drop the wooden bucket down with a splash into the timber-walled depths and draw it up again brimming with sweet, cool water. A long-handled tin dipper used to hang on a nail and thirsty passengers off the stage would gather around and help themselves.

He tore past the ruins of the windmill and came to a halt close to the charred remains of the stage station. The high platform that had once stood over the dug well had fallen in.

Ross pushed through the thick brush and peered down the square shaft. The faint glimmer that met his look told him that water was there if he could get at it. He drew back, stared about desperately.

After a moment's thought he began a methodical search, casting about like a hound nosing for a rabbit. He wanted a rope, or pieces of rope that could be spliced into a strand long enough to lower a can to the water that glimmered so maddeningly beyond his reach. Wire would serve the purpose, and there were plenty of cans. He espied a whole mound of them all but concealed in a rank growth of greasewood. They would be rusty, but anything that could hold water was all he asked.

Panic began to grip him as he doubled back and forth across the yard and corrals. If any shreds of rope or wire remained, they were too well covered by the dense brush that had taken possession of Skeleton Wells.

He came to a halt by the wrecked platform of the well, his cracked lips twisted in a grimace of rage. He had found water, and it might just as well have been a thousand miles away.

He shifted his gaze from that beckoning gleam in the well and was suddenly intent on a dust haze that drifted slowly nearer. Horsemen — several of them, to make all that dust.

Ross swung a look at the road where it angled past the upthrust of red rock that was Skeleton Butte. The old stage route to Guadalupe. Those approaching riders were following it and fifteen minutes or less would bring them to Skeleton Wells.

He was under no illusions about them. He had an uneasy suspicion they were looking for him, and if they found him he would have no further worries about water. Not that they would refresh him from their canteens.

It was not water they would give him, but hot lead from their guns, or perhaps a rope to dangle him from one of the cottonwood trees.

He flung a despairing glance at the well and went as fast as weary legs could carry him toward a greasewood-covered ridge that was one of a wave of ridges that rose higher and higher to savagely bleak hills. It was imperative for him to be out of sight before the strangers rounded the butte.

Despite the peril of the moment he managed to keep his head. His body was wracked with physical exhaustion and he was tormented with an unbearable thirst for water, but his mind was clear — functioned with the precision of a well-oiled machine. It was not the first time death had stalked him.

Another backward glance told him that the drifting dust had reached the big butte. He broke into a run and dove headlong behind a clump of greasewood.

He lay there, gasping for breath. The last fifty feet had been almost straight up and the effort had taken it out of him. He was dismayed to find that he was trembling violently and again his lips twisted in that grimace that was a distortion of a smile. For all the harsh mask of his face at that moment, one could sense a frank, open countenance and steady eyes and there was humor and gaiety in the firm mouth now set so grimly.

The clop of horses' hoofs drew up the abandoned old stage road. Ross squirmed round and lying on his stomach peered cautiously through an opening in the greasewood. Five horsemen had pulled up close to the brush-covered ruins of the stage station. The voice of one of them reached up to him.

'No sign of the feller here.'

'He'll be looking for water,' said another voice. 'His canteen was back there with his bronc . . . bullet hole through it. He'll be crazy for water and like as not would head for the Wells.'

'He was only a kid when we shipped him out on the stage that time,' argued the first speaker, a dark squat man on a bald-faced horse. 'He wouldn't be rememberin' the Wells.'

The other man shook his head impatiently. He was long and lanky and his nose was too big for the narrow, thin-lipped face shadowed by a high-peaked black sombrero. He spoke slowly, in a flat, toneless voice.

'Ross Chaine was a smart kid,' he said. 'He won't be forgetting nothing.' His hard eyes roved restlessly. 'Don't you forget what I'm tellin' you, Tony. The kid was always smart, and he's growed up to be a man now. I've heard talk of him . . . he's slick as the devil and lightning-fast with a gun. You saw what he did to Monte back up the road.'

'You should have sent me to do the job,' grumbled Tony. 'Monte always took things too easy-like. He sure bungled.'

The lanky rider gave him a hard grin. 'Looks like you'll have a chance your own self,' he said. He pushed back his sombrero. 'Hot as hell. Let's get out of here.'

Ross watched until the lazy banner of their dust dissolved into a distant haze. These were wary, desert-wise men. He dared take no chances lest they spot him in the chaparral. Anything that stirred would bring them swooping like hawks to the scene.

Finally he got to his feet, stood pondering his next move. The movement made him dizzy. Sky and earth seemed to revolve around him. He wanted to lie down again — wait for the end. He fought off the impulse. He was not going to be beaten. . . . He was a Chaine and a Chaine never quit. You had to kill a Chaine to make him quit . . . like they had killed his father.

Something caught his near-frantic eyes, a round stumpy object on the slope above him. The sight of it cleared his head, rolled back the years. He was a small boy watching with round-eyed interest while old Injun John slashed out the insides of a barrel cactus with a big bowie knife. The Apache had made him taste the watery pulp.

Ross was already scrambling up the slope to the lone cactus. He opened the large blade of his clasp knife and furiously attacked the hard spiny exterior.

It took him some ten minutes to get at the moist pulpy contents. He filled his hat with the stuff, mashed the pulp with his fingers and sucked up the water that oozed out. When he had drained the last drop he sat back on his heels and chewed pieces of the wet pulp. Water at last, such as it was. He was conscious of fresh vigor flowing through him.

Presently he hacked more of the pulp from the barrel-like trunk of the cactus, which was a big one, almost five feet in height.

As he sat there, sucking up the last vestige of water from the mash in his hat, his thoughts were busy with the five riders. But for their unwelcome appearance he might not have stumbled across the life-saving barrel cactus.

Ross repressed an amused grin. His lips were stiff and cracked. It was painful to smile, and he was a long way from being out of the woods. To know that he was so closely hounded was cause for sober thought.

Fifteen years had made little change in the tall lean man under the black sombrero. Ross had instantly recognized Harve Welder. It was obvious that the beak-nosed man was still bossing the Flying A outfit.

Ross Chaine's likeable face took on the grim hard mask of a man who was recalling unpleasant things about the foreman of Flying A. The other men were strangers to him. He only knew that the dark squat rider of the bald-faced horse bore the name of Tony, and that Tony had wished he had been sent to the ambush instead of the man whom they had found dead up the road. Ross felt he was going to remember Tony.

His mind went back to the scene of the ambush. The first bullet had missed him, taken his horse squarely in the head. As the animal collapsed under him a second bullet tore through his water canteen. Ross found himself sprawling behind a greasewood. He lay motionless, waiting for the assassin's next move, his own forty-five now in hand.

Evidently the ambusher believed his second shot had found its mark. Brush crackled from the opposite side of the road and suddenly Ross glimpsed his man. He fired, heard a startled grunt, and then more cracklings of brush as the man fled for his horse. Ross was instantly on his feet and in chase. He was not caring much about the would-be killer, but he desperately wanted the horse he was making for at top speed.

By the time he was across the road the man was in his saddle. The horse, startled by the excitement, swerved in a half circle that brought its rider within range of the long-barrelled Colt. Ross fired again, saw the ambusher topple headlong from his saddle. The horse continued its panic-stricken flight, was soon lost to view.

Sitting there by the hacked-up cactus Ross thought gloomily of his failure to kill the man before he got to the horse. He would have been saved a lot of grief. The result had been to leave him afoot and waterless. Also the horse must have headed straight back to the ranch and so carried the news to Harve Welder of the fate that had overtaken the man he had sent to do murder. As Tony had declared, Monte was too easy. Also a craven. The odds had been all in his favor, but he'd been too yellow to shoot it out.

One thing brightened the prospect. He had managed to solve the immediate problem of quenching his intolerable thirst. He had the strength now to keep on going. Another ten miles should put him close to Alamos, and with the afternoon drawing on the going would not be so unbearably hot. He recalled that it was the time of year that often brought a cooling afternoon breeze from the mountains.

Considerably cheered by the thought, Ross got to his feet, and after a prolonged and careful scrutiny of his surroundings, set off down the slope.

He crossed the dismal ruins of Skeleton Wells and headed west into the chaparral. As he had hoped, he began to feel the cooling breath of the wind. His stride lengthened and quickened.

Some two miles brought him to the rugged foothills of the Chuckwalla Range. Stunted piñons took the place of the greasewood as he began the climb.

A pair of hoary, gnarled piñons standing close together made an umbrella of shade. Ross sat down on a flat slab of rock and wiped his hot face. Thirst pangs were again assailing him. The foothills were as dry as a bone and he had passed beyond the cactus region.

He set about refreshing his memory of locations. He had a vague recollection of a narrow pass that cut through the Chuckwallas into Red Creek Valley. He tingled a bit as he repeated the name aloud. *Red Creek Valley*. The old ranch house where he was born was in that long valley where once ranged cattle marked with his father's Bar Chain iron.

His face set in grim lines. He was back to put the Bar Chain on the map again. He had always known that some day he would return to Red Creek Valley and bring to justice the men who had murdered his father.

He became aware of an odd sound that touched his ears faintly above the rustle of the wind in the piñons. The muted tinkle of a bell.

Ross jerked at his gun and sprang to his feet, stared about with puzzled, wary eyes. He was not sure from which direction the sound of the bell came. He stood there like a great cat, poised lightly on his feet, ready for a lightning leap to the cover best suited. He must know first just where the possible danger lurked.

The bell's tinkle loudened, and suddenly Ross saw a slow-moving burro top a ridge to the right of him. Astride the burro was a long-legged gaunt man with a flowing white beard.

For a brief moment amazement held Ross transfixed. He saw the venerable stranger's hand lift in a friendly gesture and grew sheepishly aware of the gun. He thrust the forty-five back into its holster.

'Peace be with you, my son.' The old man's voice boomed surprisingly, deep and resonant and mellow.

Memory rescued Ross from his profound astonishment. Long years before when on a trip to Chuckwalla Peak with his father he had seen this same man. Nobody knew anything about him, except that he was supposed to have spent a lifetime prospecting the desert hills. Perhaps there were some who knew his real name, but he was known only as The Prophet, liked and respected — a little feared.

'You are surprised, my son.' The Prophet swung a long leg over the burro's back and stood leaning on the great staff that he carried. His eyes held a hint of a twinkle.

Ross nodded. 'I've been away a long time from this country,' he responded. 'I remember you now ——'

The Prophet smiled, turned back to the burro and

lifted a canteen from the saddle horn. He removed the cap and offered the canteen to Ross. 'Drink,' he said, 'but not too much. It is good, cold water.'

'Thanks,' Ross said simply. He tilted the canteen to his lips. It was perhaps the sweetest drink he had ever tasted. He could fairly feel his parched flesh tingle with new life. The Prophet was watching him, and his eyes were very keen.

Ross lowered the canteen. 'How did you know you'd find a man down here just about crazy for water?' he asked bluntly.

'I have watched you for hours through my telescope,' answered the old man. 'I saw your agony at Skeleton Wells. I saw those wicked men looking for you.'

Ross took another pull at the canteen, a long one. He put it down on the flat rock and fished tobacco sack and papers from a pocket.

'You'd have been too late with this water if Harve Welder and his bunch had caught up with me,' he said with a grim smile.

'It was not to be,' calmly stated The Prophet. 'You have come back to your own country because it is so ordained. You are a chosen weapon and have a work to do.' His booming voice rose. 'Aye, you will scourge the evil doer from his haunts of iniquity, smite down the wicked oppressor and make clean again a land once fair.'

'I no savvy,' drawled Ross. 'You've got me mixed up with some other man.'

For a moment The Prophet seemed what he was, a very old man. The glow that lighted his face like a flame vanished, his long gaunt frame drooped. 'Surely my tongue speaks the Word,' he muttered. 'One will come with fire and sword against the wicked despoilers of the land, aye, and with destroying floods will he smite them hip and thigh.'

Ross looked at him with mingled pity and sympathy. The old man was cracked in the head, no mistake about it, but that canteen was proof there was nothing wrong with his heart. He took another long pull at the cold water. 'I'd say this country could stand a good flood once in a while,' he said laconically.

The Prophet's head lifted and Ross saw that serenity had returned to his face. He was startled by the calm majesty of the old man. 'Come' — The Prophet gestured at the burro. 'You will ride Balaam ——'

'I'm heading for Alamos,' demurred Ross. 'The Pass should be somewhere close.'

'You will rest with me tonight.' The Prophet's voice was gentle, commanding. 'Darkness will overtake you long before you can reach Alamos. You are weary and need food and rest.' He shook his head. 'You will find neither at Alamos.'

'What do you mean?' Ross stared at him.

The Prophet ignored his surprise. 'Come,' he repeated. He replaced the canteen on the saddle and seized his staff. 'Balaam is small, but he is strong.'

A broad smile spread over the young man's face as he looked at the little burro. 'I'll use my own legs,' he said with a chuckle.

They started up the rugged slope. and behind them trailed the burro, bell tinkling soft cadences. The Prophet was as nimble and sure-footed as a mountain goat. Ross watched him with growing respect — and wonder. If he had worn flowing white robes instead of much-washed faded blue overalls and equally faded blue flannel shirt, this Good Samaritan of the Hills would have made a picture of one of the prophets of old with his majestic white beard, the great staff taller than his head. An Isaiah, or an Ezekiel, thundering great prophecies, denouncing the wickedness of man.

An hour's climb brought them to a small cliff-rimmed meadow under the spire of Chuckwalla Peak. A little spring from some hidden source in the cliffs ran across the saucerlike meadow and emptied into a rock-walled pool near a tiny log cabin. Ross guessed that both cabin and pool were The Prophet's handiwork. The overflow from the pool made a miniature brook that flowed down the lower slope and vanished into a crevice. An antlered buck lifted a noble head and stared inquiringly but without alarm. A doe browsed on the short grass.

'My friends,' The Prophet said simply. He leaned on his great staff and watched the deer with a benign smile for a moment, then he turned to the burro and began stripping off the saddle.

'I can do that,' offered Ross. The old man waved him aside. 'You are tired,' he answered mildly. 'Rest, my son.'

Ross was more weary than he realized. The steep climb had drawn heavily on his depleted strength. He flung himself full length on the grass, let his gaze wander.

The cliffs that girdled the tiny meadow rose from twenty to some hundred feet in height and from where he sprawled he could detect neither entrance or exit. He knew though that the entrance had led through a passage that made a half circle between the cliffs.

His gaze went to the western rampart of pine-studded bluffs. Below them, far down the slope beyond, would be Red Creek Valley — and Alamos.

The Prophet disappeared into the cabin. After a few moments he reappeared with a long brass telescope in one hand. Ross sat up, looked curiously at the telescope.

'A good glass,' The Prophet said, noticing his look.

'You could see me down at Skeleton Wells?' Ross

stared up at him. 'How did you happen to be looking down there?'

'Every day I watch for the one who will surely come to bring succor to an oppressed land,' answered The Prophet. 'When he comes, evil men will stalk him with death in their hands.'

Ross pondered the statement. 'There's a bunch of killers on my trail,' he said finally, 'but I don't fit into your picture.' He smiled dryly. 'Fire and sword against the wicked despoilers, you said, and smiting 'em hip and thigh with destroying floods.' He shook his head. 'I sure don't fit into your picture, mister. I'm only a cowman, and I'm heading for Red Creek Valley to put my dad's brand back on the map. You'll maybe remember Jim Chaine.'

'Ah!' The exclamation came softly from The Prophet. His head lifted in a long bright look. 'Jim Chaine's boy!'

'Yes,' Ross said.

'Then you are the one for whom I look.' The Prophet's deep-set eyes glowed. 'I knew I could not be mistaken.'

Ross looked at him uneasily. 'Crazy talk.'

'Not so, young man.' The Prophet spoke solemnly. 'Do you remember a morning some fifteen years ago, when a small boy climbed into the Alamos stage?'

'Yes,' Ross said. His own voice was suddenly unsteady.

'Do you remember what that small boy told the men who were watching him?'

'Yes,' Ross said again. 'I told them that some day I'd grow up to be a man, and that I'd be back and would kill the murderers of my father.'

The Prophet nodded. 'You did not notice me, but I was there and heard the promise you made. I have never forgotten, and when the time came for you to be a man I began to watch for your coming.'

Ross could only stare at him. He had no words.

'Others remembered that promise you made. They, too, have been watching. The fame of Ross Chaine has reached their ears as it has reached mine.'

'Watching for me, huh?' muttered the young man. 'They haven't lost any time about it.' He scowled. 'A low-down killer took a pot-shot at me up the road. I had to kill him, but he got my horse. That's why you found me afoot.'

The Prophet nodded slowly, lifted a beckoning hand. 'I will show you something,' he said.

Ross followed him through the sparse growth of stunted pine and spruce to where jagged cliffs looked to the west. They came to a narrow trail that led out to a wide ledge. Ross drew a long breath. Far below lay Red Creek Valley.

The old man handed him the brass telescope. 'Look carefully,' he commanded.

Ross obeyed. A startled expression crept over his face. 'Doesn't look the same,' he muttered.. 'No life down there . . . no water in Red Creek.'

'No,' said The Prophet somberly. 'No life . . . no water in Red Creek.'

Ross shifted the telescope. 'That should be Alamos.' He spoke in a curiously shocked voice. 'But — but there's something wrong. Doesn't look the way Alamos used to look. No smoke from the houses . . . no — no life.'

'No,' agreed The Prophet. 'No smoke from the houses . . . no life in Alamos.' He lifted his arms, stood there on the ledge like a prophet of old, the late evening wind in long white hair and beard. 'Behold!' he cried, 'behold the work of wicked men!' His deep, resonant voice boomed from crag to crag. 'Behold the valley of dry bones!'

He went on, and suddenly Ross was conscious that he was listening to ancient Biblical prophecy. His flesh tingled.

'*O ye dry bones, hear the word of the Lord . . . : Behold, I will lay sinews upon you, and will bring flesh upon you, and cover you with skin, and put breath in you, and ye shall live.*'

Ross listened, fascinated, awed; and slowly the sunset shadows crept across the valley.

Chapter

2

GHOST TOWN

THE GIRL pulled the red mare to a standstill in front of the hotel. She wore a somewhat apprehensive look as she gazed about her, and sat lightly tensed in her saddle as if in readiness to whirl the mare away in hasty flight.

A gust of wind lifted the broken signboard that dangled above the hotel's porch steps. It dropped back with a dismal rusty groan that made the girl start nervously. She stared at the lettering that sun and wind and rain had partially obliterated. A handsome sign in its day, with ornate black letters trimmed with gold leaf. A forlorn relict now of a long-gone prosperity. The girl's smooth brows puckered as she studied it.

AL M S H TEL

Her lips moved, supplied the missing letters. ALAMOS HOTEL. 'She shook her head with a show of sadness and gazed up and down the short street. A street without human life, overgrown with weeds and brush, the ramshackle frame buildings pitiful reminders of a past day when men's activities formed the heart that kept its life-blood flowing. The ghost-ridden street of a dead town.

Jean Austen repressed a shiver. The place breathed of death and desolation. She had been crazy to come.

17

Her brows puckered again in a worried little frown. She began to analyze the impulse that had decided her to ride over to Alamos.

It must have been something she had overheard Harve Welder say to Uncle Buel. Harve had mentioned a name vaguely familiar to her. *Ross Chaine*. And Uncle Buel's mouth had set in the hard, thin line that was always a sure sign of angry perturbation.

Jean sat there on the red mare, gaze fastened on the hotel sign creaking dolorously under fitful gusts of wind, her thoughts back at that scene in the ranch-house office. She heard Harve Welder's flat, toneless voice. 'Looks like Monte let Ross Chaine get past him,' he said to her uncle.

Jean had never liked Harve Welder, and for some reason she had been aware of a curious horror of him as he sat there in her uncle's office.

The man continued to speak: 'We found Monte laying back in the chaparral. Looks like this Ross Chaine jasper is mighty fast with a gun.'

Something in the foreman's voice and the look on Uncle Buel's face had held her. The office door was open and the men too absorbed to notice her standing there in the dark hall. She heard her uncle's voice, deep and rich, and all the more amazing because Uncle Buel was a spindly little man to look at him on his feet. He seemed much bigger when sitting in a chair and you noticed the barrellike chest. But if you were behind him you also noticed that curious hump in his shoulders. It gave the impression that Uncle Buel's head was fastened squarely on those wide shoulders and that nature had forgotten to give him a neck. Jean knew that Uncle Buel was a hunchback, but nobody ever spoke of it, at least not in her presence.

'He'll head for Alamos,' Uncle Buel said to Harve.

and the foreman replied, 'We'll get him.' And the way he said the words made her flesh creep.

Jean had felt then that she hated Flying A's tall, lanky foreman. There was something so odiously deliberate and cold-blooded about him. His big beak nose set in that narrow, thin-lipped face gave him a repulsive vulturelike look.

'You'd better see him first,' Uncle Buel said. 'If Ross Chaine is like his dad, he'll be chain-lightning with a gun. If your guess is right, he's killed Monte — and Monte was fast.'

The foreman swore softly. 'We'll get him,' he repeated.

'Must be all of fifteen years since we shipped him out on the Alamos stage.' Uncle Buel's deep voice was reminiscent. 'He's close on twenty-six by now, and he's built himself a reputation down in Texas and in the Territory. Deputy Marshal over in the Cimarron.'

'There's talk he swore he'd be back some day when he was growed up to be a man,' recalled Harve. 'Promised he'd do some killin' and put his dad's Bar Chain back on the map.'

There had been no answer in spoken words from Uncle Buel. Only an odd rasping chuckle that had for some reason raised a prickly gooseflesh down her back. She had fled to her room, and for long hours tossed sleeplessly on her bed, wondering — *wondering*.

And now she was here in the ghost town of Alamos. For what purpose she had only the vaguest idea. Something to do with warning a young man of a great danger — of a stalking death in Alamos.

Jean drew a restraining rein on the impatient mare. 'Stop it,' she reproved aloud. 'Mind your manners, Redbird.'

Her look went again to the weather-worn sign.

Alamos. Her Uncle Buel had said that Ross Chaine would head for *Alamos*. That was why she was here — waiting. *A kid when they had shipped him away on the stage.* She recalled the foreman's words. Fifteen years ago, and he had promised to come back when he was a man and put his dad's Bar Chain iron on the map again.

Jean Austen's memories were stirring. She wouldn't have known — or understood. She must have been about five or six, but bits of the story had drifted along with the years.

She began to fidget in her saddle. She felt she could bear this waiting no longer. The place was getting on her nerves. And yet she could not leave — not before she had warned Ross Chaine.

She hated the place. The dismally flapping sign gave her the creeps. And there were other weird noises — the wind that rattled through loosened shingles and tugged at sun-blistered warped boards. Ghosts — forever walking and moaning — and — and threatening.

Jean's hand tightened on bridle-rein and she swung the mare sharply, as quickly drew to an abrupt halt, eyes widened at the lone rider in the middle of the street.

Perhaps some twenty yards separated them; and after a long moment the big golden horse, a palomino, moved with an almost prancing step toward the startled girl.

She was aware of a tall man in the saddle, a young face just now very grave and unsmiling under the flat-crowned Mexican hat with dangling chin straps of braided rawhide fastened with a silver band. He wore a blue flannel shirt in which was loosely knotted a yellow bandanna. The blue shirt was decorated with large white buttons.

In that almost fascinated stare, Jean absorbed other details — the sagging gunbelt that hugged the stranger's lean waist — the brush-scarred leather chaps over tight dark trousers.

He drew the horse to a standstill and met her wide-eyed look. She saw that he was not so boyish when seen closely. There were tiny lines there in the hard brown planes of that pleasant face; an odd and almost wary gleam in the steady, unafraid eyes.

He was suddenly smiling at her, a smile that warmed and lighted the stern set of his face.

Jean could only stare at him, her lips parted in breathless fascination. She wanted to cry out to him to put spurs to his horse and ride away from Alamos . . . wanted to warn him that ghosts of the past were stalking him for his life. The words were there, but she could not say them. She could only look at him helplessly.

He seemed to divine her fear, but misunderstood. His smile faded and concern threw a quick, fleeting shadow across his face. 'I'm afraid I startled you.' His tone was contrite. 'I'm sorry ——' His hat swept off, and the smile flowed back. 'My apologies ——'

The sound of his soft drawling voice broke the thrall that held her tongue-tied. 'Get away from here!' The words tumbled from her, sharp and thin and panic-ridden. 'They — they're watching for you!'

His head jerked up, and the hard, wary look was back in his eyes. He deliberately replaced his hat. 'I wouldn't wonder but what you're right.' A cold note had replaced the pleasant drawl. 'I don't savvy how come you're mixed up in it.'

'You are Ross Chaine?' Jean spoke impatiently.

'Yes — that's my name.'

'Then don't waste time talking. Get away from here. . . . Go back to where you came from.' She saw the question in his eyes. 'Never mind who I am. Take my tip and head away from these parts. You're not safe in Alamos — nor anywhere in the valley.'

His look went up and down the desolate street, came to rest on the creaking hotel signboard. His face hardened. 'I'm not one who runs from ghosts,' he said curtly. His gaze shifted back to the girl. 'I have the answer about you now. You must be Jean Austen ——'

'Never mind about me,' she interrupted. 'I've warned you — and now I'm going. Your own fault if you stay to — to be killed.' She lifted bridle reins.

'Not so fast.' His smile returned. 'You've changed a lot since I saw you last.' His tone was bantering, touched with approval. 'You weren't much bigger than a minute — about three or four years old.' His smile broadened. 'You must be all of seventeen or eighteen by now.'

'I'm nearly twenty-one,' Jean said half indignantly. 'Anyway, it's none of your business and I'm not staying here talking. I've warned you, and now it's up to you.'

'Did Buel Patchen send you?' He put the question grimly.

'No!' Jean faltered. 'Nobody sent me.'

'You have me guessing,' Ross said. 'What made you come to Alamos to warn me?'

'Because — because ——' She faltered again. 'Oh — don't sit there on your horse asking silly questions!'

'I maybe can guess,' Ross said, his eyes shrewd and hard. 'You've been hearing talk ——'

'You make me tired!' flared the girl.

Ross ignored the interruption. 'You've heard talk between Buel Patchen and Harve Welder,' he went on musingly, as if building a background. 'You heard enough to know that Harve Welder and his outfit are heading for Alamos. Buel Patchen has told Harve I'd make for Alamos.'

Her suddenly pale face, the fear in her dark eyes, answered him. He gave her a mirthless smile. 'I don't savvy why you wanted to warn me, but I'm mighty obliged. Right kind of you, Miss Austen.'

Jean broke out afresh at him. 'I warned you because I don't like people being killed, and there will be people killed if you stay in Red Creek Valley. Why don't you use sense . . . keep away from this country?'

'This is my country,' Ross answered quietly. 'I was born in the valley — on my father's Bar Chain ranch.'

'The valley is dead,' retorted the girl. 'Haven't you any eyes?' She gestured. 'Alamos is dead. There is nothing here for you.'

'I'll bring things back to life,' Ross said in a low voice. His head lifted in a far-away look. He was recalling the words of The Prophet, rolling from crag to crag. 'I'm home to stay,' he said. 'There will be life again in Alamos — in the valley.'

Jean drew up in her saddle, a trim and graceful girl with a wealth of dark curls under a white stetson, wholesomely nice-looking with frank dark eyes in an attractive face. Ross was aware of a small straight nose and a firm little chin, and a mouth that he felt could express graciousness and tenderness. At this moment the soft full lips were set defiantly and the lovely eyes were hard and unfriendly. 'Let me say something for myself,' she said passionately, 'I don't want you back in the valley, making trouble for Flying A.'

He looked at her thoughtfully. 'Are you running Flying A now that you are grown up?' His tone was skeptical.

'I'm the owner of Flying A,' Jean told him haughtily.

The skepticism on his face seemed to enrage her. 'Uncle Buel has always run the ranch — as long as I can remember, but don't forget that I'm the owner, Mr. Chaine, and I'm warning you now that I don't want you for a neighbor.'

'Buel Patchen won't argue that point with you,' Ross said grimly.

She gave him a desperate look. 'All right . . . Have it your own way. Don't forget you've been warned.' She lifted the reins and the red mare sprang forward, tore at a gallop down the deserted street.

Chapter

3

ENCOUNTER IN ALAMOS

Ross watched, aware of a vague regret to see her go. The street seemed to take on a deeper, more dismal solitude that filled him with an inexpressible sense of loneliness.

He climbed from the saddle and dropped the reins over the sagging hitchrail in front of the hotel. He was crazy to stay any longer in the place. The girl had warned him to expect trouble. Any moment might bring Harve Welder, eager to even things for the killing of Monte.

He glanced at the sun. Nearly ten o'clock. Buckshot Kinners and Pete Lally were due to meet him in Alamos at ten o'clock. He had written them care of the Dos Cruces post office. The presence of the two LK men would considerably dampen Harve's yearning for an immediate showdown. The Flying A foreman would not want witnesses to a cold-blooded killing.

Ross sat down on the sagging porch steps and fumbled in a pocket for tobacco sack, musing eyes on the golden horse nibbling at the grass that grew high under the hitchrail. A first-rate horse. Ross marveled every time he looked at the animal.

Engrossed as he was with his thoughts, he managed to keep watchful eyes on both ends of the street. Kinners and Lally would approach from the Dos Cruces side and more likely than not Harve Welder would come in from the west. Flying A lay that way, beyond the high ridge that shut in Red Creek Valley from the vast reach of rolling mesa that was Flying A range.

It was possible the girl who had just left him would run into them, unless she cut into one of the canyons. It was not likely she would want Harve Welder to suspect she had been to Alamos.

He lit his cigarette, his thoughts on Jean Austen. Fifteen years had transformed her into a remarkably pretty young woman. Attractive was a better word, a girl of spirit and charm. Her father and his father had been old friends, pioneers together.

Ross fastened a somber gaze on a haze of dust drifting in from the east. Kinners and Lally. He shifted his gaze, saw another haze of approaching dust. His jaws tightened and he thought of Buel Patchen. According to a coroner's jury, Bill Austen's carelessness with a gun had caused his untimely death. The tragedy had left a helpless widow and an infant girl. Mrs. Austen's own health was none too good. She was relieved when her dead sister's husband arrived on the scene and took charge of the ranch. She died within the year, leaving little Jean in Buel Patchen's care.

From that time on things had gone from bad to worse with Jim Chaine. Flying A's tentacles had spread north and south and east and west. Flying A needed water and Buel Patchen would stop at nothing to get what he wanted. Finally he was reaching for control of the headwaters of Red Creek.

Ross had always been somewhat confused about the details of the tragedy. He was going on twelve when it happened. One fact alone was stark in his memory. His father had been killed, and men had put the murdered cattleman's small son on the Alamos stage — sent him out of the country.

Fifteen years had drawn a haze over the affair, but the memory of his father's murder remained with Ross, a live, hot coal, smoldering under the ashes of time. He had promised to some day search out and punish the murderers of Jim Chaine.

An aunt in Kansas City managed to hold the boy in leash for five years, but the cow country was in his blood. He was hardly seventeen when he seized the chance to join a hard-riding outfit in the Texas Panhandle.

Ross aroused from his reflections. The dust cloud approaching from the east was less than a mile distant, and there was no doubt that the horsemen making that dust were headed for Alamos. He shifted his gaze and studied the long dun plume drifting in from the west. Two miles away, he estimated, but coming fast.

He stood there, a hint of growing worry in his eyes. He was taking too much for granted in believing the riders approaching from the east were Lally and Kinners. He was more confident about the identity of the makers of the long plume of dust in the west. Jean Austen had warned him to expect trouble from Flying A.

His misgivings grew. There was a chance he was wrong about those other men being Lally and Kinners. *Just a chance.*

He made a quick decision, swung back to his saddle and rode into a weed-choked alley between the hotel and a dejected frame building that he recalled was once the Red Front Saloon. A large barn stood back of the hotel. Ross halted the palomino for a brief scrutiny of the place. He shook his head, rode on past the barn. A hundred yards beyond lay the dry wash of Red Creek, and a huge thicket of mesquite.

Careful to avoid ground that would lift dust he pushed

the horse along at a fast walk. Dust would attract the attention of the approaching riders.

The big clump of mesquite was familiar to him. It spread over a lot of ground and under the thick, concealing branches used to be a clearing around the massive trunk. He had played Indian there with the boys of the town. They used to hide in the brambly shelter with their ponies and make big medicine for war against the hated palefaces, usually a lot of screaming but delighted little girls.

The clearing was still there, and big enough to conceal the palomino. Ross secured the animal and hurried back to the hotel. The dust clouds were much closer. Less than a quarter of a mile away. The thought of the hoofprints in the street gave him some concern. There was no time to obliterate them. He retraced his steps as far as the alley, saw with relief that the weeds covered any sign that he had ridden that way.

The cigarette stub he had tossed aside caught his eye as he made his way back. He picked it up and hurried into the hotel. The place was nothing more than a shell, windows gone, the furniture — anything removable.

Hoofbeats touched his ears. Ross wasted no more time. He wanted to have a look at the arrivals. If they proved to be Buckshot Kinners and Pete Lally he would have at his side a pair of stanch fighting men that even Harve Welder would not lightly put to the test.

He ran up the creaky stairs and into a room from which he could look down into the street. His eyes narrowed as he caught sight of the two riders. There was no mistaking the man on the black horse. That hump in his shoulders said he was Buel Patchen.

It required a longer and more careful look before he could identify Buel's companion. Tenn Patchen had

been a chunky boy when he saw him last. Fifteen years
had changed him into a burly, stupid-faced man. Ross
had never liked him. Tennessee Patchen was the son of
Buel's first wife. A bully and a coward as a boy, he was
probably a bully and a coward still, and worse, judging
from the sullen, vicious face.

The two men reined their horses close to the hotel
porch. Ross heard the younger Patchen's voice: 'That'll
be Harve and the boys . . . comin' up fast.' His eyes
roved alertly, probed at the buildings. 'If Chaine's
been here, he ain't here now. Looks like we've missed
him.'

'We'll make sure,' Buel Patchen said in his rich voice.
'You're too shiftless, Tenn. You don't take enough
trouble with things.'

'I'll take trouble enough with this Chaine,' assured
Tenn with an ugly grin. 'I remember that red-headed
little skunk.'

His father stared at him, a hint of contempt in the
look. 'I remember he blacked your eyes for you one
time,' he said. 'You were always afraid of Ross Chaine
— and you older and bigger.'

'Wasn't wantin' it said I jumped on a smaller kid,'
mumbled Tennessee. 'Hell — I wasn't scared of the
skunk no time.' He fished tobacco sack and papers from
his shirt pocket and began on a cigarette.

Buel Patchen watched him, his mouth a hard, thin
line. 'I want you to mend your ways with Jean,' he
went on. 'You know my wishes, Tenn.'

'That fool girl just don't see me,' grumbled the
younger Patchen. He lit his cigarette and glanced
down the street. 'Here's Harve and the bunch,' he
added.

His father looked briefly at the approaching riders.
'Listen to me!' His tone was cold with anger. 'Jean

doesn't like the stink of whiskey you always carry round. Mend your ways, boy. I'm not allowing you to inter- fere with my plans. Flying A belongs to Jean, but when she's your wife, the ranch will belong to a Patchen.'

'I savvy.' Tenn shrugged his heavy shoulders. 'If I don't get her one way, I'll get her another.' His smile was unpleasant. 'She'll be glad enough to marry me when I start swingin' my loop.'

'I don't care how you do it,' Buel told him curtly. 'Do anything you want with her, but make sure she's your wife damn soon. Jean's close to twenty-one and boss of Flying A. You get busy, son.'

'I savvy,' Tenn repeated. 'No call for you to worry. I'll slap the Patchen iron on that smooth hide of hers be- fore I'm done with her.' His hand lifted in a welcoming gesture. 'Hello, Harve. Looks like the skunk has given us the slip.'

Disappointment darkened the foreman's hard face as he reined his horse. 'Sign shows somebody's been here recent,' he commented with a sharp look at the hoof marks in front of the hitchrail.

Ross drew back from the window, fearful of a chance glance. There was a hard light in his eyes, a seething anger at the two Patchens for their infamous plot against Jean Austen.

He crouched there for a moment, fighting off the rage that brought a tremble to his hands. He needed to have those hands under control . . . it was a time for coolness.

He took another cautious look down into the street. Seven riders there now, counting the two Patchens. Harve Welder was speaking again.

'Them fresh tracks show somebody come in from the west. Looks like he waited here in front of the hotel quite a spell, then rode back west ag'in.' The foreman was down from his saddle and closely scrutinizing the ground. 'There's other tracks here — a bigger horse made 'em. Come in from the east, but no sign pointin' which way he went out. We've cluttered up the street with our own bronc tracks.'

'Plenty of places for a feller to hide in this damn spook town,' commented one of the riders. Ross recognized the chunky dark-browed Tony.

'We'll make sure,' Buel Patchen said. 'Scatter out, boys. Search the buildings . . . any place that can hide a man and his horse.'

Harve's worried voice interrupted him. 'I'd say there's been two fellers here for a palaver. Mebbe one of 'em was Ross Chaine and the other feller come and tipped him off about us. Ain't that the way you figger it, Buel?'

Ross pressed close to the broken window. The situation promised excitement — too much excitement.

'One guess is as good as another, Harve. If Chaine is still hanging round here some place we'll get him, dead or alive.'

'We won't take him alive,' Harve Welder said grimly. 'Ross Chaine don't miss his shots. I'm advisin' you fellers to pull trigger on sight. Don't waste time in fool talk with him. He's slick — and damn fast.'

'I owe him one for Monte,' muttered Tony Birl as he slid from his saddle and moved cautiously toward the sagging door of the saloon.

Tenn Patchen climbed from his horse. 'I'll take a prowl inside the hotel,' he announced.

'You would choose the hotel,' sneered his father. 'The hotel is the trap Ross Chaine wouldn't pick for a hideout.' He gestured contemptuously. 'Go ahead. Somebody's got to have a look and it might as well be you.'

Tenn flung him an ugly grin as he pounded up the

broken steps. The old man was sour with him because of the girl. Tenn's loose-lipped mouth set in a snarl as he hurried into the hotel, gun in hand. He'd show the old man who was boss. Just wait until he'd made Mrs. Tenn Patchen out of Jean. He'd kick the old man off the ranch for keeps.

Ross heard his heavy footsteps down in the lobby. He took time out for another look into the street. The Flying A men were all off their horses. He caught a glimpse of Harve Welder peering warily through the open door of the defunct Alamos General Merchandise Emporium. Unlike Tenn Patchen, the others were using stealth and caution as they began their search. Only Buel Patchen remained on his horse, gaze roving up and down the street.

Ross slipped from the room and made his way quietly along the hall to the rear. If his memory was good there used to be a fire-escape running down from the second story, a crude ladderlike affair. A quick look told him the upper portion of the ladder was still in place. A five foot drop at the most.

He hurried back along the hall, warned by Tenn's heavy footsteps on the stairs. The man was a blundering fool. Ross smiled mirthlessly. Tenn was bigger, a grown man, but he was still the same stupid blusterer.

A small closet stood in the hall, door sagging open. The old linen closet. Ross slipped inside, stood there, hand on doorknob, his gun ready. He saw Tenn's head appear and in another moment the man was on the landing at the head of the stairs.

A voice floated up from the street. 'No sign of the feller in here, boss.' Tony Birl's voice as he emerged from the saloon.

Tenn Patchen stood for a moment, then moved toward the front bedroom where Ross had been watching from the window.

As he passed the linen closet, Ross stepped out behind him with the stealth of a stalking cat.   Instantly his gun was pressing hard against Tenn's back.

The feel of the gun-barrel against his spine seemed to paralyze young Patchen. He stood there, frozen with terror, afraid even to turn his head.

'One little sound from you and I'll kill you,' warned Ross in a low whisper. He reached out his free hand and snatched the gun from the man's nerveless grasp. 'Hug that wall.' He emphasized the order with a prod of his gun. 'Belly up close, mister.'

Tenn obeyed. Sweat beaded his heavy face. Ross jerked his hands behind his back and bound the wrists with the bandanna he tore from Tenn's neck. He whispered softly as he worked. 'I'll kill you,' he kept warning. 'One little yip out of you — and I'll kill you.'

He unfastened Tenn's leather belt and strapped his legs with it. 'You're losing your pants, Tenn,' he chuckled. 'You're lucky at that.'

Another sharp, whispered command brought Tenn's back to the stout newel post at the head of the stairs. Tenn was in a ghastly state of terror. He mutely obeyed the gesture that told him to lie face down on the floor. Ross seized him by the bound ankles and hooked his legs over the post. 'You look like a hog strung up all pretty on a hook,' he said with another chuckle.

Voices were calling from the street, announcing failure to find the hunted quarry. Ross listened for a brief moment, gave Tenn a savage prod with his gun. 'Listen, mister — you're going to make your own speech right now. You're going to yell out loud, tell 'em there's nobody here in the hotel. Savvy?' He bent over the bound and frightened man, his eyes hard and merciless. 'One wrong word, and this gun talks.' He thrust the long-barrelled forty-five within an inch of

Tenn's face. 'Now,' he commanded. 'Yell out loud . . . tell 'em there's nobody in the hotel.'

Tenn's mouth opened, but no sound came.

'Talk up, and talk loud!' Ross spoke savagely.

Tenn made a second try. 'Nobody here in the hotel, fellers,' he bawled at the top of his voice.

'Tell 'em you've looked all over, upstairs and down,' Ross whispered.

'Been all over the place,' yelled Tenn. 'Ain't nobody here!'

Somebody shouted back an answer, told him to 'get a move on.'

'Tell 'em you're going to the gents' room and for them not to wait,' Ross whispered. He grinned, let the helpless man feel the press of gun-barrel against his head. Tenn made haste to obey. Ribald comments and guffaws greeted the explanation of his delay, and then Buel Patchen's voice: 'We're heading for Red Creek Mesa, Tenn. There's a chance that Chaine is hiding out at the old ranch.' A wrathy note tinged the sonorous voice. 'Don't be all day up there, boy!'

Ross heard the creak of saddle leather, the stamp of hoofs fading in the distance as the Flying A men rode away. He stooped again, quickly, and thrust the twisted fragment of flannel shirt between Tenn's teeth. He drew the ends back and knotted them firmly.

Tenn made gurgling sounds, tried to lift his hooked legs over the newel post.

'No chance,' Ross told him. 'You're hung up until they come back to see what's keeping you. They'll start wondering, after an hour or two.'

Satisfied that his prisoner was secure until help reached him, Ross returned to the bedroom window and took a look at the street below. Tenn's horse drooped at the ancient hitchrail in front of the hotel. Looking west he glimpsed a drift of dust. Buel Patchen and his riders, on their way to the long abandoned Bar Chain ranch house.

His face hardened as he watched the dust haze. Buel Patchen had brought disaster to Bar Chain, but the ranch was still Chaine land. He thought of The Prophet's solemn utterance. *A valley of dry bones.* He was back to put flesh on those bones, and life again would flow through the valley.

He went back to the hall. 'You're lucky,' he said to Tenn Patchen. 'If I had good sense I'd kill you.'

The horse standing at the hitchrail lifted inquiring ears when he came down the hotel steps. Ross gave him a good-natured slap and turned him loose. The Patchens were not going to have a chance to accuse him of horse-stealing. The dun would eventually find its way back to Flying A.

Carrying Tenn's confiscated gun and cartridge belt, Ross made his way back to the mesquite and got his own horse. He tossed the gun and belt into the brush as he rode away.

The palomino carried him along an old trail that followed the dry sandy wash of Red Creek. Ross reveled in the swift running-walk of the big silver-maned horse.

'I've been saving him for you, son.' The Prophet's words came back to him as he rode toward Dos Cruces. 'I've trained him with my own hands from the time he was a colt. Oro is as gentle as a kitten, as brave as a lion, and as swift as an eagle. He'll carry you all day and on through the night. He'll stay put any place you tell him and he'll come at your whistle.'

'You were awfully sure of me.'

'I heard what you said when they sent you away on the stage,' reminded the old man. 'I knew you would be back. I kept track of the years and when the time drew nearer I made ready.' He looked contentedly at the big golden gelding quietly grazing with the deer. 'I knew you would need a good horse.'

Oro was proving all that The Prophet claimed. Ross was confident the palomino could outrun any horse that wore the Flying A brand.

He swung away from the dry wash and cut over a high piñon-covered ridge. Oro took the climb with hardly a falter. Ross halted on the crest and looked at the huddle of buildings that sprawled at the desert's edge far below. Dos Cruces.

He let the horse rest while he smoked a cigarette and studied the town. Perhaps he was a fool to show himself in Dos Cruces. But there were things he must know, things that Buckshot Kinners and Pete Lally could tell him. Something had kept them from meeting him in Alamos. It was not like those two men to break a promise.

He snubbed out the cigarette and started the horse down-trail. Come hell or high water he was heading for Dos Cruces. He had pressing business in that desert cow town.

Chapter

4

CHUCHO CARRIES A MESSAGE

THE TWO MEN in Ross Chaine's thoughts sat at a small table in the far corner of the White Buffalo Saloon. The bigger of the two wore a gloomy look as he listened to his companion. He suddenly spoke softly, his voice hardly above a whisper. 'Careful, Buckshot . . . Rick's been lookin' our way kind of suspicious. You'll have him wonderin' what's got you excited.'

Buckshot Kinners made no attempt to glance across at the long bar. Rick DeSalt would only be the more suspicious. He raised his voice until his words were plainly audible for all to hear. 'I'm sayin' out loud you're loco. There ain't no such thing as a white buffalo. Any feller as claims he's seen a *white* buffalo is sure a liar.' He banged a fist on the table. 'I get doggone fed up with your stubborn notions, Pete Lally.'

The big man's face betrayed no surprise at his friend's sudden outburst. Buckshot was always quick to take a hint. He had instantly switched to talk of a white buffalo without batting an eye. It was like Buckshot to grab an idea out of thin air, or, as in this case, from the big painting that hung above the plate-glass mirror behind the bar. Pete hid a grin behind a hamlike hand and went to his friend's aid. He threw a sideways glance at the watchful man lounging negligently against the bar.

'Did you hear him, Rick?' His tone was pitying. 'The lop-eared maverick is claimin' there never was no white buffalo.'

'You bet there ain't no white buffalo!' howled Buckshot.

'There's one starin' into your fool face from that pitcher behind the bar!' shouted Pete Lally. 'The artist feller that painted her wouldn't have put in a white buffalo if he hadn't seen one. Ain't that right, Rick?'

The proprietor of the White Buffalo Saloon approached the wrangling pair, an amused look on his dark, keen face. Buckshot eyed him combatively. 'That pitcher don't mean a thing and you know it, Rick.'

'He was a *real* artist, that feller,' Pete declared. 'He wouldn't have painted in a lie, would he, Rick?'

The saloon man turned and studied the big painting critically. It ran nearly the length of the bar and showed a herd of stampeding buffalo led by a great white bull. Indian warriors rode in furious chase.

'It's an argument I can't settle,' DeSalt finally said gravely. 'I paid the artist real money for that painting.' He smiled urbanely at the pair. 'I'm inclined to agree with you, Pete. He wouldn't have lied about that white buffalo. There's room for argument when it comes to proof,' he added affably. 'What will it be, boys? The drinks are on the house.'

Pete Lally was on his feet. 'Thanks, Rick, but when Buckshot gets to talkin' so wild about white buffalo I reckon it's time we pulled our freight.'

DeSalt nodded carelessly and strolled back to the thronged bar. Pete and Buckshot got out of their chairs. 'I guess he ain't wonderin' no more about what we was talkin',' muttered Buckshot as they pushed through the swing doors to the sidewalk.

'Rick is awful sharp,' Pete rejoined. 'You fixed him

ᴀt that, Buckshot. Never seen nobody like you for being quick on the uptake. Switched that talk as natcheral as a newborn calf goes to its mammy for supper.'

They slowed down in front of a big livery barn set back from the street. Buckshot pushed up the wide brim of his hat and gave his friend an anxious look. 'Gettin' back to Ross Chaine, my mind is sure twisted in a double knot about him. He wrote us to meet him over at Alamos and that he'd write ag'in and tell us the day. We ain't been able to find us no letter at the post office.' The little man shook his head gloomily. 'It was sort of in my mind that Ross would be showin' up before now.'

'I ain't liking it,' Pete said in his slow, quiet voice. 'Ross ain't one to misplay his hand.' He stared thoughtfully at the yawning entrance of the livery barn. 'Let's ride some place. Got a notion Stack Jimson is watching us kind of sharp.'

Stack Jimson got out of his chair, an old buckboard seat placed under a cottonwood tree in front of the barn. He was an elderly, potbellied man with sharp restless eyes too closely set in his big round face. He watched the approaching men, thumbs hooked in the leather belt that held up his trousers. A trickle of tobacco juice stained a corner of his pendulous lower lip.

'Want your broncs?' His voice was a husky wheeze.

'We're ridin',' Pete told him.

'Leavin' town awful early,' commented the liveryman. 'Thought you figgered to stay over.'

'We'll be back,' put in Buckshot. 'We got a notion to ride over for a look at that trail-herd at Willow Creek. Might spot some strays wearin' our LK iron.'

Pete Lally's poker face showed no hint of surprise at his partner's statement. He nodded solemnly. 'Got to watch these drovers. Some ain't too careful about strays.'

'That's right,' agreed Jimson with a grin that showed an array of tobacco-stained teeth. He led the way into the long stable, stood lazily watching while his patrons threw on saddle gear. 'Knowin' your ways I ain't botherin' to call Pedro in to saddle up for you,' he observed.

'I like to know my saddle is on proper,' Buckshot said laconically.

'Not that Pedro ain't first-rate,' Pete added with a mollifying grin at the liveryman. 'Buckshot and me is just kind of peeculiar that way.'

'Don't need to 'pologize,' chuckled Jimson. 'Save me plenty trouble if all of 'em was like you.'

The two cowmen jogged away, horses' hoofs spurting riffles of dust. Stack Jimson watched them from his buckboard chair, sharp little eyes puckered in a thoughtful squint. Nothing out of the way in their wanting to have a look at that trail-herd. Rick DeSalt had said for him to keep an eye on them, but hell, there wasn't anything to go chasing over to Rick's place about. The obese liveryman grunted, reached into his pocket for tobacco-plug.

Pete gave his partner an amused look. 'What's the idee?' he wanted to know. 'First I've heard that we was wanting to take a look at that herd down in Willow Creek.'

'We ain't.' Buckshot's smile was grim. 'Also we don't want Stack Jimson to know we're ridin' over to powwow with Lico Estrada. Just as quick as we hit the gully you and me is headin' across the mesa to Lico's *cantina*.'

'You're awful smart, Buckshot,' admired his big partner. 'You've got brains.'

'We've got to use 'em,' Buckshot said with a mirthless smile. 'If Ross Chaine *does* show up in this part of the

country it will be like — like droppin' a chunk of dynamite plumb into hell. Things is goin' to be blowed sky
high.'

They reached the gully, followed its winding course
for half a mile and then pushed across a stretch of juniper-
covered mesa. Pete Lally broke the silence. 'Mighty
queer we never got that letter Ross figgered to send.'

'Letter-stealin' is ag'in the law,' Buckshot said darkly.

'Law!' scoffed Pete. 'Where'd you get that notion?
There ain't no law in these parts.'

'Washington's got awful long arms,' reminded his
partner.

'Won't do us or Ross Chaine much good writin' to
Washington for them to look up a stole letter,' grumbled
Pete.

A cluster of adobe buildings came into view as the
pair dropped down from the mesa to the wide mouth of
a canyon. Beyond the canyon's mouth undulated the
vast floor of the desert reaching toward the dark blue
heights of the Mogollons.

The LK partners drew rein under a cluster of china-
berry trees that shaded the weather-beaten adobe walls
of Lico Estrada's *cantina*. The long building fronted a
tiny plaza that was dominated by the crumbling mud
walls of a church. Scattered here and there were some
half score adobe dwellings.

Pete Lally gazed about approvingly, sent a smile at
the dark-faced children playing in the plaza under the
trees. 'You know, Buckshot,' he said, 'I always did think
Old Town has got the other Dos Cruces beat for bein' a
restful place to live. Sure is peaceful. I like to see the
kids playin' round.'

'Used to be called La Cruz,' Buckshot recalled. He
looked across the plaza at the ruins of the church. 'I
reckon that's the original cross up on that old tower.

Was always La Cruz until some old don feller got the notion to start the new town round on the bluffs. Used to be floods come down the canyon and they figgered the bluffs was a better place. I reckon that's how the name got changed to Dos Cruces . . . meaning the place of two crosses.'

'Thank you kindly,' chuckled Pete. He smiled down ironically at his voluble partner who was a head shorter than himself. 'Bein' borned on the Rio Grande, I was livin' here when you was playin' marbles in Kansas City, and talkin' Spanish when you was learnin' that *c a t* spells cat.'

Buckshot ignored the gibe and swung from his horse. A brown-faced barefooted boy ran up. 'Hold your horses for a penny, *señores*,' he offered with a flash of white teeth.

'Sure, sonny,' agreed Pete. He tossed the boy a five-cent piece. 'You speak good English.'

'I go to the school over in New Town.'

'Good American, huh?' chuckled Pete.

'You bet.' The boy flashed another smile. 'For this five cents I watch your horses one hour.'

'There'll be another one coming,' promised Buckshot as he turned to follow his partner into the *cantina*.

It was dark inside the inn, after the bright sunlight. Men with swarthy faces under enormous sombreros sat at little tables. The two cowmen were conscious of eyes and teeth turning their way as they paused inside the door.

A short, thickset man made a noiseless appearance from a door across the low-ceilinged room. His face wreathed in a welcoming smile at sight of the new-comers. '*Buenos dias, amigos*,' he greeted cordially.

The partners shook hands with him warmly and obeying his gesture seated themselves at a table. 'We want a little talk with you, Lico,' Buckshot said in Spanish. He glanced around significantly.

'You are with friends,' Lico Estrada assured him. He had coarse gray hair and sunken eyes that gleamed like panes of brown glass under harsh black brows. His wide-featured nut-brown face indicated a strong Indian strain. 'Only my friends come here, and my friends are your friends.' Lico gestured to the white-aproned man behind the bar. 'We will have a bottle of my best wine. It is not often I enjoy this pleasure.'

The wine came. Buckshot and Pete sipped, made appropriate signs of appreciation. Lico beamed on them, listened attentively while Buckshot briefly outlined the problem that was baffling and worrying them.

'It is possible the letter was not sent as promised,' finally commented the innkeeper. 'You are letting yourselves be disturbed for no real reason.'

Pete Lally shook his head. 'Ross Chaine is the sort that keeps his word, Lico. He's like you. He don't break a promise.'

Lico lifted a deprecating hand. 'You are too kind,' he smiled, and then gravely, 'I see your point, and I agree that you have cause to fear for your friend's safety.'

'That letter's been stole,' asserted Buckshot. 'It looks bad for Ross. Somebody found out he was headed for Alamos and laid for him.'

Lico Estrada made clucking sounds with his tongue. 'I remember his father,' he said. 'A good man, and my friend.' His intelligent face clouded. 'It is dangerous for his son to return to Red Creek Valley — and dangerous for those who would help him.'

The LK partners looked at him in silence. Lico studied them for a moment, a glow dawning in his eyes. 'You would help this Ross Chaine?' He asked the question softly.

'You've said it,' Buckshot answered laconically. Pete Lally nodded agreement.

Lico sipped his wine. He replaced the glass and the glow in his eyes grew more pronounced. 'I am your friend,' he said solemnly. 'I was his father's friend — I will be his friend, and Lico Estrada does not let a friend down.'

'Don't we know it!' Buckshot spoke fervently. 'Pete and me was awful sure we could count on you. The kid is going to need all the friends we can round up.' Buckshot broke off, shook his head gloomily. 'Providin' he's still alive.'

'One moment ——' Lico gestured, got out of his chair and went to a table occupied by three Mexicans. He spoke rapidly in a low voice to one of them. The man rose and followed the innkeeper back to the partners. Something in the bearing of the tall and rather resplendently attired stranger brought Buckshot and Pete to their feet.

'This is my friend, Don Vicente Torres,' introduced Lico. 'He arrived only a few minutes before you came in and has a piece of news that might be of interest.'

Don Vicente smilingly returned the partners' greetings and seated himself at the table. Lico continued to explain his presence at the *cantina*. 'My friend has a great rancho in Sonora and is on his way to Deming to look at some Hereford bulls he plans to purchase. I am honored that he stays the night with me.'

'You are the best of friends,' declared the Mexican with a wave of his hand. 'To be a friend of Lico Estrada is to be fortunate.'

'That calls for another bottle of my finest wine,' declared the innkeeper. He beckoned the barman.

Don Vicente looked curiously at the two cowmen. 'My bit of information may be of value — or not.'

'Shoot,' grunted Buckshot.

Don Vicente touched a match to his cigarette. 'I passed within a mile of Alamos on my way in this morning,' he continued. 'Much dust drew my attention and I saw the dust was made by a party of horsemen riding away from the town. Some time later I reached the piñon ridge above Dos Cruces and, looking back, picked up the dust of a lone rider a mile or so behind me. I carry a pair of very good glasses and took a look. The man was riding a very fine palomino and he was coming fast.' Don Vicente smiled, shrugged. 'It takes a good horse to climb that ridge with the speed of that palomino. Which is why I mentioned the matter to Lico. I asked him who in Dos Cruces owned such a grand horse.'

'I have never seen such a horse in Dos Cruces,' broke in Lico. He looked inquiringly at the LK men.

Buckshot stood up quickly. 'Might be Ross at that,' he muttered. 'What do you say, Pete?'

'Might be.' Pete Lally lifted his huge frame from the chair. 'We've got to try and head the feller off, Buckshot. If he's Ross Chaine we don't want him ridin' into Dos Cruces. Too risky.'

'Let's go,' Buckshot said crisply. 'Our thanks to you, Lico, and to you, Torres,' he added gratefully.

Lico lifted a detaining hand. 'One moment. If this rider of the palomino should be our young friend, it is best you are not seen with him by unfriendly eyes.'

'We haven't time to talk about it,' reminded Buckshot irritably. 'We've got to head him off — bring him here.'

'Exactly what I mean,' smiled Lico. 'Only we will act discreetly, my friend. We will send Chucho on a fast horse and Chucho will bring him to my place.' He drew a piece of paper and a pencil from a pocket. 'Quick — write a note that Ross Chaine will understand is from you.' Lico moved swiftly to the street door and they heard his voice calling for Chucho.

'Sounds like good sense,' Pete told his partner. 'You fix up the note, Buckshot. We'll both put our names on it.'

Lico reappeared, his expression annoyed. 'Chucho tells me he has been paid five cents to watch your horses,' he grumbled. 'He says he cannot desert his post unless he has your permission.'

The LK partners exchanged startled looks. 'Doggone!' chuckled Pete. 'Wasn't knowin' the kid's name is Chucho.' He made a beeline for the door. 'Never mind about the horses, Chucho,' he called to the boy. 'You do what the boss says.' He fumbled in a pocket and a silver dollar flashed in the air. 'There's another comin' to you if you find the man on the palomino and fetch him here.'

Chucho deftly caught the dollar in a nimble brown hand. 'You bet your sweet life.' He grinned, sped across the plaza to a ewe-necked red and white pinto dozing under a cottonwood tree.

By the time Chucho was back at the *cantina* door, Buckshot had the note ready. Chucho thrust the piece of paper inside his shirt, listened intently to further directions and was off in a cloud of dust.

'Sure is one smart kid,' declared Pete Lally.

Lico Estrada beamed his pleasure. Chucho was his grandson, he informed the cowmen. The innkeeper's eyes twinkled. 'The boy is already most *Americano* and says that when he is a man he will be the governor of New Mexico.' Lico gestured amusement. 'He has the big ideas in his head.'

'Shouldn't wonder but what the kid will be president one of these days,' chuckled Pete.

The rapid drift of dust approaching up the slope caught Ross Chaine's watchful eyes. He swung the palomino off the trail and reined to a standstill behind a thick tangle of brush.

The lone rider was forging up the hill at an astonishing speed. A small boy on a red and white paint pony.

Ross holstered his gun, grinned sheepishly and headed back for the trail. He was surprised to see the boy pull the pony to a quick halt. Ross again reined in his horse and for a moment the two stared at each other. A smile spread over the boy's brown face. He thrust a hand inside his shirt and pulled out a piece of paper.

'For you,' he said briefly. He swung the pony alongside, the paper in extended hand.

Ross took the paper, scanned the penciled scrawl swiftly. Chucho watched him, obviously enjoying his astonishment.

'The big man gave me a dollar to bring it to you quickly,' he said. 'There will be another dollar when I bring you to the *cantina* of Lico Estrada, who is my grandfather.' His tone took on an anxious note as he read hesitation in the eyes of the palomino's rider. 'You will come with me, señor? I must not lose this other dollar the big man has promised.'

'You speak good English,' Ross said.

'Sure — I am American, same as you,' retorted Chucho; and he added earnestly, 'You will come with me?'

Ross studied the note again. There was no doubting those signatures. It meant that Buckshot Kinners and Pete Lally were waiting for him at the *cantina* of Lico Estrada. His look went to the boy. 'I will come,' he said.

Chucho nodded, too overjoyed for more words. In less than an hour he had earned two dollars and five cents. Never before had he possessed so much money. Ross read his thoughts. His smile broadened. 'I will

add to those silver dollars.'   He held up a glittering coin.
'When you bring me safely to the *cantina* of Lico Estrada
who is your grandfather, this five-dollar gold piece can
make music in your pocket with the two silver dollars.'

Chucho forgot that he was an American.   He broke
into his mother tongue.   '*Cáspita!*'   His voice lifted
jubilantly.   '*Válgame Dios!*'   With a gesture for Ross to
follow him, he slapped the pony with bare brown heels
and swung round to the down trail.

Chapter
5

MEN FROM MEXICO

THE FROWN on her uncle's face brought a measure of relief to Jean. She leaned over the garden gate, anxious gaze on the men riding into the big ranch yard. Harve Welder wore a sullen look. Their expressions reassured the girl. The man they sought to trap at Alamos must have eluded them.

Surprise widened her eyes when she saw that Tenn Patchen was not with them. Not that she felt any particular interest in her step-cousin's whereabouts. Jean knew there would be no regrets on her part if she never saw Tennessee Patchen again. He had bullied her when a stupid, uncouth boy, and now he was a man he was persecuting her with odious attentions. She loathed and despised him.

She turned away from the gate, not wanting to betray any curiosity. Buel Patchen was always resentfully evasive whenever she mustered the courage to ask him questions, especially about the ranch. He had a way of looking at her with sharply suspicious eyes and his thin lips would tighten in that hard look of annoyance that for some reason she found frightening.

She heard the slam of the garden gate, the sound of booted feet coming up the flagged walk. The rasp of dragging spurs told her that Harve Welder was accompanying her uncle to the house. Buel Patchen never wore spurs.

Jean moved slowly across the grass to a bench under one of the trees. She was not going to let them see she was dying to know what they had planned to do at Alamos. She reached the bench and picked up the book she had been reading when the men rode into the yard.

The heavy footsteps on the walk came to a halt. Jean heard her uncle's voice. 'Seen Tenn around, Jean?'

She looked up from her book, saw the two men staring at her from across the lawn. 'No.' She shook her head. 'I thought he was with you.'

There followed a silence. The two men exchanged dismayed looks. It was obvious her reply startled and disturbed them. Buel Patchen spoke again, his voice unnaturally harsh. 'You're sure you haven't seen him, Jean? He should have come in a couple of hours ago.'

'Quite sure,' she answered. 'What's the trouble?'

They ignored the question, and looking at her uncle Jean saw something like panic in his eyes. She heard Harve Welder's worried voice: 'Somethin' gone awful wrong,' the foreman said. 'Tenn's had plenty time to get back here.'

Buel Patchen made an angry gesture. 'We've been outsmarted!' Growing rage twisted his face into a malevolent mask. 'Chaine must have been there... hiding in the hotel some place.'

'That's where we left Tenn,' muttered the foreman. 'I ain't likin' this, Buel. No tellin' *what* sort of hell went on after we rode away.' He swung on his heel with a jingle of spurs. 'We've got to head back to Alamos quick as we can make it.' He glanced back at Patchen. 'I'll have your saddle throwed on a fresh horse.'

'No.' Buel's eyes burned in an ashen face. 'I'm not going back there.' His voice cracked. 'Get a move on you! Don't stand there asking fool questions.'

The gate slammed behind the running foreman. Jean heard his voice lifted in shouts to the men at the bunkhouse. Her uncle stood near the steps of the wide porch. His dejection, his obvious deep anxiety, touched her. She went toward him. 'What is the trouble, Uncle? Has something happened to Tenn?'

His head swung her way. The slow movement made Jean think of an owl, only there was nothing owlish about Buel Patchen's livid face. She was frightened by his look, and still more alarmed by the question he suddenly flung at her.

'Where were you riding this morning? You went off some place — early.'

'Why ——' She faltered. 'Why — I rode over to Red Creek, down in the wash.' Which was the truth as far as it went.

'What took you down that way?' His thin mouth was tight and hard, his eyes bright with suspicion.

'Why — nothing in particular.' Again she faltered. 'I heard Tony talking about seeing some coyote pups down in the wash. I wanted to have a look at them.'

'Did you go as far as Alamos?' He shot the question viciously.

'Alamos!' Jean floundered, reached desperately for an answer that would satisfy him. 'I can't bear the sight of that awful place. What makes you ask?'

He stood glowering for a moment, then swung his head in a quick look at the yard. Some half dozen men, with Harve Welder in the lead, were sending their horses on the run toward the gate. Buel watched until only the drift of their dust was visible, then without another look at the girl he went into the house. She heard his office door bang.

Jean was conscious of unutterable relief. She stole quietly around to the back of the house and slipped into the big kitchen. The cook, an elderly Chinese, was taking a pan of bread from the oven. He gave her a benevolent smile, then looked at her with eyes suddenly keen behind their spectacles.

'Wha' foh you so white? . . . allee same flour,' he asked.

'I've a headache,' she told him. 'You're too sharp, Sing Gee.' She forced a smile.

Sing Gee shook his head. 'Me cook here long time . . . since you baby. Me know you, Missie Jean. Me think so you got more bad than headache.'

Jean shrugged her shoulders and passed into the hall and into her room. The scene in the garden had left her unnerved for some reason. The look on her step-uncle's face . . . the talk about Tenn — Alamos.

She flung herself on the bed. Sing Gee was right. It was a lot worse than a simple headache. Her thoughts were in a whirl. Something had happened at Alamos. Her uncle and his riders had been to the place and evidently left without encountering Ross Chaine. And then they must have ridden to the old Bar Chain ranch in search of him. The gloom on their faces was proof of their failure. Ross Chaine had managed to escape them. Her warning had not been in vain.

A little shudder ran through the girl. Her uncle's questioning terrified her. It was obvious he suspected that Ross Chaine had been warned. Apparently her explanations had satisfied him.

She began to speculate about Tenn Patchen. His failure to put in an appearance had something to do with Alamos. Jean had never seen her uncle show such complete fright, a fright mingled with a malevolent anger that shocked her.

She pressed her face into the pillow. Her head really was aching. She recalled the foreman's words, some-

thing about the hotel . . . something about leaving Tenn
behind in the hotel. That was where she had last seen
Ross Chaine, standing by the hotel steps, telling her
that he was back in Red Creek Valley to stay. . . . He
was so good-looking, too . . . dark reddish hair, and those
cool eyes with dancing red and green flecks on them . . .
hazel eyes . . . and he had a way of smiling that lighted
his face, and a way of talking, too, a slow drawl, un-
hurried and yet incisive.

Jean suddenly sat up, a bit startled at the picture she
was summoning. She was being foolish. Ross Chaine
was Flying A's sworn enemy, or her uncle would not be
so worried, so in fear of his return to Red Creek. And
it was plain her uncle and Harve both feared Ross
Chaine had killed Tenn. For what other reason had the
men gone tearing back to Alamos?

Twilight pressed in through the windows, and sounds
that brought the girl to her feet and hurried her out to
the garden. She leaned over the gate that opened into
the ranch yard. It was hard to be sure in that rapidly
deepening dusk and it was not until the riders drew to a
halt near the long water trough that she recognized Tenn
Patchen's bulky form. He sat his saddle limply, heavy
shoulders bowed, head slumped forward, hands tightly
gripping the pommel.

Jean saw Harve Welder slide from his own saddle, go
to Tenn and help him down. Quick footsteps from behind told her that Buel was hurrying from the house.
He pushed by the girl and through the gate and ran to
the group of horsemen. She heard his voice, harsh,
staccato, quite lacking its usual bell-like tone.

'Found him hog-tied up in the bedroom hall,' she
heard the foreman reply. 'He was hangin' face down
with his legs hooked over the stairs' post.'

'Ross Chaine's work,' Buel Patchen said in the same
harsh and violent voice.

'The skunk jumped me when I wasn't lookin',' mumbled Tenn. He loosed a string of epithets. 'Stuffed a piece of my own shirt in my mouth . . . left me strung up there like a side of beef in a butcher shop.'

Jean drew back as the three men came through the gate. Tenn leaned heavily on the foreman. They took no notice of her.

'Found his horse down in the wash,' Harve told Buel.

Tenn broke into another outburst of profanity. 'Took my gun off of me,' he complained.

'You're lucky at that,' commented the foreman acidly.

Jean approached from the shadows. 'Are you hurt, Tenn?' She felt the necessity of showing sympathy.

'None of your business.' He limped past her without a glance.

'That's no way to talk to your cousin,' reproved his father.

'I want a drink,' Tenn grumbled. 'All I want is a good long drink and something to eat. I'm damn near starved.'

They disappeared into the house. Jean watched, conscious of mixed emotions. Relief that nothing serious had happened to Tenn, an odd elation over the humiliation her step-cousin had suffered at Ross Chaine's hands.

She made her way into the house. Voices in the ranch office told her that Buel Patchen and Harve were questioning Tenn about his encounter. One thing was certain. Ross Chaine had completely thwarted their plans.

Sing Gee was beating the dinner gong. Jean went with some reluctance to the dining room. She was trying, with small success, to analyze her confused thoughts. It was wrong of her to feel as she did about Ross Chaine's escape. Her uncle regarded the man as a menace to

Flying **A**. According to Buel Patchen, Ross was a dangerous character, even worse than his father who once owned the Bar Chain ranch. And yet she had risked a lot to warn him of the plan to catch him unawares at Alamos. Ross Chaine would assuredly have fallen into her uncle's hands but for that warning.

She took her usual seat at the table. Why had she warned Ross Chaine, knowing he was Flying A's enemy? The question continued to torment her. She looked blankly at Sing Gee when he set a plate in front of her. 'Wah foh nobody come eat?' he asked crossly. 'Food all go damn cold . . . too bad . . . too bad!' He shuffled back to his kitchen muttering to himself.

Jean hardly knew what she ate. Her mind was too busy with the problem of Ross Chaine. Instinctively she found and clung to the truth about him. Her uncle was wrong. There was some hideous mistake, something hidden beyond her knowledge. She had seen and talked with Ross Chaine. He was not a bad man, as her uncle asserted. Tenn Patchen was a bad man. Instinct warned her against Tenn Patchen. The same instinct told her the truth about Ross Chaine. She was glad she had helped him. Glad — *glad*.

She was finishing a piece of cake Sing Gee had served with a dish of canned peaches when Buel Patchen came in, followed by Tenn and the foreman.

'I didn't think you'd want me to wait,' Jean said apologetically.

'That's all right,' Buel Patchen assured her with a thin smile.

Sing Gee slippered in with an armful of plates. The old cook looked curiously at Tenn. 'You allee same sick cow,' he chuckled.

'Shut your mouth!' Tenn glared at him. 'You get too damn fresh.'

Sing Gee sniffed disdainfully and shuffled out of the room. Jean darted an indignant look at her step-cousin. 'You've no business talking like that to old Sing!'

'He's been here too long. We need a new cook in this house.'

'You have nothing to say about it,' she retorted. 'This is my house.'

It was the first time she had made the flat assertion. Harve Welder seemed to choke over his soup. He put the spoon down and wiped his drooping mustache with shirt sleeve. 'Soup's hot,' he remarked laconically.

Buel Patchen's look flickered at her, then fastened on his son. 'Jean is right,' he reproved. 'You shouldn't ride old Sing. He's a good cook and he didn't mean a thing — saying what he did. You know how these old Chinese cooks are.'

'Tenn is feelin' some touchy,' Harve Welder said with a mollifying grin at the scowling young man. 'He sure got treated rough back there in Alamos.'

'I'll kill him,' muttered Tenn. 'I'll ——'

His father interrupted him. 'You take good care of your house, my dear,' he said in his rich voice. His lips smiled, but not his eyes. They were cold and watchful.

Jean sensed he was slyly testing her. She tried to speak, found herself without words. Tenn was watching her, and Harve was giving her furtive glances. She was conscious of a sudden dread of these men. Anger began to boil up in her.

She put down her coffee cup. 'I'll soon be twenty-one.' She heard her voice with some wonder. It sounded unnatural — hard, defiant. 'I should know by now how to run a house, Uncle, but it is time I learned how to run the ranch. I'm a grown woman and — and the ranch is mine. I intend to run things the way I want.'

'I've been doing pretty well for you, Jean.' Buel Patchen spoke smoothly, the smile still on his lips, his eyes more than ever cold.

'I know, Uncle.' She made herself smile, tried to soften that odd hardness from her voice. 'I am only saying I won't need a guardian after I'm twenty-one.'

'You talk like a loon,' Tenn Patchen said, with a sour look at her. 'What do you know about running a cattle ranch?'

'Shut up, Tenn!' His father's brows drew down in an annoyed frown.

'She makes me sick,' grumbled the younger man.

There was a silence. Jean heard the hurried clump of feet, the bang of the kitchen door and a man's voice speaking to the cook. Harve's head lifted. 'Tony!' he exclaimed. 'Wonder what's up.' He pushed back his chair, but the door opened and Sing Gee came in with Tony Birl at his heels.

'A bunch of fellers in the yard,' the cowboy announced. 'Mexicans.'

'What's their business, Tony?' Buel put down his knife and fork.

'The feller that does the talkin' claims he figgers to buy some cows.' Tony looked at Tenn. He grinned. 'You sure look like you was drawn through a knothole, Tennessee,' he commiserated.

'Shut your damn mouth,' snarled young Patchen. 'You couldn't have taken what I did from that killer.'

'He wouldn't have had no chance to string *me* up like a stuck hawg,' guffawed Tony.

Buel's angry exclamation stopped the argument. 'Harve, you go take a look at these Mexicans. If they're buying cattle we can maybe do business with them.'

'Sure,' assented the foreman. He left the room by way of the kitchen. Tony clattered after him.

Jean was curious about the visitors and wanted an excuse to linger at the table. She rang the bell and asked Sing Gee for a fresh cup of coffee.

Harve was soon back. He stamped in through the kitchen. 'The feller calls himself Don Vicente Torres,' he told Buel. 'Seems all right . . . has a rancho down in Sonora.' The foreman hesitated, glanced at Jean. 'They'd like supper, and if we figger to sell 'em some cows it means an all-night stay.'

'How many?' queried Buel.

'Five of 'em, all Mexicans,' Harve replied. 'How about it?'

'Tell them to come in,' agreed Buel. His voice lifted in a call for Sing Gee.

The cook thrust his head inside the door. 'Me savvy,' he said affably. 'Me fixum plenty supper heap quick.' His head vanished. The foreman gave the girl a crooked little smile and swung on his heel.

Buel Patchen looked down the table at Jean. 'You have no objections, Miss Austen?' His tone — his smile, brought the blood to her cheeks. The insult was too deliberate.

She chose to ignore it. 'Why should I object if Sing doesn't? Providing food is his job.' She smiled. 'We don't have visitors *every* day. I wonder what these Mexicans are like. Don Vicente Torres sounds rather grand. He must be a rich *ranchero*.'

'You don't need to meet them,' her step-uncle told her irritably.

'I haven't finished my coffee,' smiled the girl. 'Anyway, I want to see what the don is like.'

Harve was bringing the guests in through the front hall. Spurs jingling, sombreros in hand, they followed the foreman into the room. Buel rose from his chair, faced them with a welcoming smile. Tenn made no effort to rise. He flung the newcomers a sulky glance and returned his attention to his plate.

'I am honored,' greeted Buel. 'You will be seated, gentlemen. The cook is preparing your supper and you will soon be served.' He spoke in English, addressing the tall, elegantly garbed man who Harve's gesture indicated was Don Vicente.

'Our grateful thanks for your kindness,' responded the Mexican. He held his hat to his chest, bowed to the girl. 'Alas, my companions no spik Americano. I say their name to you.' He indicated the equally tall man by his side, 'My cosin, Don Alfredo Olveras.'

Don Alfredo Olveras bowed to Jean, smiled affably at Buel and flicked a curiously hard glance at Tenn busy with knife and fork.

Don Vicente finished introducing the other three men and they all sat down. Jean found herself between Don Vicente and his equally resplendent cousin. Her heart was beating madly under the muslin of her tight bodice. What did it mean? What was happening in Flying A's ranch-house dining room? Her head was in a whirl. She could hardly believe her eyes. Was she losing her mind?

She stole another surreptitious look at the tall dark *caballero* on her left. She was not mistaken. She would have known Ross Chaine anywhere — and this man, who Don Vicente Torres said was his cousin Alfredo, was Ross Chaine. Jean wanted to scream. She sat very still, her face as white as the muslin of her bodice.

Chapter

6

JEAN SEES A PICTURE

SING GEE appeared with a large platter of sizzling steaks. He deftly served the unexpected guests. He paused at Jean's shoulder. 'I bling piecee cake foh you,' he said with an inscrutable smile.

She understood what was in his mind. He sensed her desire to remain at the table. She gave the old cook a grateful look.

With an annoyed glance at his niece, Buel Patchen wasted no time in getting down to the purpose that had brought the Mexicans to the ranch.

'*Sí*,' Don Vicente Torres admitted in answer to Buel's blunt question, 'I was tell you 'ave *mucho* cow for make the sell. I wan' good cow for my rancho in Sonora.' He gesticulated. '*Basta!* A queek sell make all ready for you an' me, no? So I 'ave come, *señor*, for look at the cow you 'ave for sell.'

'Who sent you to Flying A?' questioned Buel.

Don Vicente mentioned the name of a Deming cattleman. Buel nodded. He knew the man. 'We can make a deal,' he said. 'For cash, of course.'

'For the cash, *sí*,' agreed the Mexican with a careless wave of his hand. 'Thees cash money weel be pay at Deming, where I wan' cow deliver pronto.'

'Why don't you drive direct to your rancho?' asked Buel suspiciously.

'I buy more cow in Deming,' explained Don Vicente. 'I 'old the cow on friend's rancho near Deming for maybe a mont'.'

'You always speak of cows,' Buel said dubiously. 'Do you mean you want only cows?'

'*Sí.*' Don Vicente's tone was firm. 'I wan' the cow for make leetle cow. I wan' buy five 'undred cow.'

Buel's eyes questioned Harve Welder. The foreman nodded. 'We can fix him up,' he said. "Sure we can. Take some time to round up that many young stock. Means combin' the canyons.' He stared speculatively at his coffee cup. 'I'd figger about a week.'

'A week!' Don Vicente showed signs of dismay. He lifted a protesting hand. 'I no stay so long as week! No! I am already *mucho* late for promise to meet beeg cowman in Deming.'

'We're both out of luck,' grunted the foreman.

Don Vicente apparently was not to be beaten by this matter of time. He looked at his tall cousin. 'It is a job for you, Alfredo,' he said in Spanish. 'You will remain here with our good friends and select these young cows for me.'

'Certainly, my cousin,' agreed Señor Olveras. 'But alas — this American language! How shall we arrange the difficulty? I do not speak this American language.'

Jean was conscious of a quick stirring of her blood. Something mysterious was indeed in the wind. This talk of buying Flying A cattle . . . Ross Chaine, posing as a Mexican and pretending he could not speak English.

With an effort she kept her eyes away from him, from all of them. She bent her head, toyed with the cake on her plate, heard Don Vicente's pleasantly accented voice translating Don Alfredo's words.

'My cosin say he weel stay for 'elp with the cow but my cosin no spik *Americano*.'

'I don't savvy Mex lingo good enough to get on with him,' Harve Welder admitted gruffly. 'Monte could speak Mex good, but he's dead.'

Buel Patchen's look went to Jean. He hesitated, said reluctantly, 'My niece went to school in El Paso. She speaks good Spanish.'

'Ah!' Don Vicente was radiant. 'You speak our Spanish, *señorita?*'

'Well enough.' The color was back in her cheeks.

'*Bueno!*' The Mexican beamed, broke into a flow of Spanish. 'All is well, Alfredo. The young lady will be your interpreter. You will stay as long as it is necessary for your task.' An indefinable note of warning crept into his voice. 'Be careful, my cosin — oh, most careful. The cows must be of the best and I beg you *not to be rash*.'

'Do not worry, Vicente.' The tall *caballero* was unperturbed. His glance flowed across the girl's averted face. 'It is very good of the young lady.'

Don Vicente looked at her briefly, a hint of amusement in his brown eyes. He returned his attention to her step-uncle. '*Bueno*,' he said in a satisfied voice. 'The *señorita* weel do the talk for my cosin. It ees all fix.' His eyes signaled the other three Mexicans and they rose from their chairs. 'We go now weeth *muchos gracias* for the nize eating.'

'You are welcome to stay the night,' cordially invited Buel.

'No, no.' The tall Mexican shook his head. 'I mooch 'urry to go Deming an' the night ees w'at you say still mooch yong, no?'

Tenn Patchen lifted a sullen face in a look at Señor Olveras who had risen from his chair. 'Don't like this monkey business,' he said to his father. 'Never had any use for damn greasers and don't like you throwin' this feller and Jean together.'

Jean flashed an alarmed look at Señor Olveras. His expression was politely questioning, the uncertain look of one who though not understanding the words is vaguely aware of an insult. Admiration for him thrilled the girl, and then doubts seized her. She was mistaken. This man could not be Ross Chaine. He actually *was* Señor Alfredo Olveras, a Mexican, and the cousin of Don Vicente Torres. She suddenly met his eyes, and her doubts faded. She was not mistaken.

As in a dream she heard her step-uncle's voice. 'I must apologize for my son, Señor Torres. He narrowly escaped losing his life in a bad accident today. He is suffering from pain and shock and is not responsible.' The look in Buel's eyes seemed to rock his son like a blow. Tenn got out of his chair, stood leaning on it heavily, his loose-lipped mouth sagging in a feeble grin. 'Reckon I'm loco,' he mumbled. 'Sure sorry I talked out of turn.' He moved uncertainly toward the kitchen door.

Don Vicente gave his cousin a curious look, tapped his head significantly. 'Our friend's son suffers from an accident.' he explained in Spanish.

There was the merest hint of a twinkle in Señor Olveras' eyes. 'It must have been a bad accident,' he commiserated politely. He avoided Jean's challenging look.

She spent a night of worry, trying to make up her mind about the pretended Don Alfredo Olveras. Was it her duty to unmask him, reveal his true identity to her step-uncle? It was plain he was up to some mischief. Don Vicente's assertion that he wanted to buy five hundred head of cattle was nothing more than a ruse to plant Ross Chaine at Flying A. Ross wanted to do some spying and no doubt the scheme was his.

Jean began to have doubts about the elegant Don Vicente Torres and his Sonora rancho. He was playing a rôle assigned him by Ross Chaine.

She tossed restlessly on the bed, too excited to sleep. She would have to make up her mind. Ross Chaine's look had told her that he knew she was not deceived. He was aware she had recognized him. Perhaps he was wondering why she had not immediately denounced him to her step-uncle. He had not shown any particular concern. Perhaps it was because of the presence of his Mexican friends. They could easily have surprised and overpowered Buel Patchen and Harve Welder.

She forced herself to think out every possible angle. The pretended deal for the five hundred head of cattle might be a cunningly conceived scheme to pull off a surprise raid. The roundup would mean the gathering of two or three thousand head. Ross Chaine would have his Mexican friends in some chosen place, ready to swoop down on the herd. The border was not too far away. The thing was possible.

Jean found herself rejecting this answer to the tormenting puzzle. Ross Chaine was planning mischief, but not against her. Stealing Flying A cattle meant he would be doing her an injury. She recalled his steady, reassuring look and took comfort.

Her bewilderment grew. He was not risking his life without good reason. She knew the Patchens and Harve Welder feared and hated the son of Jim Chaine. She had overheard their talk from time to time, always talk about the day when Ross Chaine would show up and make trouble for them. He was in the house now, probably asleep. She had only to say the word and these men would have his life.

The thought brought a shudder from the girl. She knew she couldn't tell her uncle the truth about the man who called himself Señor Alfredo Olveras.

Her mind refused to drop the matter. One thing was certain. Ross Chaine would have to explain the masquerade when she saw him in the morning. He would have to convince her of his lawful intentions. Otherwise she would insist that he leave. She would give him *that* chance — a chance to get away with his life.

She got out of bed and went to the open window. Moonlight silvered the landscape. She could see the big barn beyond the trees — the long line of tall haystacks. Uncle Buel was proud of those great haystacks — thousands of tons of winter feed. He was a shrewd and careful manager. Jean knew that he was responsible for those hundreds and hundreds of acres planted to alfalfa and grain crops. Buel Patchen was something of an engineer and had conceived and built the great dam at the headwaters of Red Creek.

A thoughtful, troubled look crept into the girl's eyes as she stared out at the moonlit night. She was not able to remember much of her father. A vague memory from baby days, that was all of him she had left. Buel Patchen had come to run the ranch after her father's death, and there had been trouble with Jim Chaine — something to do with water.

Jean went slowly back to the bed and got under the covers. She was conscious of a curious sick dread inside. What was that trouble between Buel Patchen and Ross Chaine's father? At the time it meant nothing to a five-year-old girl. She was only aware there had been trouble. Her uncle Buel would never talk about it — told her not to listen to silly stories.

As she lay there, Jean began to see a picture in her mind. A picture of a long green valley with cattle roaming the slopes. Bar Chain cattle. And now the valley was a drear desolation — the creek a wide sandy wash.

She stifled a little moan. Things were taking coherent form in her mind. Buel Patchen's great dam at the head-waters of Red Creek . . . Flying A's lush green fields fed by the waters of the West Fork. No more water went down Red Creek. The great dam turned the stream down the West Fork — and so had desolation claimed Red Creek's once fertile valley.

Jean knew now that she had the answer to Ross Chaine's presence at Flying A.

Chapter
7

A STRANGE ALLIANCE

SHE FOUND HIM leaning indolently against the high adobe wall and apparently admiring a clump of tall, sinuous ocotillos. He turned at her step, removed his hat and gestured at the ocotillos gracefully undulating in the early morning breeze.

'A beautiful thing,' he said in Spanish.

'My father planted it many years ago,' Jean told him.

Don Alfredo Olveras regarded her with a warm smile that showed a hint of white teeth. 'You speak good Spanish,' he complimented. Without giving her a chance to speak he gestured again at the scarlet-tipped ocotillos. 'A beautiful thing,' he repeated. 'They do not belong in a garden. Those savagely wild flame-tipped spears look best in their native desert hills. You should see them in a storm, writhing like tortured shapes from an inferno.'

'I have seen them,' Jean said stiffly. 'Seen them lots of times.' She looked at him steadily with unsmiling eyes. 'You needn't keep up this farce with me,' she added in a low, tense voice. 'You are Ross Chaine. Don't pretend with me.'

'Yes,' he admitted. 'I'm Ross Chaine. I knew last night you spotted Señor Olveras for a fraud.' The smile left him, and he added gravely. 'You could have told Buel Patchen.'

'Yes,' Jean said. 'I could have told him.'

'Why didn't you?'

'I've been thinking it over most of the night,' she broke off, looked uneasily over her shoulder. Buel Patchen was watching them from the porch steps. 'We mustn't seem too serious,' she said.

Ross threw back his head in an amused laugh. Jean joined him, turned a smiling face as her uncle strolled up. 'Señor Olveras says nice things about my Spanish,' she said, with a mixture of gaiety and mischief. 'I was not so polite and told him he must be very stupid not to be able to speak English like his cousin.'

Buel Patchen gave the pretended Señor Olveras a cordial nod. 'I'm the same way as Tenn,' he said smilingly. 'He don't savvy what I'm saying, but I never did like a greaser. Watch yourself with this one, Jean. Don't let him get fresh.' He went on down the path and disappeared through the gate into the yard.

Ross broke the silence, said a bit grimly, 'He'd like me a lot less if he knew what you know.'

Jean nodded. Her face was pale. 'I'm frightened,' she said. 'I've never been so frightened. Why did you do it? Why have you come here, pretending you're a Mexican?'

He was studying her intently. 'You've not answered *my* question,' he reminded. 'Why haven't you told Buel Patchen the truth about me?'

'I don't want them to kill you.' She spoke resentfully.

'Why should you care?' His tone was curious. 'I've been wondering why you took the trouble to ride over to Alamos yesterday.' He smiled. 'Haven't had a chance to thank you for that warning.'

She stared at him, a tiny frown puckering her smooth

brow. He passed very well as a Mexican, despite the auburn glint in his dark hair. It was not uncommon to see Mexicans with reddish hair. She had seen blue-eyed Mexicans.

'You're not answering my questions,' he reminded.

'I really can't,' Jean told him. 'It's all very confusing. I hardly slept a wink last night for thinking about it, trying to make up my mind.'

'You mean about telling your uncle who I am?'

She nodded. 'You needn't worry. I'm keeping your secret, Ross Chaine.'

He looked at her gravely. 'You're doing a lot of trusting.'

· 'You must tell me why you are here,' Jean said. 'Flying A ranch belongs to me. If you harm Flying A, you harm me. You can't expect me to let you do that.' She paused, glanced back at the house. 'You have had your breakfast?'

'An hour ago.' Ross lit the cigarette he had been making. His face wore a troubled look. It was going to be difficult to explain his main reason for the masquerade. It would be hard to convince this girl of Buel Patchen's sinister plans concerning her. She trusted Buel. He was her guardian and she had visible proof that he had done well by Flying A.

Ross recalled the snatches of conversation between father and son under the upstairs window of the Alamos Hotel. He had overheard enough to arouse grave concern for the girl's safety. *I don't care how you do it . . . any way you want . . . make sure she's your wife before the year is out . . . she'll soon be twenty-one — her own mistress.* And Tenn Patchen's rejoinder — its ugly implication. *I'll put the Patchen iron on that smooth hide of hers.*

She broke into his reflections. 'Don't look so grim.' He saw her nervous glance at the gate. Tenn Patchen pushed in from the yard. 'My cousin's coming. I think they want you.' She finished rapidly in a low voice. 'You've got to make believe awfully hard that you really are Señor Olveras — or they'll suspect something is wrong.'

Tenn came tramping across the grass. His perceptible limp gave Ross a secret satisfaction. He smiled politely. '*Buenos dias, señor*,' he greeted.

'Sure,' grunted Tenn, 'howdy and to hell with you.' He grinned at the girl.

Jean had difficulty in keeping her indignation from eyes and voice. She forced a light laugh. 'You're plain stupid,' she said.

'The greaser don't savvy what I say,' grinned Tenn. 'Sure gives me a kick — insultin' him to his face.'

Ross was smiling blandly, said something in Spanish. Tenn looked at him blankly. 'What's the greaser talkin' about?' he asked Jean.

She smiled sweetly, too sweetly. 'Señor Olveras wants to know about your accident yesterday. He wants to know what happened.'

'None of his damn business,' Tenn said with a sour look at the pseudo Señor Olveras. His brows wrinkled in a puzzled frown and he continued to stare at the tall man under the Mexican hat. Jean held her breath, conscious of a sudden terror. Tenn's next words reassured her. 'Harve says to tell the greaser we're headin' over to Painted Canyon if he wants to come along with us.'

Ross smiled in his best Mexican manner when Jean translated. He would be delighted, he agreed. He was indeed eager to get at the business entrusted to him by his cousin.

'You'll have to come along with us,' Tenn told the girl. He scowled. 'Sure hate for you to be foolin' round with the feller. Nothin' else we can do, though. Damn Monte for lettin' Ross Chaine get the drop on him. Monte could handle Spanish talk good as a Mex.'

'You needn't wait for us,' Jean told him. 'I've got to change my clothes.'

Tenn started back toward the yard gate. 'We'll have a bunch rounded up by the time you make the canyon. Be sure you get there by noon.'

'We'll be there,' she promised.

The gate banged behind him. Jean looked at Ross. 'I thought for a moment that he recognized you. He stared so hard.'

'He didn't have much of a chance for a good look at me yesterday,' Ross reassured. 'I've changed a lot since Tenn and I used to play Indians together.'

'Tenn spoke of your red hair,' she said. 'I don't remember you at all. I was too young, but Tenn seems to think of you as a redhead.'

'Tenn still goes by his kid memory,' grinned Ross. 'My hair never was really red, but you know how kids are. Just because I was known as that red-headed Chaine kid, I'm still red-headed to Tenn. Anyway, growing up has made my hair a lot darker.'

'I turned cold all over,' Jean said with a shudder. 'I'm terrified to think of what will happen if — if they guess.' She added half-angrily, 'I wish you would go away — before something *does* happen.'

Ross shook his head. 'I have reasons for staying.'

'I want to know those reasons.' Her breath quickened. 'You can't expect me to — to do this for you — and not know your reasons.'

He looked at her unhappily. 'No,' he said in a low voice. 'I suppose not — and yet I'd rather you didn't press me. I can only say the reasons concern you as well as me.'

Her astonishment was complete. 'Concern me?' Her tone was incredulous.

'I'll tell you this much,' he went on with some reluctance. 'I know more about Buel Patchen than you do.'

'That's nonsense,' Jean exclaimed angrily. 'I've known Uncle Buel since I was a small child. He's been almost the same as a father to me.'

'You know only one side of him,' asserted Ross. He hesitated. 'Or have you noticed another side of him lately — now that you are nearly twenty-one?' He smiled. 'I remember you told me at Alamos yesterday that you were nearly twenty-one.'

Jean was silent, her expression thoughtful. She *had* noticed something different about her uncle of late, especially when she spoke of the approaching birthday that would end his legal guardianship. His irritability at such times, his glowering looks at his son.

She broke the silence. 'I don't see how my personal affairs can possibly interest you.' She gave him a long, steady look. 'I'm afraid you really must be more frank if I'm to go on with — with this deception.'

He was silent, and she saw a look of worry shadow his face. She recalled the picture that her troubled thoughts had conjured up during the long, sleepless night. The picture that was the answer to Ross Chaine's presence at Flying A. Not an entirely illuminating answer. She was still in the dark as to what it all portended. And now the picture was clouded by his disturbing statement that she, too, was concerned with the mysterious reason that brought him masquerading as a Mexican to Flying A.

'I must be crazy,' she exclaimed. 'Anyway, I'm quite sure *you* are crazy.'

'We should be starting for Painted Canyon,' he reminded dryly.

·'I'll be ready in a few minutes.' Jean suddenly smiled. 'You haven't a nerve in your body, have you? I never knew what coolness was before. You're nothing but a piece of ice. You make me afraid.' She fled toward the house.

He watched her, fingers busy with paper and tobacco, his expression sober. She was right in demanding complete frankness on his part. He would be obliged to tell her about the conversation he had overheard between Buel Patchen and his son. There was a chance she would not scoff at the story. She seemed disturbed when he had asked if she had noticed any change in her uncle's manner of late.

He made his way down the walk and pushed through the gate into the yard. A man was saddling the same red mare he had noticed under the girl at Alamos.

Ross threw him a nod and went on toward the stable. The man stared after him curiously. He was an old man, small and wiry and bow-legged. He wore a huge drooping mustache stained at the corners with tobacco juice and there was a speculative look in his keen blue eyes as he watched the tall stranger disappear into the barn.

Ross was well aware of that speculative look. He wondered if Breezy Hessen could possibly have recognized him after fifteen years. Breezy was a hang-over from Bill Austen's time. He had always been with Flying A. A first-rate cowman in his day, a top-hand. It was obvious the infirmities of old age had relegated Breezy to the lowly post of choreman.

He saddled his horse and led the animal into the yard. Jean was already in her saddle. She had changed her skirt for a pair of well-worn overalls. Ross gave her an approving look. He liked the way she sat her saddle. He heard old Breezy Hessen's voice.

'Looks like an LK bronc you've got there, mister.'

'Señor Olveras doesn't speak English,' hurriedly broke in the girl. Her frowning gaze was on the tall roan under Ross. 'Breezy's right,' she added in Spanish. 'That's an LK horse you're riding. I know that brand. Lally and Kinners. They have a ranch south of Dos Cruces.'

Ross shook his head. 'Is there something wrong?' He put the question anxiously. 'My cousin picked him up in Dos Cruces.' He frowned. 'Is it wrong to have this horse? He is a good horse.'

'Nothing wrong,' assured Jean. 'I mean it's all right if your cousin paid money for him, or hired him.'

Ross gestured at the interested choreman. 'Tell him this horse is not stolen. Tell him a price was paid. He seems curious.'

'Breezy knows Buckshot and Pete,' smiled the girl. 'He was wondering why a stranger should be riding one of their horses.'

She explained the situation to Breezy's satisfaction and they started away. 'Breezy's been with Flying A from the time my father branded his first cow,' she told Ross. She hesitated. 'He's about the one man left in the outfit that I really trust. Breezy would do anything for me.' She laughed unsteadily. 'I shouldn't say things like that — make you think I don't like Harve and the others.'

'I'll tell you something,' Ross said quietly, 'if your father were alive today, Harve Welder wouldn't be bossing the Flying A outfit.' He looked at her, a hint of compassion in his eyes. 'I remember Bill Austen. He was my father's best friend, and like my father, he was murdered.'

Jean reined the red mare to a halt, stared up at him with shocked eyes. '*Murdered! My father — murdered?*'

'It's one of the reasons that has brought me back to Red Creek Valley. I want to bring the murderers of my father and your father to justice.' He spoke bitterly. 'I want to see them hanged.'

She continued to look at him, horror in her dark eyes. 'Who — who murdered my father?' She asked the question faintly.

'I know — but I've got to find the proof.' Ross paused, his face an inscrutable mask. 'I'm not saying more until I have the proof.'

'I've got to know!' cried the girl.

'You must trust me,' Ross said brusquely. 'You must trust me as you trust old Breezy.' A smile softened his face. 'I was scared the old-timer would spot me. Breezy is hard to fool.'

Jean looked at him thoughtfully. 'We *can* trust Breezy,' she suggested hopefully. 'I feel — well — a bit overcome with all this business. I'd like Breezy to know about you. He may suspect the truth about Señor Olveras anyway, and make trouble.'

Ross hesitated. 'I'd want Buckshot and Pete to have a talk with him first,' he finally replied.

Jean's eyes widened. 'You mean Buckshot and Pete are your friends . . . and know about this masquerade?'

'You bet they're my friends.' Ross chuckled. 'Buckshot and Pete helped think up the scheme. They and Vicente Torres and Lico Estrada.' He touched the roan's thick mane. 'Now you understand about this LK horse.'

'Yes,' she said, 'I'm beginning to understand a lot of things.' A bitter note crept into her voice. 'I — I feel like a traitor — talking to you like this.'

'You mean because of Buel Patchen?'

'Yes — and it's an awful feeling. I know you hate him. He hates you, and he'll do you harm if he can. Kill you, perhaps.' She spoke unhappily. 'I don't understand what it is all about. I only know that my uncle fears you more than any other man alive. And you hate him — and Buckshot and Pete hate him. I've seen the way they look at him, as if he were something poisonous.'

Ross kept his eyes away from her. He knew she was fighting desperately to keep the tears back. He said quietly, 'Buckshot and Pete are good men. They wouldn't be down on your uncle without cause.'

'That's what worries me,' Jean confessed. 'And now you come along and it gets worse and worse. There are things I don't know, or understand . . . terrible things . . . and I feel like a traitor because of a dreadful certainty that my uncle is to blame. I want to take his side but something won't let me. Buckshot and Pete are too honest to be against him without good reason.'

'It's time you knew the truth about your uncle,' Ross said in a hard voice.

'Go on,' she said in a voice as hard as his own. 'Don't keep anything back. I've a right to know.' Then, sensing his reluctance, 'Buel Patchen is only an uncle by marriage. He married my mother's sister and she's been dead for years. Tenn is the son of his first wife.' She made a wry face. 'I'd hate to think Tenn was a relation of mine. I despise him.'

'You make things easier,' Ross acknowledged. He would say no more, despite her half angry insistence. The situation was a difficult one. He felt the need of advice from Buckshot and Pete. Jean had said she trusted the two LK men and Ross felt she would believe from them what she would doubt from himself. If all went well, he was to meet them at the old Bar Chain place that night. He had already framed a suitable excuse that should satisfy Buel Patchen of the need to go to Dos Cruces Old Town for further instructions his cousin Vicente had promised to leave for him.

He told Jean of the plan in his mind. 'I wish you could go with me,' he said. 'I'd like you to have a talk with Buckshot and Pete.'

'I've *got* to go with you,' Jean declared. 'I must know the truth. Buckshot and Pete will tell me — if you won't.'

'I'd rather they did.' Ross was frowning. 'Don't see how you can get away from the ranch without arousing suspicion.'

'I can manage it . . . I've *got* to.' Her chin lifted. 'I'm not Buel Patchen's prisoner.'

Ross smiled skeptically. 'I don't see Buel Patchen letting you go out for an evening ride with Señor Olveras,' he pointed out.

She was thinking hard, and suddenly her face lighted. 'I've got it . . . I'll take the hounds for a coyote chase. I've done it lots of times. There'll be no reason for them to suspect I'm meeting you . . . that I'm riding to Bar Chain with you.'

Ross considered the suggestion doubtfully. 'It may be late before we get back to the ranch. After midnight.'

Jean brushed the objection aside. 'I'll say I got lost and had to wait for the moon. There's a late moon. It's easy enough to get lost in this country,' she added.

They left the mesa and followed a trail that twisted down a rugged slope. Jean gestured with her quirt. 'Painted Canyon,' she said. 'Harve's been busy, judging from the size of the herd he's gathered.' She broke off, looked at her companion curiously. 'Is this all a game? Is Don Vicente really buying five hundred head of cows?'

'No,' replied Ross. He gave her an enigmatic smile.

She halted her horse, her expression indignant. 'You mean it's only a ruse to get you onto the ranch? It's not fair to the boys — making them round up a lot of cattle for the fun of it.'

His smile widened. 'You asked if Don Vicente is buying the cattle. I said *no* because the purchaser happens to be myself. I can't appear in the deal openly, so I'm buying the cows under cover of Don Vicente's name.'

Jean stared at him. 'It's very mysterious,' she said finally. 'What are you going to do with the cows?'

'Do you remember what I told you at Alamos?'

'You said you were back in Red Creek Valley to stay.'

He nodded. 'To stay!' he echoed. 'There'll be cows again in Red Creek Valley, all of them wearing the old Bar Chain on their hides.'

'In the valley?' She looked troubled. 'There's no grass in the valley. It's dead . . . the Bar Chain is dead.'

'I'm here to bring life back to the valley.' He spoke grimly. 'The Bar Chain will live again.'

'In the meantime where will you find range? You can't range cattle in the valley — not yet.'

'Buel Patchen agreed to make delivery in Deming,' Ross reminded. 'Don't you worry. I've ten thousand acres of range under lease near Deming.'

She looked at him, a hint of a smile on her lips. 'You've got nerve, Ross Chaine,' she said. 'But it's the kind of nerve I like.' A note of wonder crept into her voice. 'It's a crazy thing I'm doing, making myself your ally.'

'You won't give me away to Buel Patchen?'

'Not in a hundred years.' Jean's chin went up. 'After all, they're *my* cattle you're buying. Not Buel Patchen's.' Her smile broke into an amused laugh. 'I'd like to tell old Breezy, though. He'd laugh himself to death if he knew of the trick you're playing on Buel Patchen.'

'I wouldn't tell him too soon,' warned Ross. 'We've got to be sure of Breezy.'

'Maybe you're right,' Jean assented as they started their horses across the tule-covered flats. 'I won't risk your secret, Ross.'

He gave her a quick glance, unutterably pleased by the sound of his name on her lips.

They would have been surprised at Breezy Hessen's deep cogitations about Jean's Mexican friend and the roan horse that wore the LK brand. Breezy was doing some hard thinking, and when Breezy got down to a job of real thinking he usually found what he was looking for.

It took him an hour to come to a decision, but finally his mind was made up. He went to his bunk, retrieved an ancient long-barrelled Colt from the blankets, buckled on his gun-belt and slipped the big forty-five into its holster.

'Figgered to fool me,' he muttered to himself as he made his way to the horse corral. 'Huh! I'm mebbe stove up some, but I've got plenty brains left and I reckon time's come to use 'em.'

He got a rope over a vicious-eyed rangy buckskin, threw on a saddle and rode out of the yard. The gleam in his eyes would have told anyone who knew him that Breezy Hessen was in a fighting mood and *going places*.

Chapter

8

RENDEZVOUS AT BAR CHAIN

THE OLD RANCH HOUSE stood back in a grove of trees, a reproachful reminder of fifteen years of neglect. Weeds choked the garden and fallen trees, and over all lay the stillness of death and desolation. There remained hardly a pane of glass in the windows, but the walls were still sound. Jim Chaine had built them sturdily of stone and adobe and good yellow pine logs. The wings formed three sides of a square and represented Bar Chain's growing periods. What was now the kitchen had been the original ranch house, its adobe walls more than three feet thick. A wife and baby boy had called for another wing and Jim Chaine's bull teams had hauled the pine logs down from the high mountains. Years later his Mexicans had cut rough granite slabs for the third wing and placed the beams of polished yellow pine in the ceiling of the big living room.

Memories of those days when he was foreman of Bar Chain lay heavily on Pete Lally as he rode into the yard and drew rein near the sagging gate in the high patio wall.

'It's sure a crime,' he said to his companion. 'Bar Chain was murdered along with poor Jim. It gives me the creeps, Buckshot, just to look at that old house with its windows all shot out.'

Buckshot stared at the house looming darkly under the starlight. 'Looks awful sick,' he agreed, 'but there's a change due, now that Ross is back in the valley.' His glance went to the palomino he had on a lead-rope. 'Let's take a look in the barn.'

Pete shook his head. 'We've got to find a safer place for that horse. No tellin' but what Patchen keeps this place scouted. The barn won't do, Buckshot.'

'Used to be a hideout cave in the gully down below the spring house,' recalled Buckshot, harking back to the days when he was Bar Chain's top-hand rider. 'Remember, Pete? Me and you helped fix it up for Ross when he was a kid. You give him that skin from the bear you shot to lay on the floor. Used to play there a lot, Ross did.'

'Let's take a look-see,' suggested Pete. 'That cave would be a bang-up hideaway for this palomino horse. Was awful well hidden in a tangle of cat's-claw.'

They followed along the high patio wall and came to a prostrate gate in the yard fence. An owl rose silently from a post and drifted away on soundless wings. Buckshot swore softly as he pushed through the opening. 'Went floatin' off like a ghost,' he muttered. 'What's wrong?' he added with a quick glance over his shoulder at Pete who was following with the palomino.

'Reckon it was the owl startled him,' Pete said in a low voice. 'Threw up his head the way a bronc does when he hears somethin'.'

They held their horses motionless, eyes fixed on the palomino. No sound broke the stillness and the horse showed no further sign of nervousness.

'Must have been the owl,' finally agreed Buckshot. He started his horse and the two men rode on through the wild tangle of trees and brush that stretched for several hundred yards in front of the ranch house.

Neither of them saw the shadowy form that moved across the yard they had just left. The palomino, following on Pete's lead-rope, twitched sensitive ears. Pete and Buckshot were too engrossed in locating the old cave to notice.

It took them close on half an hour to work their way into the cave hidden behind the thicket of cat's-claw that covered the side of the gully.

'Room enough for a dozen broncs in this place,' Pete said in a satisfied voice. 'Wouldn't nobody ever think to look for a horse here.'

'Let's get back to the yard,' Buckshot said. 'About time Ross is showin' up — if nothin' ain't happened to him.'

'Ross is awful smart,' Pete reminded in his slow, quiet voice. 'He ain't one to get rattled easy.'

'There'll be hell to pay if Buel Patchen gets wise to this Olveras bus'ness,' prophesied Buckshot. 'I used to think Jim Chaine was the coolest hombre in ten states, but Ross has him beat.'

They found their horses and rode back to the big yard. Something stirred near the corral fence as they reached the fallen gate, a harsh, whispering voice struck at their startled ears.

'Hold your broncs dead still an' keep your hands in sight.'

The partners obeyed, checked their horses to a standstill, stiffened in their saddles.

'Won't be no trouble if you don't start none,' assured the unseen whisperer.

Buckshot found his voice. 'What do you want?' he asked. 'Who in the hell are you, skulkin' back there in the shadows?'

'I'm wanting some answers to some questions.' The hidden speaker had moved closer. Something familiar in his voice brought a startled grunt from Pete Lally.

He called out angrily, 'What's the idee, Breezy? Are you loco?'

'You know me, Pete, an' you know I ain't no play-actor. I mean bus'ness an' don't you get foolish an' go for your gun.'

'All right, all right,' soothed Pete. 'We're just some surprised, Breezy. We've always got along good together, even if you are on the Flying A payroll.'

'Sure,' agreed Buckshot. 'Speak your mind, Breezy. We're listenin'.'

There was a silence. They sensed that Breezy was having some difficulty in finding suitable words for his question.

'I want a yes or no. Is Ross Chaine back in the valley?' Breezy put the question in a hard, rasping voice that showed he was in no mood for equivocation.

Another silence, a long one. Pete and Buckshot exchanged troubled looks. It was Pete who finally spoke.

'We don't tell Flying A what we know about Ross Chaine.' Mild reproof tinged his deliberate voice. 'You should know us better than that, Breezy.'

'I ain't a fool,' retorted the old cowboy. 'There's a feller at the ranch that calls hisself Señor Olveras. I know he ain't. He's Ross Chaine, an' I figger to find out just what he's up to — ridin' round with Jean an' pretendin' to be a Mex. Answer that one, Pete Lally.'

'If this Olveras feller is Ross Chaine like you claim, he's up to no harm so far as the girl is concerned,' Pete answered. 'You know I don't lie, Breezy. You can take my oath that Ross don't mean any harm to the girl or to what belongs to her.'

Breezy pondered for a moment. 'You mean it's Buel Patchen he's after?' His voice crackled with suppressed excitement.

Buckshot Kinners answered him. 'You've been with

Flying A a lot of years, Breezy,' he said acidly. 'You take your orders from Buel Patchen and for all we know it's him that sent you gunnin' for us tonight. We ain't answerin' your question.'

'I had to do it, fellers,' Breezy's voice was almost pleading. 'Buel Patchen's my boss, like you say. I had to get the drop on you afore you got hostile an' went for your guns. You'd kill me quick as a wink if you thought I was hornin' in to spoil Ross Chaine's play.'

Their grim silence was answer enough for him. He broke into a torrent of words. 'I'll tell you somethin'. I've stuck with Flying A ever since Bill Austen's death on account of Bill's gal. I wasn't leavin' her alone with that damn wolf she calls her uncle, which he ain't. I'm the only real friend Jean's got on that place an' I'm stickin' with her come hell an' high water.'

'You mean that, Breezy?' Relief touched Pete Lally's deep voice.

'Sure I mean it!' shouted the old Flying A man. 'You just said on your oath that Ross ain't meanin' harm to the gal, nor to what's hers. I'm believin' you, Pete. I'd sooner take your word than a gove'ment bond. If it's them Patchen skunks Ross is after I'm sidin' him.' His shadowy form moved in close to them and they saw the gun in his hand slide into sagging holster.

The partners got down from their horses. Breezy gripped their hands. 'We'll shake on it,' he chuckled. 'I'm hell bent for any play that'll bust the Patchens loose from Flying A.'

'How did you get track of us?' queried Pete in a worried tone. 'Didn't know we left sign pointin' to Bar Chain.'

'Picked up your sign in Dos Cruces,' Breezy explained. 'Was in the White Buffalo an' Rick DeSalt said you'd been in for a drink an' just left. I moseyed over to Stack

Jimson's livery barn. Stack said you'd come an' got your horses an' rode off. Hadn't been gone fifteen minutes, he said. So I got busy huntin' sign. Picked you up headin' west into the valley. Wasn't no trick to keep you in sight.'

Buckshot's hand lifted in a gesture for silence. The three men listened tensely. 'Horses!' Buckshot said. He gave his partner a worried look. The same thought was in their minds. Ross was to have come alone to the rendezvous, but those approaching hoofbeats warned that more than one rider was entering the yard — an ominous sign that spelled trouble.

Pete's big hand gripped Breezy's arm fiercely. 'You're sure nobody trailed you from Dos Cruces?' He bent his face in a hard look at the Flying A man.

Buckshot muttered a low exclamation. 'It's all right, Pete.' He was staring across the yard at two shapes that suddenly stood out under the starlight. 'One of 'em is Ross . . . but who in hell is the other feller?'

Breezy took a look and they saw amazement spread over his weathered old face. 'By damn . . . it's Jean with him!' Before they could stop him he was hurrying across the yard at a run, leather chaps slapping at his bowed legs.

Jean stifled an astonished cry as she recognized the Flying A man. She stared with incredulous eyes. He came to a standstill, amazement still plain on his face as he returned the look.

Pete and Buckshot hurried up, curiosity, bewilderment in their eyes. Ross relaxed. The sight of Breezy Hessen had startled him. He was mystified, but reassured by the presence of the two LK men.

'Miss Austen wants to have a talk with you,' he said in a matter-of-fact voice. 'She knows who I am,' he added. His look went questioningly to the Flying A man who was breathing hard, astonished gaze still fixed on the girl. 'What's Breezy doing here?'

'Breezy is all right, Ross.' It was Buckshot who spoke. 'Breezy is sidin' with us in this fight.' Amusement touched his voice. 'He spotted who you were back at the ranch. Says he knew the moment he got a close look.'

'You bet I spotted you,' grinned Breezy. 'I'd know Jim Chaine's boy any place.' His gaze returned challengingly to the girl. 'You sure got me guessin',' he added reproachfully.

'I had to come, Breezy. There are things I must know.' She slid from her saddle, stood looking gravely at the old Flying A man. 'Maybe I'm crazy, but I don't think so.'

'Not crazy, gal ... just wakin' up.' Breezy's voice was a hard rasp. 'Been a heap o' trouble pilin' up for you what with Buel Patchen's schemin' an' that whelp of his swingin' his rope for you.'

Jean's face paled under the starlight. She looked uncertainly at the intent faces watching her. Pete Lally broke the silence.

'No call for you to get scared, Jean,' he said in his deliberate, reassuring voice. 'We're your friends and we aim to do some house cleanin' for you. We'll maybe stir up a stink but you won't be hurt none. You bank on us, Jean.'

She smiled up at him. 'I believe you, Pete.' She drew a long breath. 'I — I've had a feeling there is something terribly wrong — something I couldn't put a finger on. It's worried — frightened me.'

Buckshot Kinners, always practical, made a suggestion. 'Let's get back some place in the trees. Kind of open out here in the yard.' He looked at the Flying A man. 'You watch the horses, Breezy. Hold 'em close to the patio gate and keep a sharp lookout.'

Ross swung down and holding Jean's hand, followed the LK partners through the patio gate into the garden.

The girl stared about curiously as they went up the path to the porch steps. 'I haven't been here since I was a baby,' she confided to them. 'Uncle Buel always told me to keep away from Bar Chain. He used to frighten me . . . told me the house was haunted.'

Buckshot glanced back at her. 'About time you quit callin' that wolf your uncle,' he said harshly.

Ross felt her hand tremble in his. He pressed it reassuringly. Her eyes lifted in a quick, grateful look.

They sat down on the wide porch steps, and Pete Lally turned a quizzical gaze on Ross. 'How's the cow deal makin' out?' he drawled. 'Looks like Señor Olveras has got Buel Patchen fooled proper.'

'The deal is moving fast, Pete,' Ross replied with a laugh. 'We'll have the herd started for Deming in a day or two, at the rate Harve Welder gathered cows today.'

Buckshot laughed softly. 'Got news for you, Ross. We had a talk with Don Vicente this mornin' . . . met him at Lico's place. He said to tell you his vaqueros will be waitin' for the cows in Tres Piñones Pass. He's scared Buel Patchen will tumble to you and go back on the deal.'

'*Bueno!*' Ross grinned, then looked at Jean, who was listening attentively, a hint of worry in her eyes. 'You're thinking about the money Don Vicente is to turn over for the cows?'

'They are my cattle,' she answered a bit defiantly. 'Buel Patchen is my guardian, but they're my Flying A cattle. I'll soon be of age and I hate to see all that money get into his hands.'

Ross hesitated, said slowly, 'Buel will never see that money, Jean. Or if he does, he won't keep it long.'

Jean was puzzled. 'Don Vicente agreed to pay for

them on delivery at Deming,' she reminded. 'If nothing happens to keep them from reaching Deming,' she added dubiously.

'Them cows will get to Deming, you bet,' Buckshot assured her with a cold smile. 'Don Vicente's vaqueros will take care of *that* part of the deal. Buel's outfit won't have a chance to help themselves. They'll go along with the cows like good little boys.' His eyes questioned Ross. 'Don't savvy how you can stop Buel from gettin' Don Vicente's money for 'em though.'

'I've figured it out,' Ross explained. 'One of three men will be in Deming to get the cash from Don Vicente, Buel Patchen, or Tenn — or maybe Harve Welder. Whichever one, it doesn't matter. The money will be taken from him before he gets home.'

'Sounds like highway robbery,' commented Pete Lally gravely.

'It *is* robbery,' asserted Jean in a dismayed voice.

Ross gestured carelessly. 'Sounds a bit high-handed,' he admitted. 'Not robbery, though. Just a little precaution to keep Buel Patchen from stealing what is yours, Jean. You'd never see the color of that money if Buel gets his paws on it. You will see it if we take it away from him and place it in the Deming bank for safekeeping until you are of age and can claim it.'

'I'll take back what I said.' She gave him an oddly searching look. 'No wonder Buel Patchen is afraid of you.'

Buckshot's voice broke the silence that fell. 'Tell her about that talk you listened to in Alamos,' he said to Ross. 'It's time Jean knows what Buel is up to.' He looked at the girl and she saw that his eyes were blazing. 'Buel's been stealing you blind for years, and he's planning worse things. He's fixin' to get hold of Flying A for his own.'

The shock of his words seemed to turn the girl to stone. She sat motionless on the step, her face pale under a glimmer of starlight through the trees. 'What was it you heard in Alamos, Ross?' She spoke with stiff, cold lips.

Ross told her of the conversation he had overheard between Buel and his son. She listened without comment until he finished.

'I'm not surprised,' she said after a brief silence. 'Tenn has been getting worse every day.'

'He's a skunk,' declared Buckshot Kinners savagely.

'Worse than a pizen rattler,' agreed his big partner. 'You and me should be havin' a talk with him, Buckshot.'

'Usin' bullets for words,' growled Buckshot. He swore softly but feelingly. 'Excuse me, Jean. Just thinkin' of that Patchen hombre fills me to burstin' with profane langwidge.'

She smiled faintly, touched by their very real anguish and wrath on her account. 'I could swear myself,' she told them. 'Don't mind me, Buckshot. Swear all you want.' She was studying Ross intently as she spoke. 'Did you expect to find me mixed up in your plans when you came back to Red Creek Valley to put Bar Chain on the map again?' she asked.

'Not to this extent,' he confessed. 'I wouldn't have known how bad things are with you but for that talk I overheard in Alamos. I didn't know how you would feel toward me, but as I told you, what I learned in Alamos is one of the reasons that determined me to visit Flying A. I had to warn you.' His voice hardened. 'Showing up at the ranch as Señor Olveras helped kill two birds with one stone. Buel is going to have the shock of his life when he learns those cattle will soon wear the Bar Chain on their hides. You'll be on your guard — now that you know their miserable plot.'

'You haven't told me enough,' Jean faltered. 'You said my father was — was murdered — like your father.' Her voice broke. 'Why — why do you think he was murdered? — And who murdered him?'

'You tell her, Pete.' Ross seemed suddenly reluctant to talk.

'Folks said how your pa was shot accidental when he was crawlin' through a wire fence with his rifle.' Pete's skeptical tone showed his own disbelief of the story. 'Bill Austen was never one to be careless with a gun. I seen the wound and it just couldn't have happened like Harve Welder claimed.'

'Harve Welder!' Her eyes dilated. 'You mean ——'

'I'm not sayin' Harve killed him,' Pete went on. 'I'm only claimin' it wasn't no accident that killed your pa. We ain't knowin' the truth, but shouldn't wonder but what Harve could tell us — if he wanted to talk.'

Jean looked thoughtful. 'Buel Patchen wasn't with us at the ranch,' she said. 'He was living in Socorro. Mother sent for him.'

The LK partners exchanged looks. Ross made no comment, but a hard gleam sprang to his eyes. Jean studied their faces. 'You're hiding something from me,' she exclaimed.

Buckshot answered her. 'Been talk goin' round that Harve and Buel used to be pardners down on the border some place. Accordin' to this talk they was mixed up with a rustlin' outfit runnin' cattle across the border . . . had to hightail it away from there in a hurry when the gang was broke up.'

'Oh!' Jean's tone was shocked.

Buckshot continued. 'Harve headed over this way and your pa hired him. It wasn't until after your pa was shot that Harve got to be foreman of Flying A. Buel come along, like you said, and he made Harve foreman.'

'That's the story, Jean,' Pete Lally affirmed in his deep kindly voice. 'You're a grown woman now and can do your own thinkin'.'

'Yes,' she said in a low voice. 'I can do my own thinking.' Her look went to Ross. 'Has this story anything to do with your father — his — his murder?'

He nodded. 'We think so, Jean. It all ties up.' He paused, added quietly, 'My father was shot down on these steps. Nobody saw the killer, but he must have been somebody my father knew and apparently trusted.'

Jean repressed a shudder, glanced about uneasily. 'Buel told me the place was haunted,' she said again. 'He used to frighten me with a story about a great tall figure all in white seen under the trees in the moonlight.'

Ross kept his eyes away from Pete and Buckshot, but he sensed their secret amusement. They knew as well as himself what had given start to the rumor that Bar Chain was haunted. The LK partners were friends of The Prophet and had not betrayed their knowledge that he was the supposed ghost. It was just as well to let the rumor persist. It was all part of The Prophet's plan. The ghost story had served a good purpose, saved the old ranch house from molesting hands.

Jean was speaking again, her voice puzzled. 'What became of your father's cattle, Ross?'

'Stolen,' he answered laconically.

She questioned Pete Lally. 'You were the foreman here?'

The big man reddened, looked uncomfortable. Ross spoke for him. 'Pete wasn't to blame,' he said. 'No use going into it now. It was devil's work. The man who planned it had the brains of a devil.'

'And you can never get them back?' Jean's mind was on the stolen cattle.

'Not a chance . . . not after fifteen years.' Ross suddenly smiled at her. 'I'm not worrying about the stolen cattle. I'm back in this country to do another job.'

She remembered what he had told her in Alamos. *I am home to stay . . . there'll be life again in Alamos . . . in the valley.*

'It's a big job,' she said. 'You will do it. I'm sure of it.'

They sat there on the porch steps for nearly an hour while the three men discussed plans. Jean listened attentively. Some of the things said sent chills of apprehension through her. The proof they desired still seemed out of reach. A link was missing in the sinister chain of events that had wrought death and destruction in the valley. She heard the name of Rick DeSalt mentioned, and they spoke of Lico Estrada. She knew Rick DeSalt was a saloon man, a friend of Buel Patchen's. She knew too that Lico Estrada lived in Old Town — that he owned the *cantina*. She gathered that Lico was a man these men trusted.

The late moon lifted, sent a silver gleam through the trees. Ross looked at the girl. 'Time you're heading back to the ranch,' he said.

Breezy came from the shadowed wall with the horses. 'Was beginnin' to think the ghost had got you,' he grumbled crustily.

Somewhat to Jean's surprise Ross made no move toward his roan horse. 'Aren't you coming?' she asked.

'Breezy will see you home,' he replied. 'I'd have trailed you back, but there's no need now you've got Breezy. Gives me a chance to pull off a little business I've in mind.'

She looked at him wonderingly, saw the moonlight reflected dancing gleams in his eyes — laughter lurked in them. 'You're up to something,' she accused uneasily.

'Maybe,' he admitted with a sudden smile. He paused, added thoughtfully, 'You and Breezy better rig up a story for Buel if he's on the lookout for you and wants to know where you've been.'

'I'll say I got lost . . . and the hounds made for home without me.' Jean laughed, glanced at Breezy. 'How did you find me, Breezy?'

The Flying A man chuckled. 'I'll tell 'em I was headed for the ranch from Dos Cruces an' run smack into you, bawlin' your eyes out 'cause you got lost an' was scared the coyotes would gang up on you.' His tone sobered. 'Can prove I was in Dos Cruces if Buel acts up. Was in the White Buffalo an' spoke to Rick DeSalt. Rick can back me up if Buel gets nosey.'

'Alibis for both of you,' Ross said with a contented nod. 'All right, you two. Get going.'

Jean hesitated. 'What about you? Buel will wonder what has happened to Señor Olveras.'

'Señor Olveras will be safe and sound in his room when Sing Gee rings the breakfast gong,' reassured Ross. He looked at Breezy. 'If Buel asks if you saw me in Dos Cruces you tell him you did. Tell him you saw me heading over to Old Town. I'm supposed to be in Old Town.'

'I'll fix it,' promised Breezy. He rode off with the girl, a wide grin on his weather-beaten face.

Ross watched them disappear across the moonlit stretch beyond the trees, then turned and met the inquiring eyes of Pete and Buckshot.

'What's this bus'ness you figger to pull off?' Pete asked bluntly.

'Seems like a good chance to give the Patchens something to think about,' Ross drawled. 'It's my idea to divert their attention from Señor Olveras in case they get suspicious.' He glanced off toward the barn. 'You brought Oro along with you?'

'We've got the horse hid out in a safe place,' reassured Buckshot. 'Didn't say nothin' about him in front of the others. Ain't good sense to let too many folks in on a secret. You won't want it known where you've got the horse hid out.'

'Where's that?' queried Ross. 'I'm riding in a hurry. Let's get him.'

'Back in the old cave in the cat's-claw, where you used to play when you was a kid,' chuckled Pete.

Ross grinned. 'You're a couple of old foxes,' he told them admiringly.

Leading their horses the three men started across the yard and were lost to view in the tangle of trees and brush beyond the broken gate.

Chapter
9

CONFERENCE AT FLYING A

Tʜᴇ ʀᴇᴛᴜʀɴ of the hounds without the rider who had gone with them on a coyote chase passed unnoticed until the arrival of Rick DeSalt. Their noisy greeting of the visitor drew Buel Patchen out to the porch in time to see Rick pull his team of sleek bays to a halt at the hitching post in front of the house. A sharp word from Buel sent the hounds slinking away. DeSalt climbed from the light buggy and tied the horses to the big ring in the post.

'What brings you from town so late, Rick?' Buel called from the porch steps. His puzzled gaze followed the hounds as they disappeared into the darkness. 'Something on your mind?'

'Plenty.' The saloon man paused to remove his long dust coat and throw it into the seat of the buggy. Something in his voice drew Buel's attention from the hounds. He gave DeSalt a sharp look as the latter mounted the steps.

'Harve around?' DeSalt drew out a case and selected a cigar. He returned the case to his pocket without offering one to the other man. He knew Buel was a nonsmoker.

'Sure. He's in the office. We're going over some tally sheets.' Buel's tone was uneasy. 'What's wrong, Rick?'

He led the way into the house and pushed through the office door. Harve Welder glanced up from the tally book spread before him on the table. If he was surprised to recognize the late visitor, no sign was visible on his poker face. 'Hello, Rick.' The foreman nodded and returned his attention to the tally book.

DeSalt sat down in a leather chair studded with big brass nails. 'You can stop fooling with your tally sheet, Harve. I've got things I want to talk to you and Buel about.'

'Just a minute,' muttered the foreman. His pencil checked down the column of figures, lips moved in a silent count. He put the stubby pencil between the pages and closed the book. 'Three hundred and twenty-six,' he said aloud, looking at Buel. 'With good luck tomorrow we'll have the rest of the Mexican's stuff in by night. Means we can start the drive the next day.'

'What's Harve talking about?' DeSalt spoke smoothly enough, but his eyes were cold and watchful behind the veiling wisps of cigar smoke.

'Some cows I'm selling to a Mex from down Sonora way,' explained Buel. 'It's a cash deal on delivery at Deming, and I'm needing the money. You know that, Rick. You know I've got to raise cash — and damn soon.'

'You won't need cash if you'd listen to me,' said DeSalt.

'Now that Ross Chaine is back in the country I can't risk waiting,' Buel retorted angrily. 'That option won't be worth the paper it's written on if Chaine gets wind of it. Right now it's as good as gold, only it takes gold to handle it.'

'Get rid of Ross Chaine and we won't need any cash,' persisted DeSalt. 'With him out of the way all we've got to do is to move in on Bar Chain and take it lock, stock, and barrel.'

'I don't follow you,' grumbled Buel Patchen. 'We've got to show some kind of paper — a deed that can go on record. It's cheaper to take up that option his aunt gave me. She'll go for the money like a hungry trout jumps at a fly.'

'A deed signed by his aunt won't hold water,' DeSalt reminded. 'She was his guardian when she signed that option, but Ross has been of age years since. A deed for Bar Chain won't be worth a damn.'

'She hasn't seen Ross since he ran away from her,' Buel told him with a thin smile. 'I had a piece printed in a Socorro newspaper about him being killed in a saloon brawl. She thinks Ross is dead and that the property is hers. I wangled a new option out of her to sell for five thousand cash.' Patchen swore softly. 'I should have raised the cash then and there and got the deed from her. We'd be sitting pretty now, Rick. We'd have grass growing in that valley again and all of Bar Chain range turned over to Flying A.'

Harve Welder broke his silence. 'That's right,' he agreed in his flat voice. 'Only one thing stopped you, Buel. You was hopin' we'd get Ross first so he couldn't queer the deal.'

'I should have risked it,' muttered the hunchback. 'We'll get Chaine yet. Sure we'll get him.'

'Right now there are hundreds of people who know Ross Chaine is alive today,' Rick DeSalt said cuttingly. 'You're a fool, if you think a deed signed by that woman is any good. Only Ross can sell Bar Chain.'

Buel looked at him coldly. 'You talk too fast, Rick. The woman's next thing to a half-wit. The deed she signs will be dated ten years back, while Ross was still a kid. The woman won't know the difference. And nobody else will ever know the truth, except us three — and Tenn.'

DeSalt puffed meditatively at his cigar. Suddenly he shook his head. 'I'd drop that deed business until you're sure Ross Chaine is dead. Forget it, Buel, and watch your step from now on. Ross Chaine is back — and that means trouble for all of us.'

'I know he's back,' retorted Patchen angrily. 'We've got a dead man to prove it. You know what he did to Monte.'

'I know what he did to Tenn,' smiled the saloon man. 'He did plenty.'

'Who told you about that Alamos business?' snarled an angry voice from the hall door.

DeSalt looked round coldly at the speaker. 'Hello, Tenn. Talking to me?' His tone was reproving. 'You don't have to yell.'

Tenn came further into the room. 'Who's been shootin' off his mouth about that mixup?' He kept his voice down.

'Breezy was in the White Buffalo this morning.' DeSalt's smile was sardonic. 'He gave me a good laugh with that story. I treated the old longhorn to a drink on the strength of it.'

'I'll treat him,' yelped young Patchen. 'He's too damn smart . . . always has been. You've got to give him his time.' Tenn glowered at his father. 'He's too stove-up and useless, anyway.'

Buel shook his head. 'Jean wouldn't stand for firing old Breezy,' he demurred. 'You wait a bit, son. We'll take care of Breezy when the time comes.' He gave his son a significant look. Tennessee grinned, subsided into a chair and fumbled in a pocket for his tobacco sack.

'Have a cigar,' invited DeSalt. He held out the case. 'No hard feelings, Tenn.'

'I ain't finished with Ross Chaine yet,' boasted the young man. 'He'll be dog meat when I get done with him.'

His words recalled the matter of the hounds to Buel Patchen. Jean had said she was taking them for a coyote chase. He had watched her ride away in the growing dusk, the hounds trailing her. The hounds were back but he had not seen Jean, nor heard her in her room.

He spoke sharply. 'Seen Jean around, Tenn?'

'Not since she went off with the hounds. Reckon she's here some place.' Tenn shrugged his burly shoulders and put a match to his cigar.

'Take a look in her room,' Buel Patchen said, still more sharply. 'The hounds are back, but I haven't seen her come in.'

Tenn complied, grumbling. They heard his impatient voice, calling the girl's name, and then a moment's silence followed by the quick pounding of his booted feet as he ran along the hall back to the office.

'She ain't in her room,' he reported excitedly.

'See if her horse is back in the barn,' ordered Buel.

Harve Welder's voice halted Tenn at the door. 'Her red mare ain't in the barn,' he said. 'Not unless Jean's come in since I was over there an hour ago.' The foreman paused, wrinkled his brows thoughtfully. 'Breezy wasn't in for supper,' he added. 'He don't usually stay out so late. He sure had no bus'ness goin' off like he done. He should have told me he was goin' to town.'

'Like as not the old coot got pie-eyed drunk,' chortled Tennessee.

Harve shook his head. 'Breezy ain't one to get drunk,' he demurred. 'I ain't likin' this, Buel. Kind of queer, Jean and Breezy not showin' up.'

Rick DeSalt broke into the conversation. 'I told you I saw Breezy in town,' he reminded. 'He didn't stay long in my place but Stack Jimson said he saw him heading toward Old Town.'

'Forget him,' grunted Buel. 'Breezy can take care of himself. He most likely got into a card game in Estrada's Mexican joint . . . always goes there when he's in a gambling mood.'

'That don't explain how come the dogs got in without Jean,' commented Harve. He frowned. 'She's awful reckless when she gets to runnin' coyotes. No tellin' but what the mare put her foot in a hole and got throwed.' The foreman stood up and reached for his hat. 'I reckon I'll get the boys and go take a look. There's a chance Jean's layin' some place, bad hurt — or worse.' He clattered from the room.

Buel's head lifted in a curiously speculative look at his son. 'You go with Harve, boy. It's a shocking thought, but he's right. Jean may be hurt — or *dead*.'

Tenn stared back at him and suddenly his heavy lips twisted in an ugly leer. 'A hell of a lot you'd care,' he sneered.

'Get out, fool!' exploded his father. His hand closed over a horseshoe paper weight. 'Get out!' he repeated furiously and hurled the horseshoe.

Tenn dodged the missile and ran into the hall. They heard his low laugh, taunting, derisive.

Buel relaxed in his big chair. His hands were shaking, his eyes hot with wicked anger. Rick DeSalt looked at him curiously over his cigar. 'I wouldn't worry too much, Buel,' he said smoothly.

'I'd hate for anything to happen to her.' Buel spoke hoarsely. 'I'm the same as a father to her. Of course I worry.' He controlled himself with an effort. 'You see, Rick,' he went on more quietly, 'Jean and Tenn plan to get married very soon. An accident would be most unfortunate at this time.'

'Naturally,' agreed DeSalt. 'The girl will soon be of age — her own boss.' His smile was significant.

'You make me sick,' fumed the hunchback. He changed the subject abruptly. 'You haven't told me yet just *why* you came?'

'Some things going on in town that have me puzzled,' explained DeSalt. 'For one thing, Kinners and Lally seem to have a lot on their minds . . . been hanging round over in Old Town. They don't know it, but I've been having them watched.' DeSalt laughed softly. 'I told you about that letter they never got from Chaine. They don't know how to figure it out . . . been over to the post office a score of times.'

Buel Patchen chuckled. 'Won't be any trouble from that pair of old-timers,' he declared. 'Not unless they get in touch with Ross Chaine, and Ross won't dare show his face in Dos Cruces.'

DeSalt seemed dubious. 'I'm not so sure they haven't connected with Chaine,' he worried. 'There's been a high-toned Mexican hanging round at Lico Estrada's *cantina* . . . claims he's up from Sonora on a cattle-buying trip.'

Buel's head lifted in a sharp look. 'Sounds like my Torres hombre,' he said.

'That's the man.' DeSalt frowned. 'He sees a lot of Lally and Kinners.'

The sound of voices came to them through the open window. Buel listened for a moment. Harve was getting the boys out of the bunkhouse. His look went back to Rick DeSalt. 'Torres wants breeding cows,' he said. 'It's possible he's got a deal on for some LK stuff.' Buel paused, his expression suddenly puzzled. 'He told me he was in one big hurry to get to Deming. He went off the same night and left his cousin to rep for him, an hombre named Olveras.'

'Stack Jimson said Torres had a bunch of vaqueros with him,' commented DeSalt. 'I guess one of 'em was your Olveras man.'

'Maybe so,' agreed Buel. 'What has me puzzled is your talk of Torres being in Dos Cruces. He was headed for Deming when he left here last night.'

'You've got me wrong,' smiled DeSalt. 'I didn't say Stack has seen him in Old Town today.'

Buel looked relieved. 'Well, what's eating you, Rick? As far as I know Torres is all right. If he's not, I'm being played for a sucker — roundin' up five hundred head of cattle for a drive to Deming.'

DeSalt grinned. 'Maybe I'm jumpy about Chaine. It's like having fork-lightning wandering round on the loose. Ross Chaine's going to hit and we don't know when or where.' He chewed savagely on his cigar. 'I'd like to have a look at this Olveras,' he added.

'He's not here,' Buel told him. 'Olveras went to town right after supper. Said he wouldn't be back till most breakfast time.'

'I wonder what took him to town?' speculated DeSalt.

'He claimed Lico Estrada would have a letter from Sonora for him.' Buel's eyes narrowed. 'What's wrong in him going to town, Rick?'

DeSalt grinned again. 'Just that batty feeling I have about Ross Chaine. I don't feel safe while he's on the loose.'

'What has Chaine got to do with Olveras?' Buel asked irritably. 'You make me tired with your fool suspicions.'

'I'll ask you one,' countered the saloon man, 'Supposing Olveras is *Ross Chaine?*'

'You're crazy,' retorted Buel. 'I know a Mex when I see one.' He gave his friend an exasperated smile. 'If you get back to town, you can look Olveras up at Estrada's place and size him up for yourself.'

DeSalt got out of his chair. 'I'll do that, Buel. Maybe I'm jumpy about Ross Chaine, but I'd be a damn fool not to admit he's smart. He's got a lot of tricks in the bag and he'll use them.'

'You're getting me jumpy, too,' grumbled Buel as he followed his visitor out to the porch.

DeSalt shrugged into his long dust coat. 'I've told you what I think of Ross Chaine,' he replied coldly. 'Do you want your neck stretched, Buel?'

A startled oath exploded from the hunchback's lips. 'Damn you, Rick!'

'Damn is right!' DeSalt's smile was sardonic. 'You and I — and all of us will be damned to a fare-you-well if we don't watch out for Ross Chaine.'

Chapter
10
THE LONE RIDER

BUEL STOOD THERE on the steps, head sunk low on his misshapen shoulders, mixed anger and fear in his eyes as he watched the buggy melt into the night. Despite the chill in the air his face was beaded with perspiration. He pulled out a handkerchief and wiped his forehead and went slowly into the house. Rick DeSalt was right about Ross Chaine. The man was dangerous, a menace to be ruthlessly destroyed. Already he had eluded them twice, and the first encounter had cost Monte his life. The second encounter had resulted in Tenn's humiliation. Chaine could have killed Tenn. The fact that he had chosen to be merciful was a weakness that might prove his own undoing. Buel knew that on his side there would be no mercy — only ruthlessness — only death.

Rick was wrong about Olveras. Buel knew a Mexican when he saw one, and Olveras was a Mexican. No doubting that fact. Also there was no reason to suspect him. Torres had left him behind to pass on the cows Harve was rounding up for the drive to Deming. Buel could not for the life of him discover anything wrong with either Olveras or Torres. He had no intention of allowing Rick's suspicions to spoil a profitable deal.

His thoughts went to Jean. Was Harve's guess right?

Was the girl lying out there in the chaparral — her neck broken? Buel's hard thin lips drew back over his teeth in a cruel smile. Fate would have struck the blow that he had hesitated to strike. He had done a lot of thinking about the approaching day that would make Jean Austen mistress of Flying A — her own boss. There was too much of her father in Jean. She possessed all of Bill Austen's independence, his strong, resolute spirit. She was fearless and forthright — not easily deceived. She would demand her rights.

Buel's hand, lying on the desk, clenched into a hard fist. He saw trouble, looming large and dark on the horizon. The dawn that ushered in Jean Austen's twenty-first birthday promised disaster unless certain plans matured. The easiest solution would have been her marriage to Tenn, a solution that seemed destined to fail, despite Tenn's boast that he would slap the Patchen brand on her smooth hide. Buel was under no illusions about his uncouth son. Tenn was base to the core. He would not hesitate to attempt force if the girl persisted in refusing his attentions. Also he was under no illusions about Jean. She would kill Tenn. No doubt about that. She would kill him. She was too smart and spirited to cower under any form of brutality. And the law would hold her blameless.

Again the hunchback's lip lifted in that cold glimmer of cruelty. If Harve's guess proved correct, the problem was solved. If not — there still remained time to arrange a little accident . . . a cut saddle girth . . . a runaway horse — a girl dragged to death at the end of a stirrup. There were many little ways of arranging a plausible accident.

Buel's clenched fist tightened until the knuckles showed white under the hairy brown skin. Suddenly his head lifted in an eager look at the open window. The late moon was well up, and something moved out there under the silver-dappled trees. A lone horseman. Harve, or Tennessee, bringing news of the girl.

He got out of his chair and went quickly out to the porch. The lone rider was closer. Not Harve or Tenn. His sharp look made certain of that. Harve's tall frame always had a sideways sag when in the saddle, and Tenn's heavy body slumped clumsily like a bag of meal. This man rode with careless grace and the horse under him moved at a swift running-walk. Olveras, returning from Dos Cruces. But the Mexican's horse was a roan, and this stranger was riding a pale gold horse with a silvery mane and tail. A palomino.

Buel drew back in the shadows, conscious of a sudden fear. The lone rider saw him and before the startled rancher could retreat further into the house the palomino was rushing toward the steps.

'Just a moment!' The stranger's voice was coldly crisp. 'Stand as you are, Patchen!'

Buel made no attempt to push through the door. The gun in the lone rider's hand was a threat he could not force himself to ignore.

The man spoke again. 'You know me, Patchen?' There was a hint of hard laughter in his voice. 'You didn't see me in Alamos the other day. Well, here I am.'

'Ross Chaine!' Buel's voice was a whimpering growl.

'The same Ross Chaine you shipped out of the valley fifteen years ago.'

'What do you want?' Buel was losing his first panic. He thought he heard the sound of approaching hoof-beats. He must keep the man here until the outfit's return.

'I don't need to tell you what I want,' Ross replied with a short hard laugh. 'I'm back to stay, Patchen. You know what that means.'

'We should have a talk,' Buel suggested. His straining ears told him he was right about those approaching hoofbeats. Ten minutes would bring Harve and the boys. 'We should have a talk,' he repeated. 'Get down from your horse, Chaine. I've got a bottle of rye in the office and we can talk things over peaceably, as man to man.'

'I won't even say thanks,' Ross said in his quietly scornful voice. 'You're not a man, Patchen. You're a killer wolf and I'm out to nail your hide to the barn door.'

'Don't talk like a fool.' Buel's voice took on something of its usual bell-like tone. Those hoofbeats were getting nearer every moment. With an effort he kept his eyes on the palomino's rider. A single glance might warn him of the net spreading for his capture. 'Get down from your horse,' he repeated. 'You're welcome here, Chaine. More welcome than I can tell you.' Buel's laugh was genuine. 'You'd be surprised.'

'Don't fool yourself,' Ross said in his quiet voice. 'I'm not staying to be surprised. I've got ears, too, Patchen.' His tone hardened, struck at the other man like flailing whips of steel. 'I should kill you where you stand, shoot you down like a mad dog. I'm not that sort of killer, Patchen. You're going to die, and soon, but you'll die according to the law — hanged by the neck till you're dead. It may not have been your hand that shot down my father, but you were one of the cowards back of the murder. Nothing will stop me from getting at the truth and the truth is going to hang you and all the others.'

The hoofbeats were unmistakably closer. Buel hardly dared breathe. He wanted to let out a yell that would bring Harve and the outfit on the run. The menace of the gun, the threat of death in his visitor's eyes, held his tongue in an iron leash. Ross spoke again:

'Come down the steps,' he said. 'Quick — or I *will* kill you.'

Buel obeyed, halted close to the tall golden horse. Ross gestured with his gun at the grove of trees. 'Keep moving.'

Buel walked along in front of the horse, careful to keep his hands in sight above his head. His spine cringed at what might happen if he made a wrong move . . . the roar of the forty-five — the heavy bullet smashing the life from him. He failed to see Sing Gee peering from the corner of his kitchen. He would have been startled at the fierce exultation in the old Chinese cook's eyes.

Ross saw the cook and correctly interpreted the look on his face. Sing Gee was enjoying Buel Patchen's humiliation, was obviously hoping for the worst to happen to the man he hated. Sing Gee was Jean Austen's friend.

Satisfied there was no danger of interference from the old Chinese, Ross hurried his terrified prisoner deeper into the grove of trees.

'All right, Patchen,' he said suddenly. 'Get down on your belly between those two saplings, and no noise from you.'

Buel obeyed, stretched out full length, face down on the ground. Ross swung from his saddle, two short pieces of rope in his hand. He pulled Buel's arms around one of the saplings and tied the wrists together with one of the ropes, then drew his legs closely around the second sapling and bound the ankles with the remaining rope.

'I'll have to tie up your mouth, Patchen,' he said with a mirthless chuckle. 'Who's being surprised now, I wonder?' He stuffed Buel's handkerchief into the man's mouth and knotted the ends tightly. 'I'll be a long way from here by the time they find you.'

Ross gave a final tug at the knotted ends and stood up. Sounds from the yard told him the Flying A men were back. He guessed that Buel had sent them out in search of the long-overdue girl. It was possible Jean and Breezy had run into them. Ross was not worried. Jean and Breezy had a good story ready.

He stared down at the bound and gagged man lashed to the two saplings. 'Listen, Patchen' — he spoke with cold emphasis. 'I heard that talk between you and Tenn in Alamos the other morning, so listen hard. If anything happens to Jean Austen I'll know who's responsible. You leave the girl alone, Patchen. It's a warning. I've sent a sealed note to the United States Marshal. If anything happens to the girl and I'm not alive to get you, the marshal will know where to look.'

Without another glance at the man Ross swung up to his saddle and rode on through the trees and was soon following a deep gully that angled southeasterly toward the Dos Cruces road.

As soon as he dared, he put the horse to a fast run. His night's work was not yet finished. He had seen Rick DeSalt heading for Dos Cruces away from the ranch. The opportunity was not to be missed. He wanted a word with the suave saloon man.

Rick's bays were making slow progress across the wide wash of Red Creek when the lone rider drifted out of the willows. Rick's hand slipped inside his coat. Moonlight lay cold on the gun leveled at him and reluctantly Rick's hand came away empty, lifted with its mate above his head.

Ross spoke softly: 'Climb out, Rick.'

DeSalt glowered. 'Who the hell are you? Is this a holdup?'

'You know who I am — and I said *climb out.*' Ross spoke curtly, his voice edged with impatience.

'Ross Chaine?' DeSalt's face took on a greenish tinge under the moonlight.

'I'm in a hurry,' Ross said. 'Climb down from that buggy.'

DeSalt made an awkward descent between the high red wheels and at another curt command he turned his back to horse and rider.

'Keep your hands up high,' Ross said. He pressed the Colt hard against DeSalt's spine, reached over with his free hand and deftly removed a small derringer from the man's inside coat pocket. 'You can turn around now.'

'What do you want with me?' DeSalt asked sullenly.

'I want to know about a letter that Lally and Kinners didn't get,' Ross answered. 'What do you know about that letter, Rick?'

'Not a damn thing,' retorted DeSalt. 'I'm not the postmaster in Dos Cruces.'

'Jed States is postmaster and that amounts to the same thing,' Ross said. 'You own the store he runs, and you own him.'

'You're talking through your hat,' sneered Rick.

'It's the . truth,' insisted Ross. 'You own the Dos Cruces Merchandise Store and you own Stack Jimson's livery stable. Stack and Jed take your orders and they're a pair of sneaking spies.'

'You know a lot.' Rick DeSalt forced a smile. 'I don't see the point in you holding me up with a gun for this fool talk. Why don't you drop in at my place if you want to talk to me? Might be a good idea if we got together,' he added. 'You've got brains and nerve, Chaine. We'd make a team.'

'Walk into my parlor, said the spider to the fly.' Ross laughed. It was a hard, bitter laugh. 'I'm not a fly, Rick, and if I ever walk into your parlor it'll be to drag you out and stamp on your face.' He paused, added slowly, 'I've just been having a talk with your partner over at Flying A. I told him I'm here to hang the murderers of my father and Bill Austen. Does that mean anything to you, Rick?'

The Dos Cruces saloon man licked dry lips. 'You can't prove anything on me,' he muttered finally.

'I'll let you do the worrying,' Ross retorted. 'In the meantime, Rick, remember that tampering with United States mail can put a man inside looking out.' He gestured with his gun. 'Lie down and play dead, Rick. Scrape your belly over that hump of sand.'

'Damn you ——' DeSalt choked off his protests and stretched out on the sand, face down. 'What are you up to?' he mumbled.

'I'm taking your team and buggy down the road a mile or two,' Ross told him. 'You'll find them hidden out in the brush some place, if you look hard enough. By the time you get back to town I'll be a long way from here, Rick.'

The saloon man smothered an oath. Ross spoke sharply. 'Keep your head down. I'll be watching, and I don't miss my shots.' He climbed into the buggy and drove away, the palomino following at an easy trot. DeSalt lay very still, listening until the grind of the buggy wheels in the sand faded into the distance.

He got to his feet, stood there, swearing. Unless he regained possession of his team and buggy he was confronted with the dismal prospect of a long walk. It was all of ten miles to Dos Cruces from Red Creek Wash. DeSalt hated unnecessary exercise and the thought of those weary miles made his feet ache.

It took him an hour to come up to the buggy half hidden behind a creosote bush, and another fifteen minutes to locate the horses hidden a hundred yards apart in a gully. The animals wore their bridles but the rest of the harness had been stripped off. Horses and buggy were useless without the harness.

DeSalt spent another fifteen minutes in a futile search of the bushes. He gave up finally and, shortening one of the long driving lines into a bridle rein, climbed onto one of the horses, and was promptly bucked off. The bays were buggy horses and had never felt the weight of a man on their backs.

He got painfully to his feet. The hard fall had jarred him, and he had landed in a clump of cholla. The agony of the vicious little spines in his hands and legs brought the tears to his eyes. Also, to make matters worse, the second horse, excited by the bucking incident, had broken loose and galloped into the night after its fleeing mate.

Cursing the man responsible for his misery, DeSalt went limping through the moonlight, pausing frequently to worry at the torturing cholla spines with his fingers. The sun would be up long before he could reach the comfort of the White Buffalo and the soothing ministrations of Doc Webb.

Chapter

11

SMOKE IN THE MOUNTAINS

DAWN WAS PAINTING the mountain peaks when Jean got out of bed and went to her window. She stood for a few moments, stared at the changing colors with unseeing eyes. She had slept badly and she was still confused about the events of the preceding night. According to Buel Patchen's tale, Ross Chaine had mysteriously appeared on a palomino horse and brutally attacked him — left him bound and gagged under the trees. The thing did not seem possible. Jean and Breezy had left Ross with the two LK partners at the Bar Chain. Ross could not have reached the ranch ahead of them and done the things claimed by Buel Patchen. Also he was riding a roan horse when she accompanied him to the old Bar Chain ranch house. And he was wearing the elegant garb of a high-caste Mexican. Buel Patchen's story was too fantastic. The mysterious lone rider of the palomino horse must have been another man, and not Ross Chaine.

There was no doubting part of his story. Somebody had handled him roughly, left him tied up with a hand-kerchief stuffed in his mouth. It was not until hours after her return with Harve and the boys that they found Buel. In a way the affair had saved her from too close an inspection of the story concocted by Breezy and herself. Buel was too sick to give her any thought.

'We got scared when you didn't get back with the hounds,' was all he said. 'You ride so reckless we got to thinkin' that maybe your mare had put her foot in a hole and thrown you for a broken neck.'

'I got lost until the moon came up,' Jean said, repeating what she had told Harve. 'Breezy ran into me, on his way home from town.'

'Sure did,' confirmed Breezy. 'Lucky thing I showed up, the way the gal was — all ready to bust into tears. Shakin' all over like a leaf she was, an' thinkin' every shadder was a wolf or an Injun.' The old cowboy chortled.

Jean pretended indignation. Breezy's romancing made a convincing background for their story. 'You're being plain mean,' she accused. 'I wasn't scared, and I didn't need your help nor anybody's help.' She smiled at the circle of faces. 'Thanks just the same for looking for me, and I'm sorry I caused so much trouble.'

'Next time you fix to go runnin' coyotes at night you tell me,' grinned Tenn. 'Ain't wantin' my little bitsy sweetness get her neck broke.' He winked at his father, scowling up from his big office chair. 'I'm your stickum-close burr clover from now on, young un.'

She had left them and gone hot-cheeked and angry to her room, and now, standing at her window, unseeing gaze on the sunrise, Tenn's words, and the ugly gleam in his eyes came back to her frighteningly.

Her thoughts went to Ross Chaine, and, suddenly feverish with anxiety, she hurriedly bathed and got into her clothes. She would soon know if Buel was right about the identity of the mysterious lone rider. If Señor Olveras was around, it meant that Buel was wrong. She knew what Buel didn't know. She knew that Señor Olveras was Ross Chaine.

His smile greeted her when she entered the long raftered room where they sat at breakfast. He was in his chair at her end of the table. Buel Patchen occupied his high-backed chair at the opposite end, with Tenn at his right and Harve Welder at his left. The foreman used a small cabin outside the garden for his living quarters and office, but usually took his meals with the family. As a consequence the talk invariably centered on ranch affairs, the hay crop, the price of cattle, the virtues and sins of the outfit. Without the men suspecting she was all ears, Jean had acquired a knowledge of ranch business that would have surprised them. Ever since her return from the boarding school in El Paso she had deliberately sought to familiarize herself with the thousand and one details of a big cattle ranch.

Sing Gee shuffled in from his kitchen and favored her with an inscrutable smile. 'Can fix you nicee flied egg,' he said. He placed a saucer of peaches in front of her. 'Maybe you likee steak, flied potatoes, allee same others?'

Jean was young and healthy. Despite her sleepless night she realized she was hungry, somewhat to her surprise. 'The steak,' she told the cook. 'And hurry up with the coffee, please, Sing.' She smiled up at the tall man in the resplendent garb of a Mexican *caballero*. 'You missed a lot of excitement last night, Señor Olveras,' she said in Spanish. 'Or were you already back from town and asleep in your room?'

Ross looked at her, politely interested. 'I returned very late from Dos Cruces,' he replied. 'But what is this you tell me about the excitement last night?' He gestured at the other men who were watching him, suspiciously. 'Alas, they do not speak my Spanish and so cannot tell me about this excitement.'

Buel Patchen broke in, his voice unnaturally gruff, 'Ask Olveras if he saw Rick DeSalt in town last night.'

Ross shook his head regretfully when Jean translated the question. 'Alas again, but no, I did not see this Señor DeSalt in town.'

Jean translated for the benefit of her uncle and the others. Buel showed a curious relief. He nodded, smiled thinly at Harve. 'I told you Rick was all wet about Olveras being Ross Chaine.'

'I reckon that's right,' agreed the foreman. 'Olveras couldn't have been in two places at once, so it sure proves Rick is all wrong about him bein' Ross Chaine.' He took a long drink from his coffee cup and wiped his mustache with shirt-sleeve. 'And Breezy claims he seen Olveras in Lico Estrada's *cantina*,' he added. 'Rick is sure loco.'

Ross looked at Jean with politely questioning eyes. She obligingly translated, her tone mirthful. 'It seems Mr. DeSalt was here last night and he was suspicious about you, señor. He thought you might be a man known as Ross Chaine — a very dangerous character.'

The 'señor' smiled indulgently. 'This is very amusing. A good joke indeed.' He leaned back in his chair and let out a loud laugh.

'Señor Olveras says it's very amusing,' Jean told the others. 'It is a joke that makes him laugh.'

'No joke about last night,' growled Tenn. 'I'll slap the ears off the damn Mex if he laughs at what Chaine done to the old man.'

'Señor Olveras doesn't know about last night,' reminded Jean coldly. 'None of you speak Spanish and you haven't told him about last night.'

'Well, go ahead . . . tell him,' Tenn said peevishly. 'We'll all be watchin' him close.'

The 'señor's' amazement and indignation as he listened to the girl's story were convincing enough, even for the distrustful Tenn. Jean herself was aware of a growing perplexity. Of course she knew that Breezy had not seen Ross at the *cantina* of Lico Estrada. Ross had told Breezy to say he had seen Olveras if anybody questioned him. What mystified her was Buel's claim that Ross had appeared at the ranch on a palomino horse when she knew that Ross must have been at the old Bar Chain ranch house. The thing made her dizzy. She longed to ask Ross in Spanish for the truth. Instinctively she downed the impulse. It was too risky and would be unfair to Ross. These men were watching him with hair-trigger suspicion.

Sing Gee shuffled in with a small steak sizzling on a plate, and fried potatoes and a fresh pot of coffee and a plate of hot buttered toast. 'Velly good steak,' he chanted, 'velly tender, allee same buttah.' He chuckled, flicked an oddly inscrutable smile at the tall man in the Mexican clothes, and went slippering back to his kitchen.

Harve Welder broke the silence. 'Tell the Mex we're startin' the drive soon as we've et breakfast,' he said. 'We can make the camp at Oxbow Creek come sundown. Plenty of cows there to make up the herd an' we'll be fifteen miles on the way to Deming.'

Jean conveyed the information to the 'señor,' who bowed assent. 'Don Vicente will be pleased indeed that we have so quickly gathered the cows,' he answered. For a brief moment Jean fancied his eyes were trying to convey a message to her. She couldn't be sure, because Tenn's watchful look was on her. She hoped desperately there would be an opportunity for a few words before Ross rode away with the outfit. She knew from the moment that Harve mentioned the Oxbow Camp that she would not be allowed to make the trip. She would not be needed. Curly Bristow was in charge of Oxbow and Curly could speak Spanish.

Tenn was suddenly speaking and his words confirmed her fears. 'No call for you to be trailin' the outfit, Jean,' he said with a satisfied grin. 'Won't be no chance for the Mex to get spoony with you today.'

'Don't talk like a fool,' she retorted sharply. She bent her head, wondered if Ross noticed the color warming her cheeks.

'I wouldn't trust him alone with you as far as I could swing a dogie by the tail,' chortled Tenn. 'These Mex birds are all the same.'

'That's enough, Tenn.' His father gave him an angry look. 'Harve won't need you along,' he added. 'I want you to stick around close, son. It's about time you got busy on that job we were talking about.' Buel's glance strayed briefly to the girl.

'Sure.' Tenn grinned. 'I savvy.' He rubbed his unshaven chin thoughtfully and suddenly pushed back his chair. 'If I ain't goin' with Harve I reckon I'll go get a shave an' slick up some.' He stood looking at Jean, his ugly grin widening. 'Maybe we can go have that picnic up in Bear Canyon,' he added. 'You ain't puttin' me off *this* time, Jean.'

He swaggered out, not waiting for an answer. Ross smilingly gestured an *adios*, but Jean saw a slight tensing of the jaw muscles. She looked quickly at Buel, but he was talking to the foreman. It was obvious that neither of the men had noticed the fleeting betraying expression on Ross Chaine's face. They would have immediately suspected the truth — that he understood English . . . that he was not Señor Olveras — but Ross Chaine — the man they feared and would destroy.

Harve Welder got out of his chair. 'I reckon we'll be starting,' he said. 'Tell the Mex to git a move on, Jean.' He went out, and after a moment, Buel stood up, his gaze fixed on Ross. 'Tell him there's a man at

Oxbow who savvys Mex talk,' he said to Jean. 'Shouldn't be any trouble there. Harve's going on with the herd to Deming,' he added. 'He'll take payment for the cows from Torres.' Buel moved slowly to the hall door, glanced back at the pair at the table. 'Harve's in a hurry to get started.' He spoke impatiently.

Jean reached for the coffee pot. 'Señor Olveras wants another cup,' she smiled. 'He'll be out in a few minutes, Uncle.' She hoped Buel would not notice the unsteadiness of her hand as she poured the coffee.

They heard his slow footsteps in the hall, a pause while he took his hat from the rack, and then the slam of door. Ross spoke quickly in a low voice: 'I don't like leaving you here — alone.'

She shook her head, brow puckered in a tiny frown as she stared at him. 'Were you here last night? Was it you who tied Buel up?'

'Yes.' For a moment his eyes danced, then almost fiercely, 'I can't leave you alone at Flying A.'

Again she disregarded his words. 'It's incredible! You couldn't have been here. We left you at Bar Chain.' She smiled faintly. 'Are there two Ross Chaines?'

'No,' Ross said. 'Only one Ross Chaine, and he's a very worried man, Jean. Worried about you.'

'Buel wouldn't dare harm me.' Jean's tone was positive.

'I saw the look in Tenn's eyes when he spoke of the picnic,' Ross said in a hard voice.

Jean shrugged slim shoulders, glanced down at the thirty-two snuggled into the holster of the belt she had buckled on for the ride Harve Welder's plans had spoiled. 'I can shoot straight,' she told Ross with a faint grimace.

He looked at her, his eyes hard. 'You're too sure of yourself. You're a lamb in a den of wolves. Don't you realize that — yet?'

'Stop worrying about *me*,' retorted the girl. 'Do some worrying about yourself.' Her voice was unsteady. 'I'm frightened every minute you are here . . . frightened for you.'

'Buel doesn't suspect . . . not after what happened to him last night.' The dancing imps of mischief were back in his eyes.

She shook her head, unconvinced. 'Something will happen. Harve Welder is not easy to fool. He doesn't say much, but he thinks a lot — and he keeps looking at you so hard. I was terrified — the way he stared at you before he went out.'

Voices reached to them from the yard, the trample of horses — and the quick hammer of booted feet on the flagstoned walk. Jean put a hand on his. 'Be careful,' she begged. 'I — I *will* be alone — if anything happens to you.' She broke off, got to her feet as the hall door slammed.

'Hell, Jean! What's keepin' that damn Mex? Harve's gettin' on the prod, says for you to tell the damn greaser to come on the run.' Tenn Patchen's hulking frame suddenly bulked in the doorway, anger red in his face, suspicion in the look he flung at Ross.

'Don't be so rude, Tenn,' reproved the girl. 'Señor Olveras is a guest, and not somebody for Harve to order around.'

'Well, get him started then,' grumbled Tenn. He stood aside, waited for them to pass into the hall. 'I ain't givin' him a chance to do any good-bye kissin'.' He grinned.

Her cheeks pink, she hurried down the hall. Ross followed with Tenn trailing at his heels. It was obvious they were not to be allowed any more time together.

Despite Harve's sulky look at her, Jean insisted upon accompanying the outfit as far as Coyote Creek. She was in the mood for a ride, she told the visibly annoyed foreman. Breezy had her red mare waiting.

'I figgered you'd mebbe want to ride along with 'em for a ways,' he chuckled.

She saw that he had his own rawboned buckskin waiting, and she saw, too, the quick exchange of looks between Ross and the old cowboy.

Tenn joined them as they rode out of the yard. 'Reckon I'll ride along with you, Jean,' he said, leering at her. 'No tellin' what might happen with that Chaine jasper runnin' round on the loose. The damn skunk might figger to kidnap you if he catches you alone.'

'You needn't come on my account,' she protested. 'I'm not afraid of your Ross Chaine with Breezy along.'

'Breezy ain't comin'.' Tenn scowled at the old man 'You get back to the yard and mind your work.'

'I want Breezy — and he's coming,' flared Jean. 'You leave him alone, Tenn.'

He said no more, but kept his horse ranged alongside hers. Ross spoke softly in Spanish. 'I don't like it. He's planning trouble.'

'I'm not afraid of him,' Jean replied. 'He's a coward.'

'All the more dangerous,' worried Ross. 'I should have killed him, that day in Alamos.'

Tenn caught the last word, which he understood. 'What's the Mex sayin' about Alamos?' he asked the girl suspiciously.

Her mind raced. 'Alamos?' Her answer came, and she gestured at some stunted cottonwoods at the edge of a dry wash. 'He was talking about those cottonwoods . . . alamos means cottonwood in Spanish.'

'I savvy that much Spanish,' grunted Tenn. He continued to watch Ross suspiciously. Jean was aware of cold chills running up and down her back. She wondered if the unfortunate mention of Alamos was reviving Tenn's memories of his humiliation in the hotel. Recognition of the man riding on the other side of her might suddenly come. She could bear it no longer, drew the red mare to a standstill. They were perhaps a quarter of a mile in advance of the more slowly moving herd.

'I won't go any further,' she said, and then in quick Spanish to Ross, 'I'm afraid for you. I must take him away before it's too late. He's beginning to remember — things.' Her glance went nervously to the cloud of dust hovering above the herd. Harve Welder and Tony Birl were riding point. 'Be careful with them . . . they'll kill you if you give them a chance to suspect.'

Ross managed to keep a politely affable smile on his face while he listened to her. His heart was heavy with premonitions on her account. He could not refuse to continue on with the herd to the Oxbow camp. A wrong move would unmask him and all indeed would be lost. With an effort he kept the rage and despair from his eyes, kept that smile on his face for the distrustful Tenn's benefit. The play must go on awhile longer. He removed his hat with a sweeping gesture, held it against his heart and bowed courteously as a gallant Mexican would when bidding *adios* to a lady. His words, though, were words of warning. 'You'll hear from me *soon*. Keep close to the house . . . don't go out alone with him . . . you're in danger.' His smile went to Breezy. There was nothing he could say to Breezy, nothing that Tenn couldn't understand. But there was significance in that smile, in his look, and the momentary answering flicker in the old cowboy's eyes told Ross that he understood the unspoken message. Breezy would stick close to the girl.

'The Mex sure puts on plenty high-toned dog tellin' you good-bye,' sneered Tenn. 'Good thing me and Breezy is here or he'd sure try to kiss you.'

Jean ignored him. She was staring across the mesa at the saw-toothed peaks of the Chuckwallas. 'What's that smoke over there?' She spoke in English, was suddenly horrified as Ross turned his head and looked. Fortunately Tenn had not noticed the 'señor's' apparent understanding of her words. Her quick gesture at the peaks had distracted his attention from Ross. Breezy was staring, too, at the little puffs of smoke.

'Injun smoke talk,' the cowboy said. 'Mighty queer. Ain't seed smoke talk sence Geronimo was put away.' He paused, shook his head, added in a puzzled voice, "Tain't Apache talk at that. Cain't make it out a-tall.'

'Oh, hell!' exclaimed Tennessee. 'Just smoke — that's all, and don't mean a damn thing. Come on, Jean, if you're headin' back home, let's go.'

She was watching Ross, saw the sudden tautness of jaw muscles as he stared intently at the curious puffs of smoke. She sensed he read meaning in those puffs.

'What is it?' she asked in Spanish, her voice low.

He did not immediately answer, and then suddenly the little puffs of smoke were gone. Ross looked at her and she saw that his eyes held a bleak light. 'A friend,' he said curtly. 'Do not worry. It was a message to me.'

Tenn's heavy voice broke in. 'Hell,' he grumbled. 'Let's ride, Jean, and tell the damn greaser for me that I hope he keeps on traveling till he hits the border. Tell him I'm all set to break his damn neck if he ever shows up at Flying A again.' He swung his horse, head craned watchfully back. 'Come on, kid.'

She threw Ross a quick smile. '*Adios, amigo!*' The red mare sprang forward, was off in a dead run. Tenn swore, raked his horse with his spurs and set out in chase.

Breezy held his own horse back for a moment. 'He's a damn polecat, Ross,' he said bitterly. 'I'll tell you this, if he gits too much for her to handle I'll sure blow

his light out, if I swing for it.   Don't you worry, son.
I got your message an' I'll stick close.   You get busy, an'
tell Buckshot an' Pete they'll find me on the job.'   With
a grim nod he gave the rangy buckskin his head.

Ross watched from the little knoll where he held his
roan horse, waiting for Harve to come up.   Far in the
lead rode the girl, the red mare running at reckless
speed.   A hundred yards behind her was Tennessee, a
clumsy rider; and overtaking him with every stride of
the long-leaping buckskin rode old Breezy Hessen, sitting
his saddle with the careless ease of a born horseman,
the wide brim of his hat flattened by the wind, voice
shrilly uplifted in the yipping yell of his salty breed.

Ross took comfort in the sight of him overtaking and
passing Tenn Patchen.   The old-timer was a watch-dog
to be relied upon.   Breezy was on his guard now.   Tenn
would not hesitate to kill old Breezy.   After all he was
only an *old* watch-dog, and Flying A was a den of wolves.
What could Breezy do to fend off the danger that threat-
ened the lone lamb?

His gaze traveled across the vast stretch of mesa and
fastened on Chuckwalla Peak.   He would have liked to
send back an answer to that smoke talk.   The Prophet
would be waiting, scouring canyons and valleys and
desert with his long brass telescope.   No chance now,
with the herd so close, and the foreman's watchful eyes
on him.

Harve Welder and Tony Birl drew up on the knoll.
The lanky, taciturn foreman gave him a bleak nod.
It was Tony who spoke, addressing Harve.   'Tenn
shouted for us to watch him close when he hightailed it
past us after the gal.   I think Tenn's so damn jealous
of the Mex he's gone kind of loco.'

The foreman spat out a stream of tobacco juice, gave
Ross a keen glance.   'I ain't so sure he's loco.   There's
times when this feller has me guessin'.'

Tony put a match to the cigarette his fingers had twisted into shape, a scowl on his hard dark face as he gazed back at the approaching herd. 'How come he has you guessin'?' he wanted to know. 'He's nothin' but a Mex. Ain't no harm in him far as I can make out.'

Ross listened with the polite curiosity of a man who does not comprehend the language. The foreman's sharp glance again flickered at him. 'I was thinkin' about Ross Chaine,' he explained in his toneless voice. 'Chaine's an hombre to keep you guessin'. Take that ruckus at the ranch last night. Chaine shows up out of nowhere, hog-ties the boss almost in front of our noses. The boss says we wasn't a hundred yards away when Chaine walks him off to the trees and ties him up.'

'Sure took nerve,' agreed Tony. Admiration tinged his voice. 'No wonder he got Monte like he did. Chaine was too smart for him.'

'He's too smart for most folks,' Harve said gloomily. 'I know a lot about him. He was poison to them rustlin' gangs over in the Territory, and he'll sure be poison to us if we don't get a rope on his neck damn soon.'

'Or empty our guns into him,' grinned Tony. 'Hot lead's a lot faster.' He stared thoughtfully at the tip of his cigarette. 'Don't savvy yet how come you an' Tenn is all worked up about this Mex feller. What's he got to do with Chaine?'

'If you wasn't so stupid you'd savvy what I mean,' grumbled the foreman. 'I've just been tellin' you there's a chance this Mex feller *is* Ross Chaine and that it was him that pulled off the play at the ranch last night.' Harve was looking hard at Ross as he spoke, a hostile gleam in his cold eyes, his hand unostentatiously close to gunbutt.

Tony grunted incredulously. 'You're plenty loco,' he derided. 'Breezy says he seen the Mex in Estrada's *cantina* last night. You cain't pin that play on him — make out he's Chaine.' He guffawed, slapped a dusty leather chap. 'You sure give me a laugh.'

The foreman's eyes continued to bore at Ross, hard, hostile, suspicious. Slowly his expression changed. No man could have stood that test and not shown some betraying flicker of facial muscles. Not even Ross Chaine could have listened to their talk without batting an eye. He would have betrayed himself. This man's indifferent manner was proof he understood no English.

Harve spoke regretfully. 'I reckon he's a Mex all right. Was just tryin' him out, but he's a Mex and we ain't due for any trouble. Was some fearful we was headed for a trap and have the cows took from us. Would be like Chaine to figger some damn trick to raid us.' He looked at Ross again, gave him a friendly smile and held out tobacco sack and papers. 'Have a smoke, señor?'

'*Gracias.*' Ross smiled politely. '*No quiero cigarillo.*' He gestured the 'makings' aside. '*Gracias,*' he repeated.

Harve returned the tobacco to his pocket and glanced at the cattle, now within a hundred yards. 'Time we got to movin',' he said curtly, and rode on down the short slope.

For the moment neither man was looking at Ross. He drew a deep breath, let it out in a long, long sigh of relief. He had the feeling of a man who had been standing on the brink of a precipice with hands reaching out to push him off. With an effort he straightened his face from its suddenly grim lines and put on again the polite nonchalance that as Señor Alfredo Olveras he must wear until the end of the play somewhere beyond Oxbow Creek.

Chapter
12
THE CAMP AT OXBOW

THE MOOD possessed Don Vicente Torres. He drew his horse to a standstill in the shade cast by a great sycamore. 'Estevan! Quick — my guitar.' He began to hum a little tune, lifted hand beating out the time.

The pair of hard-visaged vaqueros following him down the wide floor of the canyon jumped their horses forward and drew alongside. Estevan unslung the guitar from his shoulder and handed it over to the impatient Vicente.

'It has come!' exclaimed the young *ranchero*. He strummed a note, frowned, shook his head. 'But no — the thing eludes me still!'

The two vaqueros reined their horses away to a respectful distance, eyes wary under the shadowy brims of their high steeple hats.

'It is good we are with him when he suffers these moods,' murmured Estevan. It was a thought he had expressed on other similar occasions.

'We are his eyes, his ears,' muttered Diego, as he had often done before. His gaze roved alertly. 'He is always this way, when a new pretty one takes his fancy.' Diego's tone was not without affection. Like Estevan, he had a fondness for their gay and sometimes too-reckless señor.

The guitar twanged, and Vicente's voice lifted in song:

> Chaquita — thy eyes like stars
>   of the night
> Shine down on my heart, bring joy
>   with their light.
> Oh, sweet one, oh jewel, thy
>   lips I'd claim!
> Chaquita — Chaquita, what
>   bliss — thy name!

Don Vicente lowered the guitar and looked with dancing eyes at his companions. 'It is good, my friends. Say you not so?'

'Never have you done so well,' Estevan stanchly declared.

The fierce-eyed Diego remained silent. Vicente frowned. 'Come, come, have you no praise, Diego?'

'It is well done, as Estevan has said.' The vaquero's tone was stiff. 'Perhaps too good for the inspiration.' He gestured eloquently. 'I have seen this granddaughter of Lico Estrada, but perhaps it is of another Chaquita that you sing.'

'Bah!' exclaimed Vicente. 'You have no eyes, my Diego!'

'My eyes are better for other things,' muttered the vaquero. His rifle lifted. 'They keep watch, my señor.'

Vicente and Estevan reached for their own guns, eyes sharply probing the alder thicket indicated by their companion's leveled rifle.

'A boy!' Estevan exclaimed softly.

'Chucho!' Diego lowered his rifle. 'The grandson of Lico Estrada.'

Don Vicente handed the guitar back to Estevan and started twisting a cigarette into shape. He was at once the practical man of affairs. 'You have alarmed the boy,' he said to Diego. 'That rifle of yours does not look pretty from the other end.' His voice lifted in a friendly hail. 'You seek us, Chucho?'

Chucho's bare heels slapped the sides of his red and white pony. 'For you,' he said as he rode close to Don Vicente's side. He held out a piece of paper. 'The two old ones gave me a silver dollar to find you.'

Vicente read the penciled scrawl. 'This is good!' he exclaimed, smiling at the attentive vaqueros. 'Listen.' He read the message out to them.

> Your cousin will be at the Oxbow camp at sundown. Wants help.

The lack of signature apparently caused Vicente no concern. 'A message from Buckshot Kinners,' he told Estevan and Diego.

Chucho's nod confirmed the assertion. 'The two old ones wait at the *cantina*,' he said. 'There will be another silver dollar for me if I take them a writing from you.' His eyes sparkled.

Don Vicente nodded benignantly. 'You shall have it, Chucho.' He fished out a pencil and hastily scribbled a line on the blank side of Buckshot's note which he thrust at the boy. 'And now, another silver dollar if you know your way to Cañon Los Gatos.'

'Sure I do,' Chucho answered in English. 'Means Cat Canyon, in American.'

A dollar spun from the *ranchero's* hand. Chucho deftly snatched the coin, his face ecstatic. 'I am rich,' he gloated. 'I will some day be governor of New Mexico — and very grand.'

'Come to Mexico,' chuckled Don Vicente. 'You shall be president.'

'I am *Americano*,' Chucho said with a finality that forbade further temptation.

'It is all the same.' Don Vicente gestured carelessly. 'Mexican or *Americano*, a good man is a good man anywhere.' He paused, frowned thoughtfully. 'For the silver dollar I have paid, you will go to Cañon Los Gatos where you will find a camp at the spring under the high red cliff. Say to Carlos Montalvo, who waits there with my vaqueros, that I want them to ride at once for the Flying A camp at Oxbow.'

Chucho repeated the message. 'It is done,' he promised and added, 'Will this Carlos Montalvo have another silver dollar for me?'

'Do not be too greedy,' sternly reproved Don Vicente. 'Dollars can burn the fingers.'

'Not mine,' Chucho retorted. 'I put them in a bank.'

The *ranchero's* expression relaxed. 'A smart boy,' he smiled. 'I will leave a five-dollar gold piece with your sister Chaquita for you.'

'Long may you wave!' shrilled Chucho. 'That is good *Americano*,' he explained.

'On your way,' chuckled Don Vicente. 'Do not let the dust catch up with you. The word to Carlos Montalvo is most important.'

Chucho nodded, kicked his pony into a fast run and was lost to view below the alders. Don Vicente swung his own horse down the trail. 'Come,' he said curtly.

The two vaqueros put their horses in motion. Don Vicente glanced back at them, saw the curiosity in their eyes. 'We go to this camp at Oxbow,' he told them. '*Por Dios* — this is fun.'

Estevan and Diego exchanged gloomy looks. Their señor's fantastic ideas sorely tried the patience at times. They should have all been in Deming these two days past, but no, the señor must neglect his own most important affairs because of his interest in the young *Americano* he had chanced to meet at the *cantina* of Lico

Estrada. The thing was incomprehensible, like many other of his adventures. But what could one do save follow where their gaily reckless señor led; be his eyes, his ears — his faithful defenders.

Mesquite and cat's-claw threw restless shadows across the yellowing sunlight when the trio rode up the left bank of Oxbow Creek and halted at the shallow ford where a lone horseman waited on the opposite bank. Still further, perhaps a hundred yards distant, was a barbed wire corral, and a small adobe cabin, its roof thatched with tules. Near the cabin door a man bent over a camp fire, stirring something in a black kettle with a long-handled spoon. The sound of bawling cattle told of an approaching herd below the ridge on the far side of the camp.

A smile of recognition warmed the face of Don Vicente as he looked at the waiting rider on the opposite bank. He sent his horse splashing across the shallow stream.

'This is good,' he laughed. 'You have worked fast.' He laughed again. 'You look astonished, *mi amigo*.'

'Keep to the Spanish when you talk to me,' warned Ross with a quick glance over his shoulder. Harve Welder had topped the ridge and was pushing his horse at a lope down the long slope. Behind him suddenly appeared a line of tossing horns and the cattle came pouring clamorously over the crest in a thirst-maddened rush for the creek.

'Don't forget your cousin speaks no English,' reminded Ross with a grim smile. 'The foreman of this outfit is not any too sure of me, so don't take chances, Vicente. We're sitting on dynamite.' He went on in Spanish, 'Astonished is no word for it. I thought you were in Deming by now. What's the idea?'

'Our good friends, Buckshot and Pete,' smiled Don Vicente. 'We have had talks, yes, and those two are wise — like foxes. They say to me, "Vicente, we leave our young friend in big hell of a mess. It is a hundred to one those wolves find out that Señor Olveras is Ross Chaine. They will tear him to small bits and feed him to the coyotes." '

'It's been touch and go,' admitted Ross with a shrug. Another quick glance told him that Harve was heading their way.

Vicente nodded, his expression grave. 'So ——' he gestured. 'I stay close and today I get a note from Buckshot. The note said you will be at Oxbow and that you need help. So I am here, and before midnight, others will come, Carlos Montalvo and a half score of his riders.'

'Who is Carlos Montalvo?'

'Carlos is my half-brother, and chief of my vaqueros — a fighting man.' Vicente's eyes flashed. 'If there is trouble here, we will be more than ready.'

Ross was watching Harve Welder out of the corner of his eye. He saw the foreman suddenly halt his horse and look back at the camp cook who had hailed him. Harve seemed to hesitate, swung a glance at Ross and the Mexicans, then turned his horse and rode back to the cabin. Ross spoke quickly. 'I don't know how Buckshot and Pete knew I would be at Oxbow with the herd today. They must have had a man watching, or maybe Buckshot was on the job himself.'

'They are greatly worried about you,' Vicente murmured, his eyes on the foreman. 'They keep closer to you than you suspect.'

'Here's the layout,' Ross went on hurriedly. 'It's a load off my mind to have you here, Vicente. You can take over with the cattle and leave me free. I've got to get back to Flying A . . . it's a matter of life and death and won't wait.'

'We ride the wind together, my friend,' the Mexican said simply. 'What you say will govern my actions.'

'You're a damn good man,' Ross told him.

'I am a Torres,' smiled Don Vicente. 'The first of our name in this land rode with Cortez. We do not give friendship lightly. You are my friend, and as I am a Torres, your fight is my fight.'

Ross knew he meant it. 'I won't forget, Vicente ——' He broke off. A man on a blazed-nose horse had joined the foreman and the pair were riding toward them. 'Be careful,' he warned the Mexican. 'There's a man here who understands Spanish. He's coming with Harve now.'

'I will forget nothing,' Vicente reassured. He gave the foreman a genial smile. 'Ha, Señor Welder,' he greeted in English, 'we meet again.'

Suspicion bristled from the lanky foreman like quills from a porcupine. His nod was curt. 'Wasn't lookin' for you at Oxbow, mister. How come you ain't in Deming by now? You was to meet us in Deming — with the money for the cows.'

'A change of plans,' smiled Don Vicente. 'Alas, news comes from Sonora that my cousin must return in haste . . . a matter of life and death.' The Mexican looked at Ross, said solemnly in Spanish, 'My poor cousin! I pray you may be in time. God ride with you, Alfredo. You have my sympathy.'

Harve glanced inquiringly at the man on the blazed-nose horse. 'What's he tellin' him, Curly?'

'Sounds like there's somebody sick or dyin', or somethin',' replied Curly Bristow. 'This Olveras feller has got to hightail it back to Sonora.'

Don Vicente nodded, 'It is so,' he confirmed. 'My poor cousin must leave you at once, and so I have come to take his place.'

'Well ——' Harve's tone was more friendly. 'Don't see that it matters a damn to me which of you sticks round.'

'*Bueno!*' Don Vicente gestured carelessly. 'It is settled, then. My own vaqueros will soon arrive to help,' he added.

Harve pricked up his ears. 'That right, señor?' He stared thoughtfully at the Mexican. 'In that case you can take delivery in the mornin', as quick as we've got the herd made up for the drive to Deming.'

Only Don Vicente noticed the almost imperceptible flicker in Ross' eyes. He shook his head, answered regretfully, 'Not so, Señor Welder. My money is in the Deming bank. It is the bargain that you deliver the cows to me in Deming. The money will be there for you.'

The foreman looked disappointed. 'Seems like fool bus'ness for us to go all the way to Deming when you've got your own outfit on hand,' he pointed out.

'It is the bargain.' Don Vicente spoke firmly. 'My men will help, but I will not accept responsibility for the drive. It is up to you, señor, to see that the cows reach Deming.' He looked at Ross and explained the argument in quick Spanish.

Curly Bristow, long-limbed and angular, listened with frowning attention. 'He's tellin' the other feller what you said about him takin' over on the spot,' he told Harve in an aside.

'Looks like we're stuck to go all the way to Deming,' the foreman grumbled. 'I'll take you along, Curly. You're the only one of us can talk the lingo.' He drew Bristow aside. 'Ain't carin' for the set-up awful much,' he went on in a low voice. 'I'll be in a hell of a mess if this Mex outfit gets the notion to take the cows away from us and run 'em west across the border.'

'The feller looks straight enough,' commented Curly. 'No sense taking chances, at that.'

'I'm not taking chances,' declared Harve. 'There's most a dozen of us, with you along. I reckon we can handle this Mex outfit if they try any tricks on us.'

'Sure we can,' grunted Curly.

'I'll send Tony back with word for the boss,' Harve said as the pair turned to rejoin the others. 'You go tell him I want him to start soon as he's et supper. Fix him up with a fresh bronc, Curly.'

Ross overheard the remark. His thoughts raced. Something would have to happen to Tony. The man must not be allowed to get back to the ranch with the news about Señor Olveras. He spoke to Don Vicente. 'I've got to get away from here in a hurry. Tell him I want a fresh horse.'

'Sure,' agreed Harve, when Don Vicente explained the situation. 'We'll fix him up. He can leave the horse at Stack Jimson's livery barn. I cain't sell him a Flying A horse, but he can buy him a good one from Stack.' He looked at the roan under Ross. 'What about this horse he's ridin'?'

'I will turn him over to my men,' Don Vicente said with a quick look at Ross. 'Will you please arrange for this fresh horse, señor? My cousin is in haste to ride.'

'Ain't he stayin' for some supper?' queried the surprised foreman.

Don Vicente shook his head. 'Alas — this sad news . . . it is a shock. His one thought is to reach the side of his loved one.'

Ross indeed had the look of a man ridden hard by anxiety. His eyes were feverish with impatience. He gave the Mexican a curiously startled glance. Don Vicente spoke better than he knew, or had his agile mind pounced on the truth? There had been no time to tell him of his fears for Jean Austen. Vicente must have guessed.

'Sure tough luck,' sympathized Harve. 'At that he can make Dos Cruces in a couple of hours. He can eat there while Stack's getting a horse ready for him.' He rode off at a trot toward the corral, voice lifted in a loud shout to Bristow. 'Throw a rope on that brown mare, Curly. Olveras is sweatin' blood to be on his way.'

Ross and Vicente started their horses and followed him to the corral. Behind them trailed Estevan and Diego, eyes roving warily under hat brims.

'I do not like this,' muttered Estevan. 'I will be pleased when Carlos Montalvo and the others come. I do not trust these gringos.'

'Our señor is a true Torres,' grumbled his Yaqui half-brother. 'He is not happy unless playing tag with danger.' A smile glinted in Diego's fierce eyes. 'We would not have him different, eh, my brother?'

'*Por Dios!* It is the truth. He puts the spice into life.'

Don Vicente hailed them. He spoke guardedly, eyes on Curly Bristow. 'He speaks our language, so watch your tongues,' he warned. His eyes danced. 'And do not act so like dogs in a pack of wolves.'

Ross stripped his saddle gear from the tired roan horse and in a few moments the brown mare was ready. He swung into the saddle.

'I will ride with you to the ford,' Don Vicente said. He glanced at Curly Bristow. 'Beyond the long ears of our friend.'

Side by side the two rode from the corral. They passed the cabin, where Harve Welder was talking to Tony Birl. The foreman's hand lifted in a careless parting gesture. Tony grinned. 'Tenn Patchen won't mind a bit when he hears the Mex is headed back for the border. Tenn sure hates Olveras' guts. Kind of queer the way Tenn got uneasy when Olveras was round. You could almost see him sniff, like a dog does when he smells danger an' don't know just what's got him worried.'

'The girl, I reckon,' commented Harve. 'Tenn figgered they was some spoony.'

'Mebbe so.' Tony wrinkled his brows. 'I ain't so sure you've hit it, Harve. It ain't just the girl. It's somethin' kind of onnatural — like as if a ghost was scarin' Tenn ever'time he saw the Mex.' He shrugged dusty shoulders. 'Well, I'll go eat and then hightail it for the ranch.'

Ross had not missed Tony's interested look. He gave Vicente a thin smile. 'He thinks it's *adios* for Señor Olveras,' he said. 'He's got a surprise coming.'

Don Vicente nodded. 'You go back to the Flying A?' His tone was placid. 'I guessed as much.'

'I must get the girl away from that place, Vicente.' He paused. 'Listen — don't let Harve balk on the cow deal.'

'Do not worry.' Don Vicente gestured carelessly. 'You want those cows in Deming. It is done.'

'Harve may get suspicious.'

'We will take good care of him, and his men. They all go with the cows to Deming.' Don Vicente's eyes danced. 'Ha! It is good fun!'

'The longer Harve and his outfit are in Deming, the better for me,' Ross told him soberly. 'Things are working up, Vicente.'

'I will be back,' promised the Mexican simply. 'The men of the Torres rancho will fight by your side, my friend.'

'*Adios!*' Ross lifted a hand in parting salute and sent the brown mare splashing across the ford.

Don Vicente made no move to immediately return to the camp. He sat there in his saddle, smoking tiny cigarettes, his expression grave, thoughtful. The twi-light deepened. Lights sprang from the cabin, and suddenly, a vague, bulking shape came drifting through the fast growing darkness toward the Mexican. He snubbed his cigarette against saddle horn, spoke politely as the lone horseman drew close.

Tony Birl halted his horse, stared at him suspiciously. 'What are you waitin' here at the ford for?' he asked. 'Cook won't keep supper any too long. He's awful short-tempered.'

'My 'eart ees sad,' Don Vicente replied. 'I find comfort in my thoughts, not in food.'

The cowboy guffawed. 'You go eat a good steak You won't feel so sad about your cousin.'

The Mexican looked at him strangely. 'You 'ave eat the good steak, eh, my frien'?' He shook his head solemnly. 'There is old saying, "Eat, drink, an' be merry — for tomorrow we die" — or ees it tonight?' he added with a hint of grimness in his voice.

'Oh, hell!' grunted Tony. He kicked his horse into motion, went splashing across the ford. The Mex was sure loco.

Chapter
13

ACTION IN THE CHAPARRAL

THE OXBOW was actually a tributary of West Fork Creek, which in turn was once a lesser branch of Red Creek until Buel Patchen's great dam diverted the headwaters and transformed the former Arroyo Colorado into a desolate dry wash fringed with stunted desert willows and mesquite that managed to send roots down to subterranean pools.

As he recrossed the shallow stream some two miles above the camp, Ross found himself almost admiring the diabolical cleverness that had laid waste the prosperous ranch wrested from the wilderness by his sturdy pioneer father. More than the ranch had suffered. The ghost town of Alamos bore mute testimony to the ruthless ambitions of Buel Patchen and those who secretly conspired with him. Settlers had moved into the broad lowlands of Red Creek Valley, small farmers, growers of hay and grain, fruits and vegetables. Jim Chaine had encouraged them, and Alamos, once a lonely little stage station, flourished, a place of neat homes and gardens and shady cottonwood trees. Jim Chaine himself had backed the building of the Alamos Hotel, put money into Ole Johnson's general merchandise store. He had been the first to subscribe money for the little schoolhouse, and had generously supported the mission church.

Buel Patchen's dam had changed it all, and under its black curse discouraged men had moved on with their families. The desert could bloom, when there was water in plenty, but without water the struggle was hopeless. So they moved on, and the little town of Alamos faded, withered, became a ghost town, a tragic symbol of man's dreams — and man's greed.

A small shape drifted like a puff of wind-blown smoke from under a bush. The brown mare snorted.

Ross wrenched his thoughts away from the dismal past. He'd run smack into something a lot more deadly than a jackrabbit if he allowed his mind to wander from the grim demands of the present.

He halted the mare and studied his surroundings, ears alert for any sound that would betray the approach of Tony Birl. Tony had to be stopped from reaching the ranch. The chances for a surprise were good. The surprise must be complete. The Flying A man would not hesitate to shoot if he saw Ross before Ross saw him. Tony was under the impression that Señor Olveras was well on his way toward Dos Cruces. To find him headed for the ranch would instantly arouse his suspicions.

Stars winked brightly down from the moonless sky. Ross could see the vague outline of the Chuckwallas darkly massed against the horizon. He thought of The Prophet — the smoke talk — Jean's curiosity. She had guessed there was a message in those little puffs of smoke. He had pretended not to hear her question. She would have misunderstood, lost her faith in him, cried out against him.

His jaws set in long hard lines. The Prophet had pointed out the way. A seemingly ruthless and terrible means to an end, a savage weapon to swing at the enemies of Bar Chain — the enemies of Red Creek Valley. Even Buckshot and Pete had exchanged uneasy looks when he outlined the plan to them. Gradually their doubts vanished as they listened, began to realize the tremendous possibilities. Not ruin and chaos, but a new hand all around — honest cards fairly dealt.

The mare's ears pricked up sharply. Ross pulled her quickly off the trail to the concealment of a thick clump of cat's-claw. He got down, tied the mare securely, drew his gun and ran to a mass of tumbled rock near the bend in the trail. He crouched behind a greasewood that had found roothold in soil blown by the winds and caught and held in the crevice of a huge split boulder.

He had not long to wait. Tony swung around the lower bend, his horse moving at an easy lope. Ross lifted his gun, was about to speak when the concealed mare nickered softly. She wore the same Flying A brand that marked Tony's horse. They were friends — pals of the same corral.

That low nicker of recognition was enough for Tony. Like a flash he was down from his saddle, crouched from view behind a bush-screened boulder. The horse halted, looked around inquiringly, then broke into a trot toward the cat's-claw that hid the brown mare.

Silence settled over the scene, a long, taut stillness through which Ross could hear the faint ticking of the watch in his pocket. He still possessed an advantage over the Flying A man. Tony would begin to have doubts. The fact that a horse had nickered out of the dark did not necessarily mean the presence of a man. The horse might be a riderless stray. Ross knew he had only to sit tight long enough and Tony would presently allow his growing doubts to allay his fears of an ambush.

Five minutes passed. There was a stirring in the bushes across the trail, the scrape of boot-heel. Ross grinned at the ruse. Tony was hoping to draw fire and so settle the question of an ambush.

More minutes dragged while Tony considered things. Ross patiently waited. The man would have to make a move. He would not endure the uncertainty longer than was reasonably necessary to satisfy himself that his fears were groundless.

Suddenly the bushes crackled again and this time Ross saw Tony, a vague dark shape against the boulder. Another long silence. Evidently reassured, the Flying A man moved back to the trail, stood fully revealed under the starlight. As his head turned to look at the thicket of cat's-claw that had swallowed his horse, Ross stepped quickly into the trail, his feet soundless as a stalking cat's.

'Your first guess was best, Tony,' he said softly. 'The mare didn't lie.'

The man's stocky figure stiffened. He slowly turned his head, showed a shocked face.

'I'll be damned . . . it's the Mex.' His tone was bitter.

'Drop your gun, Tony.'

'Damn you.' The gun dropped from Tony's hand. 'You ain't no Mex a-tall! You're Ross Chaine!'

Ross picked up the fallen gun, stuck it in his holster.

'I am Señor Alfredo Olveras,' he corrected with a low chuckle.

'Pertendin' you no savvy American talk!' sneered the angry Flying A man.

Ross studied him with hard eyes. He had overheard this man wish that Harve had sent him to do the job that had cost the blundering Monte his life. Tony had already murdered him in his thoughts. He was a cold-blooded and callous killer. The world would be well rid of a bad man if Ross squeezed a little harder on the trigger of his forty-five. An illegal execution, in the eyes of the law, but practical justice in a land where the law was still the law of Judge Colt.

Tony watched him uneasily.   He licked dry lips.
'What you goin' to do with me?'

'I'm trying to make up my mind,' Ross answered
simply.

'You ain't killin' me in cold blood.'   Tony spoke
huskily. 'It'll be *murder*.'

'You don't think of it that way when you're doing the
killing,' Ross said harshly. 'My father was shot in cold
blood. Maybe your hand pulled the trigger, Tony.'

The man seemed to cringe as if Ross had struck him.
Beads of sweat sprang on his face. 'It's a lie!' He
mumbled the words. 'You're loco — talkin' thataways.'

His abject fear startled Ross, fanned smoldering coals
of suspicion to hot flames of certainty that brought a
tremble to the hand clenched over gun-butt.   Tony
knew the truth, could name the men who had killed his
father — killed Bill Austen.

All the stored-up bitterness and grief of fifteen years
must have been in the look he gave the Flying A man.
Tony cowered, flung up an appealing hand, mouthed
incoherent words.   And suddenly the hot, blasting anger
that was shaking him like a leaf left Ross.   The cool,
well-ordered mind was in control again.   He spoke
quietly.

'I'm not killing you, Tony.   You're too valuable.
I'm keeping you safe — *very* safe.'

A voice broke in from close behind him, a flat, toneless voice. 'Much obliged, Señor Ross Chaine, an'
mind your manners, mister.'

Ross felt the hard press of gun barrel in the small of
his back.   He stood rigid, horrified.   The voice spoke
again. 'Take his smoke-pot, Tony.'

The cowboy moved swiftly, unutterable venom in his
eyes as he snatched the Colt, deftly recovered his own
gun.   And suddenly Ross saw the newcomer's face, the
sardonic face of Harve Welder.

'Figgered some monkey bus'ness was up,' drawled the Flying A foreman. He laughed silently, cold sneering eyes on Ross. 'You pulled off a right smart play, but you wasn't smart enough, Chaine.'

Ross could only look at him. He had no words at that moment. These men would kill him. He was sure of that. He knew too much. Harve must have over-heard what he had said to Tony. Harve knew his own life was at stake — knew he must destroy the man who had surprised the secret from Tony.

It was Tony who broke that bleak silence. 'Let me finish him off,' he said viciously. His gun lifted. 'I owe him one for Monte. I got a damn itch in my trigger-finger.'

Harve's look silenced him. 'I'm runnin' this show,' he said.

The cowboy sulkily holstered his gun. 'How come you got wise an' follered me?' he wanted to know.

'One of them things you call a hunch,' Harve answered with his thin-lipped grimace. 'Nothin' you can pin a word to, Tony. Just plain hunch that somethin' smelled bad. Figgered it would be smart play to trail along after you for a piece. Was beginnin' to call myself a damn fool for notions when I come up in time to show an ace card.' His silent laugh again shook his long, lank frame.

'He was all set to blow my light out,' lied Tony with a venomous look at Ross. 'He's a sidewinder, Harve. We should orter fix him here an' now.'

'I heard what he said to you,' Harve told him coldly. 'He was fixin' to keep you *very* safe.'

'I savvy.' Tony shrugged wide shoulders. 'Was figgerin' I'd talk, huh?' He spat into the dust. 'Don't you git to worryin' I'd ever talk, Harve.'

'I'm makin' certain you don't get the talkin' crave,' Harve said gently.

The unmistakable note of warning in the foreman's voice brought an ugly look from the cowboy. He muttered an oath, turned on his heel abruptly. 'I'll go git a rope down from my saddle,' he said.

'Where's your horse?' queried Harve.

'Back in that cat's-claw, where he hid the mare.' Tony disappeared in the chaparral. In a few moments he was back. The starlight showed a mixture of bewilderment and annoyance on his hard dark face. 'The broncs ain't there in the cat's-claw,' he announced. 'Sure is hell where they've got to.'

Harve Welder's head turned in a look at him, and in that fleeting instant of inattention Ross plunged at him in a headlong dive. His outstretched hand gripped the foreman's wrist, forced the gun down as Harve squeezed the trigger. A yell of pain followed the explosion. Somebody had been hit. Ross was too busy to wonder. He wrapped his arms desperately around the aghast Harve.

The foreman was strong and tough. Recovering from the first shock of surprise he fought to break Ross' hold and regain possession of his fallen gun. Ross tripped him and they went down, rolled over and over in furious struggle.

The anguished yell had come from Tony Birl. For a moment he stood motionless, stared dazedly at his bleeding right hand. Harve's wild bullet had nipped off the tip of his forefinger.

The foreman's muffled yell aroused him. He jerked gun from holster and ran toward the struggling men, circled them, watching for an opportunity to send a bullet into Ross. They were moving so fast he was unable to get in a shot for fear of hitting the wrong man.

'Smash his head!' gasped the foreman.

Tony stepped in close, took a wild swing and went down on his face as Ross jabbed him in the groin with a spurred heel. The gun barrel cracked hard on Harve's elbow, brought an anguished yell from him. Ross snatched the forty-five from Tony's suddenly limp hand and sprang to his feet.

The two Flying A men slowly got up. Harve's scratched and bleeding face wore an incredulous look. Tony clamped a hand over his bruised groin, stood groaning, his dark face twisted with pain.

'You should have let Tony squeeze that trigger the first time,' Ross said the moment he had breath to speak. His eyes blazed at them. 'Keep your hands up.'

Harve said nothing. He suddenly looked like an old and defeated man.

'I should kill the pair of you,' Ross went on in a tight, rage-choked voice. 'Better for you if I did, but you're going to do some talking before you die — before the hangman puts his rope over your necks.'

The gaunt old foreman found his voice. 'You can go to hell,' he said.

Ross fixed cold eyes on the pain-wracked Tony. 'You'd hate to feel that rope tighten over your neck, eh, Tony? You'd want to talk — tell some things you know.'

The man's face took on a gray look. He flicked a sidewise glance at Harve. 'You — you ain't scarin' me none,' he gasped.

'Harve will kill you if he ever gets the chance,' Ross told him. 'He's not trusting you any more. He knows you're yellow.'

'You're a liar,' Tony muttered between gritted teeth. His head suddenly lifted in an amazed stare at something behind Ross. He added in a stifled voice, 'I'll be damned.'

Harve Welder was staring, too, his thin lips parted in the fierce snarl of a balked old he-wolf. Ross heard a low, amused laugh, the politely ironic voice of Don Vicente Torres:

'True words, my frien'. Hanged and damned. *Sí!* You no lie.' The Mexican was suddenly close by the side of Ross. Behind him loomed the shapes of Estevan and Diego.

'A pretty fight,' Don Vicente went on. 'I had not the heart to interfere.' He looked sharply at the two Flying A men. 'Ha — you tackled a mountain lion, which was a mistake, my frien's — a very bad mistake.' His voice sharpened. 'Estevan — Diego, tie up these dogs ... make the knots tight.'

The vaqueros moved quickly to obey. Ross lowered his gun, stared hard at his Mexican friend. 'How in the hell did you get here?'

Don Vicente laughed softly. 'Ha — it ees the 'unch, as the Señor Welder would say. I watch ... I tell the faithful Diego and Estevan to watch. And so ——' he gestured eloquently, 'we arrive ... we find the mare — the 'orse, in the cat's-claw. We remove them ——' he broke off, smiled at Tony's bitter curse. '*Sí*, my frien' ... that ees why you no find the 'orse. We 'ave the beeg laugh w'en we see your funny face.'

'I wasn't giving myself one chance in a thousand,' Ross said with a rueful grin. He flexed an aching arm gingerly. 'You were a bit slow getting into action, Vicente.'

'You took that one chance, and won,' smiled Don Vicente. His voice hardened as he looked at the scowling Flying A foreman. 'You took the long chance that won, but you also saved the lives of these dogs. By now they would be dead — *very* dead.'

Diego looked round at Ross, his smile grim. 'It is not too late to make them very dead,' he said in Spanish. There was longing in his voice.

Ross shook his head. 'I want them alive.'

Diego's dark face showed disappointment. He jerked

another tight knot in the cord that bound the foreman's wrists behind his back.

'What will you do with them?' Don Vicente inquired in Spanish. He frowned, fingered trim black mustache thoughtfully.

'It's a mess,' worried Ross. 'I wanted those cattle in Deming.' He gingerly rubbed his scratched cheek. 'We can't move those cows from Oxbow without Harve on the job. His men won't stir without him. If he doesn't show up at the camp by morning there'll be hell to pay.'

'Carlos Montalvo and his vaqueros can take care of them.' Don Vicente assured him with a careless gesture.

'I wanted those Flying A men a long way from the ranch,' Ross continued. 'It's a mess, Vicente. They'll wonder what's become of Harve — send word to Buel Patchen that he's missing.'

'Señor Patchen must not hear about it,' agreed Don Vicente. 'We must use our brains . . . they are good brains.' He chuckled.

Ross came to a decision. 'Only one thing to do. Your Carlos Montalvo must keep every last man of the Flying A outfit at the Oxbow camp.'

'Carlos will tie them with their own ropes,' replied the Mexican with a hard laugh. 'It is done, my frien'.'

'How many men, including Carlos?' queried Ross.

'Eleven . . . all of them so tough that not even a wolf can sink tooth into their hides. Torres vaqueros are bred that way.' The Mexican's teeth glinted under the starlight. 'With Estevan and Diego and myself, we make fourteen, more than enough to hold your gringo vaqueros safe at Oxbow.'

Ross shook his head, his gaze on the two bound Flying A men. 'You have another job, Vicente. These two men are valuable to me. They can tell me things i must know. I want them kept safe.'

'Where more safe than at the Oxbow camp?' argued Vicente.

Ross glanced at Harve and Tony. They could not understand Spanish, but there were names for which there was no Spanish. He motioned for Vicente to follow him beyond earshot. 'I'm thinking of Buckshot and Pete,' he said. 'Can you get these men over to the LK ranch? They'd be safe enough there.'

'No more safe than at the Oxbow,' insisted the Mexican. 'It is a long way to the LK, and it is best for me to be with my men. We will keep these Flying A gringos safely corralled for you, my friend.' His eyes glittered. 'Not one shall escape. You will have your free hand.'

Ross surrendered. There was truth in the Mexican's contention. The Oxbow camp was remote. It was hardly possible anyone would learn of the calamity that had overtaken the Flying A riders. More than half of Buel Patchen's men would be under the watchful eyes and guns of Don Vicente's tough-minded vaqueros. Any chance visitor would share the same fate. It could be done, and he needed only a few more days.

'I'm leaving it to you, Vicente,' he said. He looked off at the two prisoners. 'Keep Harve and Tony in close confinement, but not together. That small shack back of the corral would do for Harve.' He paused, active mind racing. 'You'll have to use surprise . . . get the drop on them, take their guns, knives, anything they can use for a weapon. You can use that wagon-load of barbed wire we noticed, rig up a fence that should hold them.'

'*Por Dios!*' exclaimed the Mexican. 'Do you teach a newborn calf where to find its milk?' He chuckled goodhumoredly. 'My friend, I well know the virtues of barbed wire.'

'You're tackling a job,' warned Ross. 'You'll have a bunch of wildcats on your hands.'

Don Vicente made his careless gesture, then suddenly grave, 'You are in haste to be on your way. Come, I will show you where we hid the mare.' He called to the vaqueros to follow with the prisoners and led Ross around the bend in the trail and into a little gully. The horses, six of them, were tied to the gnarled branches of a juniper tree.

Ross climbed into his saddle. '*Adios, señores.*' His grim smile flickered at the two sullen-faced Flying A men as he swung back to the trail.

The late moon was showing a red tip above the dark wall of mountains. As if in salutation to the queen of the night sky, a coyote gave tongue from some distant knoll, a short, sharp bark that instantly swelled into a yipping chorus. Then a sudden stillness, broken only by the thud of the mare's hoofs, the creak of saddle leather.

Much had happened in half an hour. A life nearly lost, Harve Welder and a good half of his riders in custody — and 'Señor Olveras' again on his way to the succor of a lonely and endangered girl. Ross began to hum a little tune as he rocked along on the easy-gaited mare.

Chapter
14
A CALL FOR HELP

PERHAPS it was instinct that made Jean want to avoid
being alone with Tenn Patchen. Something told her
that a crisis was fast approaching. Now added to the
loathing and contempt she had for him was a new emo-
tion — *fear*. She had never felt afraid of Tenn. Her
tongue had always been more than a match for her slow-
witted step-cousin. The past twenty-four hours had
curiously changed the man in a way that frightened her.
She sensed danger in him. His look made her flesh
creep.

She reached the ranch yard a good hundred yards in
the lead and slid from her saddle. Breezy brought his
horse to a halt alongside and took the mare's reins.

'You sure come a-kitin',' he said. There was no
mirth in the brief smile he gave her, and he added in a
low voice, 'I savvy, Jean.'

'I'm afraid,' she said with a little catch in her breath.
'He — he looks so mean. He frightens me.'

The old cowboy glanced at the approaching Tenn who
was viciously quirting his horse to a mad run up the
avenue. 'You git away from here,' he advised.

Jean started toward the patio gate. She was too proud
to run. She was not going to let Tenn see that she was

afraid of him. She walked quickly, quirt dangling from her wrist.

Tenn was coming faster than she realized. His horse flashed through the gate and cut across the yard in front of the girl. She was forced to stop for fear he would run her down.

'Why didn't you wait for me?' He flung himself from the saddle and confronted her, heavy face flushed with anger. 'I yelled loud enough.'

Jean shrugged, looked at the winded, sweat-lathered horse. 'You're awfully hard on a horse, Tenn. Look, you've quirted blood from the poor beast.'

'None of your damn bus'ness!' he said furiously.

'That's a Flying A horse,' Jean said in a hard little voice. 'My property, Tenn. I won't have you mistreating my horses.'

'I'll treat 'em any way I damn please!' he shouted. 'You, too, if you ain't careful.' He slashed the horse savagely with his quirt. The animal squealed, broke into a panic-stricken run across the big yard. Tenn grinned at her. 'That's me,' he said, 'Treat-'em-Rough Tenn Patchen.' His hand was suddenly on her arm, a hard cruel grasp. 'I'm done with your snippy ways, kid.'

'Let go of me!' Jean hardly recognized her own voice, thin and taut, so sharp-edged with anger. She lifted the rawhide quirt and slashed at the hand on her arm. Tenn drew back with a startled oath. Taking advantage of his momentary daze she ran for the patio gate. He shouted something, started in pursuit, came to an abrupt standstill, his face turned in a look back at Breezy Hessen.

The old cowboy grinned at him, slowly pushed his long-barrelled gun into its holster. 'I was sayin' this ol' shootin' iron sure needs a workout. Ain't fired her off for a coon's age.'

'I heard what you said.' Tenn was breathing hard. 'You said you'd shoot my damn guts out.'

'You got funny ears,' cackled Breezy. His eyes, though, were not smiling and his hand hovered suspiciously close to the worn black butt of the big Colt. 'You should git 'em cleaned out good,' he added with another cackle.

Tenn stared at him for a moment. Breezy's eyes met the look squarely. There was a message in their chill depths that seemed to daunt the younger man. With a stifled oath he swung on his heel and pushed through the patio gate.

Buel Patchen was standing on the porch steps. 'You damn fool,' he said as his son stamped up. His big head weaved from side to side on his humped shoulders, the motion of an enraged bear. 'You're a hell of a lover!'

'I'll break her . . . I'll tame the little wildcat.' Tenn's voice was hoarse with balked passion. 'She's gettin' too smart, yippin' about Flying A horses being her property.'

Buel nodded gloomily. 'I've seen it coming, son. Jean's all set to stampede us out of here, soon as she's of age. She's got too much of her father in her to handle easy.'

'You leave her to me,' grunted Tenn.

'Time's getting short,' reminded his father. 'You've bungled the job, son. You're too damn clumsy.'

'I'll fix her,' Tenn assured him with an ugly grin.

Buel Patchen said with terrible finality, 'If you don't, I will — in the only way left. There's too much at stake. . . . And there's Ross Chaine to be reckoned with. I can't wait on your blundering attempts to marry the girl. She'll have none of you.'

'She'll marry me,' blustered Tenn. 'Won't be nothin' left for her to do.'

'She'll kill you,' his father said. His tone was contemptuous. 'I'm not sure I'd grieve.'

Tenn snorted, gave his father an angry look and strode

up the steps. The door slammed behind him. Buel
Patchen went slowly down the flagstones to the gate.
Breezy was unsaddling Jean's mare. Buel stood watching until the chore man carried the saddle into the
harness-room and led the mare off to the barn.

Buel's gaze followed him speculatively, then suddenly
he went quickly to the harness room, the hand in his
pocket clasped over his knife.

He was out again in a few moments and moving briskly
back to the patio gate, but not before Breezy's sharp eyes
saw him.

The chore man paused in the stable doorway. He
had not noticed Buel in the yard when he led the mare
across to the barn. His puzzled gaze went to the harness-
room. His eyes narrowed. He had left the door open.
Now it was closed.

Vaguely disturbed, Breezy crossed the yard and went
inside the harness-room. He stared around uneasily,
wondering about Buel Patchen. There had been something almost furtive in his manner as he disappeared
through the garden gate. Buel had not wanted Breezy
to know of his visit to the harness-room. The closed door
had betrayed him.

The old cowboy took up his cleaning rag, moved to the
girl's saddle, hanging from its peg, and began to wipe
off the dust. He paused, muttered under his breath,
stared with startled eyes at the cinch. The latigo had
been neatly sliced, high up on the under side. A casual
glance would not have noticed the damage.

Breezy swore softly, feelingly, as he stared at the
knife-cut. It was a diabolical piece of work. The leather
would have held long enough to pull the cinch tight.
Nobody would have suspected the latigo had been
tampered with. Jean might have ridden for miles, and
the cinch remain tightly in place. But Jean was a bold,

daring rider, and the red mare frisky and high-spirited. Any sudden strain would part the cut leather.

The cowboy's face reddened with the anger that flamed within him. He had the answer now about Buel Patchen's sly visit to the harness-room. It was an answer that horrified him. Just what to do, he did not know, except to quickly replace the cut latigo with a fresh one and say nothing about it. Buel would not know that a new latigo replaced the one he had damaged. He would be waiting, and hoping for the worst to happen. In the meantime there was Ross Chaine. Ross had promised he would be back — soon.

Old Breezy set to work with feverish haste. He must replace the cut latigo before Buel could suspect his tampering had been discovered. Any moment might bring Buel back to the yard, anxious to see if Breezy had noticed anything wrong.

He made the change quickly, thrust the damaged latigo inside his shirt and went outside. The coast was clear. No sign of Buel. Breezy closed the harness-room door and returned to the barn.

His shrewd guess that Buel would be back for a look proved correct. He heard the click of the patio gate. He went to a knothole near the stable door and peered out. Buel Patchen was sauntering toward the harness-room. Breezy saw him look at the closed door. Apparently satisfied, the hunchback retraced his steps and disappeared into the garden.

Jean saw her step-uncle from her bedroom window. She leaned out, called to him softly, 'Uncle Buel.'

He looked at her, smiled. 'What's wrong?' His bell-like voice took on a note of concern. 'You look kind of pale.'

'I want you to tell Tenn he must leave me alone,' the girl said in a fierce, low whisper. 'I can't bear it any longer. I *won't* bear it,' she added desperately.

He stood watching her, his smile gently tolerant. 'Tenn is set on marrying you, Jean.' He shook his head regretfully. 'I was hoping you'd fall in with the idea. Seems like it would be the sensible thing . . . hold us all together here on the ranch.'

'I won't bear it any longer,' she repeated.

His eyebrows lifted. 'What will you do?'

'I'll go to El Paso, or Santa Fe . . . . Stay away from here until I'm of age and — and my own boss.'

'You are your own boss right here on the ranch,' he said, a hint of reproach in his voice. 'You shouldn't be talking that way to me, after all I've done for you.'

Her stony silence to this visibly disturbed him. His face darkened for a moment, then again he was smiling, his eyes full of beaming good humor. 'I'll tell Tenn to lay off,' he promised. 'In the meantime, think it over about him. You'd be a lot more contented married, and you'd make a man out of Tenn. He'd settle down — be a good husband.' His voice took on a longing note that would have deceived anyone except Jean herself. 'I'd kind of like to see some little folks running round the place. It's time I'm grandpa, Jean.' He moved on past the window. 'Buck up, girl. Tell Breezy to throw your saddle on Redbird this afternoon and go for a good ride some place. Take the hounds along . . . You'll maybe jump a coyote.'

His suggestion of a ride did not appeal to Jean. She was, for the first time, afraid to go out alone for fear Tenn would follow her. She sensed there was danger in being alone with him. She would not give him the chance.

She kept to her room for the rest of the day. Sing Gee brought her some food on a tray. 'You sick?' She was conscious of his sharp eyes probing her.

'I don't know. I guess so.' Her tone was listless.

The old Chinese shook his head. 'You not sick . . .

you heap scared, you bet.' His slippered foot reached out and softly toed the door shut. 'You lissen me,' he whispered, 'you go way flom here plenty damn quick. Tenn Patchen no good . . . he bad fellah — allee time make eyes same as pig at you.'

Jean said, 'I've got to get away, Sing Gee. But I — I'm afraid they'll stop me.' Her voice was unsteady.

The cook's thin hand touched her gently. 'Maybe can do something. Me tell Bleezy. He velly good man.' He nodded, smiled encouragingly and shuffled from the room.

The thought of the two old faithful ones, standing by to help as best they could, somewhat cheered her. She found herself tempted by the tender little steak Sing Gee had brought her. She ate it with relish, finished the meal with the apple pie and hot coffee. The food did her good. She felt stronger, mentally and physically.

Twice during the afternoon, Buel had knocked on her door, suggesting that she go for a ride. He was strangely insistent about it. She wondered if it was a plot to give Tenn a chance to catch her out alone. It was not a pleasant thought to have about Buel Patchen. Odious as it was, Jean could not down it. Ross Chaine had told her about the conversation between Buel and his son the morning of the affair in Alamos.

Sing Gee returned for the tray, beamed approvingly at the empty dishes. 'Velly good,' he said. His voice lowered. 'Me catchee Bleezy. He say tell you he savvy . . . he say you keep allee same dless foh lide maybe damn quick.'

Jean nodded. 'I'll be ready,' she replied. 'Tell Breezy — any time — but he must be careful. They'll kill him if ——' She faltered. 'I'm afraid, Sing. He's — an old man.'

'Hoh!' Sing Gee chuckled. 'Him plenty good man, allee same me. You keep leady foh quick lide.'

'I'll be watching,' promised the girl. She paused, looked at him with troubled eyes. 'Sing — don't let them suspect you helped me. They might ——' Again she faltered.

The old Chinese cook's face was a bland mask. She had no means of knowing how her concern for his safety warmed his heart. 'Me no catchee tlouble,' he assured her, and softly closed the door behind him.

Jean got out of her dress and into a pair of blue over-alls and boots and a mulberry-colored flannel shirt. She took down her gun-belt from its peg in the closet and buckled it around her waist, examined the thirty-two Colt in the holster. She had some money in a drawer. Five-dollar gold pieces, a twenty-dollar piece and two tens. Nearly a hundred dollars. She put the coins in a small buckskin bag with a drawstring and tucked the bag inside her shirt.

Her clock told her it was after nine. She put on her white Stetson, blew out the lamp, sat down in a chair by the window and pushed up the shade. It was pitch dark, with a sprinkle of stars showing through the trees.

She began to wonder where it would all lead to. She was running away from her own home. The thought hurt her, sent a wave of anger through her. She was running away from Flying A — her own ranch — fleeing in fear from men she had known and trusted since she was a child. The thing was incredible, but a stark and hideous fact. Only flight could save her from she knew not what terrors.

An hour passed. All was silent in the house. Moon-light began to sift through the trees. Jean heard the far-off yipping chorus of coyotes. The hounds answered; and then again the silence.

The long wait there in the dark room fretted her. She began to speculate wildly. The Patchens had become suspicious, were keeping too close a watch on Breezy. They knew the old man was loyal to her. He was a hang-over from the days of her father, the only man left of the old outfit.

She sat there, her heart beating, her mind racked with anxiety. The hounds broke into an uproar that as suddenly hushed. The minutes dragged with torturous slowness, yet their passing sent apprehensive chills through her. Time was so precious. She must be far away before daylight — and the discovery of her empty room.

Something seemed to move, out there in the elusive moonlight. Jean watched, hardly dared to breathe. Or was it only a bush, stirred by the night wind?

The shadow moved again, became a shape — a man — a *tall* man. She stifled a little cry. *Ross Chaine!* He had promised to see her again — soon. She had not dreamed it would be *so* soon.

She continued to watch, not yet daring to attract his attention. He was standing motionless again, and again seemed to melt into the shadows of the trees.

A second shape stole up, stood by the taller man. Jean recognized Breezy. She stood up from the chair. In another moment she would have been through the open window. A sound behind her held her feet in a sudden paralysis of fear.

She knew, even before she heard his voice, that Tenn Patchen had come into the room. She had forgotten to lock the door after Sing Gee had left with the supper tray. She had kept it locked all through the day. Her own carelessness — and now — Tenn Patchen.

'Looks like you're all fixed to go ridin',' he said, real surprise in his heavy voice. He was too stupid to guess the truth.

Jean still faced the open window. She saw the shapes

under the trees suddenly melt back into the shadows, guessed that Tenn's voice had reached to them.

She slowly turned and looked at him, her face a cold white mask in the moonlight that drifted in through the window. 'Get out of my room.' She spoke quietly, but with a contempt that gave the words the bite of a whip across his face.

'Feelin' spunky, huh?' He was suddenly close, brought her the reek of whiskey. 'I'm taking that spunk out of you,' he said thickly.

Jean's hand went down to the thirty-two in her holster. She was too late. Tenn's big fingers closed over her wrist. He towered over her, a wide grin on his face. 'How about it, kid? Is it goin' to be Mrs. Tenn Patchen? You'll want to be, when I'm done with you.' He pulled her roughly into his arms. She screamed. 'Ross . . . *Ross!*'

Chapter

15

GUNS ROAR

Ross RODE UP the gully that ran its twisting course back of the ranch-house trees. He got down from his saddle, tied the mare to the gnarled root of a big bush and made his way cautiously into the grove. Except for a single lighted window the house lay dark and still under the moon.

The hounds sensed his presence, gave clamorous tongue and raced toward him. Appalled by their noise he came to a standstill, spoke softly to the leaping shapes. Instantly they quieted, and after suspicious sniffs and whines of recognition, trotted back to the house, tails curled high in the satisfied manner of hounds when duty has been done.

Ross continued to wait under the tree. He wanted to make certain that nobody in the house was investigating. Apparently the quick cessation of the barking had convinced anyone who heard the noise that the hounds had taken a false alarm.

Reassured by the deep stillness, Ross moved on through the trees, circled the house and reached the yard. He was undecided about what to do. He only knew that Jean Austen's peril was very real.

He knew from the lighted window that Buel Patchen was still in his office. He dared not risk showing himself to the man. The unexpected sight of Señor Olveras would make Buel suspicious, put him on his guard.

For long moments he crouched in the shadow of the high fence, mind busy on the problem of getting word to Jean. Lamplight glowed faintly from the long bunkhouse across the yard. He wondered if Breezy slept there. He wanted desperately to see Breezy. The old man was his only hope of getting a message to the girl.

Hugging the protecting shadow of the fence Ross circled the big yard and approached the bunkhouse on the further side. Voices reached him. He halted, listened intently. A poker game.

He crept closer, looked in through the low window. The room was dimly lighted by a coal-oil lamp on the table around which sat the poker players. Five of them. A sixth man lay snoring in his bunk. Breezy was not there. Obviously the old chore man had his own quarters.

Ross cautiously withdrew, made his way back along the fence toward the barn. Something seemed to move from the yawning black mouth of the stable.

Ross froze in his tracks, stood watching, hand on gun-butt. Slowly the vague shape drew closer, was suddenly revealed in the moonlight. Only for a moment, then it seemed to drift back into the blackness of the yawning stable door.

The brief glimpse had been enough for Ross to recognize Breezy. He shrewdly guessed there was purpose in the old man's curious behavior. He had seen Ross — wanted him to come to the barn.

He moved more quickly now, found himself in the pitch darkness of the stable, heard Breezy's hoarse whisper.

'Kind of suspicioned it was you when I heard the hounds yelpin' and then stop so sudden.' Breezy's hand gripped the younger man's arm. 'Ross — they're gittin' set to murder the gal. Me an' Sing Gee was fixin' to git her away tonight.'

Ross listened in grim silence while Breezy told him about the cut latigo. 'We wasn't knowin' you'd be back,' the cowboy finished. 'So Sing an' me fixed it up with her to be ready when I come to her window for her. I've got her red mare hid down in the gully on the other side of the horse pasture. Got my own bronc there, too. Figgered I'd hightail away from this wolf den with her. There's a stage leaves Mendoza at seven in the mornin'. Jean figgers to take it to Santa Fe.'

'Let's get moving,' Ross said curtly. A thought struck him. 'Can you fix me up with a fresh horse, Breezy?'

'You bet . . . . Got a black back in the stalls. Mean as hell, but can run all day.'

They led the black across the horse pasture to the gully where Breezy had sequestered the other horses. Ross got the brown mare and changed his saddle to the black. He begrudged the time it took. Breezy saw his anxiety. 'Buel ain't gone to bed yet,' he pointed out. 'I've been watching his window. He's got awful sharp ears.' The old cowboy was in high spirits. 'Sure am tickled you come along, Ross. Jean's goin' to be mighty s'prised.'

They turned the brown mare loose in the pasture and made their way stealthily into the garden. Breezy left his companion for a look at the office window. He was back in a few moments. 'Buel's still settin' up,' he grumbled.

The two men stood, silent, tense, eyes on the dark window that Breezy said looked from the girl's bedroom. They suddenly saw her slender shape as she rose from her chair, saw, too, a second shape appear in the doorway behind her, heard Tenn Patchen's voice — her scream.

Old Breezy went berserk, exploded with the suddenness of a dynamite cap. 'You low-down pup!' he shrilled. 'Let go of her!' He sprang toward the window.

The surprised Tenn glimpsed him, saw the big gun in his hand. With a startled oath he backed away from the girl. Another man was close on Breezy's heels, a tall man — *Señor Olveras*.

The truth bit deeply into the man as he backed away toward the open door. Señor Olveras was *Ross Chaine*. Jean had called out his name. It was Ross Chaine, leaping for the window.

Tenn was not armed. He had shed his gun-belt along with his coat and shirt. He wore only his trousers. He increased the speed of his backward flight to the door, careful to keep the girl between him and the threatening guns of the men now almost within hand's reach of the window. His voice lifted in a loud yell as he tore into the hall.

Jean was already scrambling out of the window. Ross reached up a helping hand. She slid down from the low sill. She was trembling, breathless with fright and excitement. Ross swept an arm around her waist, started to hurry her away. She heard a hoarse exclamation from Breezy as he swung on his heels to follow, felt the hard muscles of Ross Chaine's arm tighten. He halted abruptly.

Jean looked, eyes wide with dismay. A squat, hump-shouldered shape stood in the shadows. Moonlight touched the long barrel of a shotgun leveled at them. A voice came from the man behind the shotgun, a low, bell-toned voice that rang with sardonic mirth.

'I've got you, Chaine,' Buel Patchen gloated. 'Drop your gun. You, too, Breezy.' His musical voice was suddenly the deep growl of an angry bear. 'You heard me, Chaine. This gun is loaded with buckshot .... Won't be my fault if the girl gets some of it.'

Jean heard the forty-five thud on the ground at their feet. She knew Ross had no alternative. Her heart turned to ice. She heard other sounds. The hammer of booted feet running from the bunkhouse, curses from Tenn Patchen as he pounded up the walk from the side-porch door. A gun-belt was buckled around his naked waist.

'I'm killin' him now,' he said. His gun lifted.

'No!' Buel Patchen spoke sharply. 'Not yet, Tenn.'

'I'm rememberin' what he done to me that time in Alamos,' Tenn said angrily. He shook his gun at Ross. 'Always thought there was somethin' wrong about this Señor Olveras game. Should have figgered it out you was Ross Chaine.'

His father's voice interrupted him. 'You thought I was in the office all evening, huh, Breezy?' He laughed softly. 'I was on to you, Breezy . . . I knew you were up to making trouble.'

'You low-down murderer!' Rage shook the old cow-boy's voice. 'I seen what you done this mornin' to Jean's saddle.' He jerked the damaged latigo from a pocket and threw it on the ground. 'Fixed it so she'd have a accident, you damn polecat.'

Jean understood now why Buel had been so insistent about a ride. She looked at him, loathing in her eyes, saw his thin lips tighten in a deadly smile.

'Close the fool's mouth,' Buel Patchen said harshly. He kept the shotgun pointed at Ross. 'He's lived too long.'

The garden gate slammed open to the push of the men running in from the bunkhouse. Tenn swung his gun at Breezy. The horrified girl saw a thin stream of fire pour from the black muzzle, saw the old Flying A man stagger and fall. Even as the crash of Tenn's gun ap-palled her ears, Breezy's hand grasped the ancient long·

barrelled Colt still lying on the ground where he had dropped it at Buel's command. He squirmed sideways and pulled the trigger. 'That's for the girl,' he grunted as Tenn reeled back under the shock of the heavy bullet. The gun fell from Breezy's suddenly limp fingers. He lay very still.

Deep quiet held the scene for a long moment. Tenn stood leaning against the wall, a look of silly surprise on his heavy face, then slowly his knees buckled under him and he slid to the ground.

One of the cowboys ran to him, bent down for a look. 'He's dead. My Gawd, boss, Tenn's dead!' The man straightened up, looked back at Buel. 'Tenn's dead,' he repeated in a hushed voice.

His companions stood in a group near Buel, eyes hard and unfriendly as they looked at Ross, curious and puzzled when they went to the girl standing so close to him.

'The Mex,' one of them muttered. 'What the hell!'

Buel still kept the shotgun leveled at the pair. He shook his head. 'You're wrong, Dater. You're looking at Ross Chaine and he's going to hang for the double murder of my son and Breezy Hessen.' His cold eyes fastened on Jean. 'The girl, too. She's as guilty as the man. She planned for him to kill Tenn.'

'You beast!' flared Jean. 'You — you dreadful, lying murderer.'

The men exchanged uneasy glances. They had not actually witnessed the shooting. One of them, Dater, picked up the gun Ross had dropped. He examined the chamber, looked up at Buel curiously.

'He used the other gun, Dater. The one layin' near Breezy. Threw it at Breezy after he shot him.'

The men were not disposed to argue the matter. 'Wasn't close enough to see the play,' Dater admitted. 'I cain't swear to nothin'.' He continued to stare doubtfully at Buel.

'Me too,' said another man. 'Too much shadder back here to see good an' we was all of us just headin' in through the gate.' The speaker's hard look fastened on Ross. 'Don't seem like good sense to waste time on this killin' snake when there's plenty trees handy.'

His companions were crowding close to Ross and Jean, guns threatening. Buel lowered the shotgun, shook his head.

'We'll have no lynching on this ranch,' he said reprovingly. 'The law will punish them.' He looked hard at Jean. 'I hate this business, girl. You've been the next thing to a daughter to me.' He wagged his head. 'The law won't hang you like they will him, but it will put you in prison — yes, in prison for a long, long time.'

'You beast,' Jean repeated. Her hands beat fiercely at the crowding men. They gave way and she ran to Breezy, fell on her knees by his side. He was dead, she saw at a glance. Her eyes were suddenly wet as she looked at him. It seemed to her that a smile was on his lips, a satisfied, contented smile. Breezy had died with gun blazing in his hand, died in defense of Bill Austen's daughter. He would not have had it different. That odd little half smile told Jean a lot. She bent down, kissed the still warm cheek.

Buel Patchen's hand was on her shoulder. 'Get up!' He spoke gruffly.

She brushed his hand away fiercely, stood up and faced him. 'You murdered my father, too,' she said bitterly. 'How blind I've been all these years!' Her look went to Ross standing there like a rock, his face a hard mask. Two men were at his back, knotting a short tie rope over his wrists. The sight caught at her heart. She was afraid she would faint. There seemed no way out for him. Despite Buel Patchen's smooth talk of turning him over to the law she knew the end for

Ross would come more swiftly — more surely. Buel would see to it that Ross did no talking. He would close her mouth, too. Jean was in no doubt about her cold-blooded step-uncle's intentions. Ross and she would never see the inside of a courtroom as prisoners on a trumped-up charge.

'Turn him loose!' she begged. 'I'll do anything you want . . . only let him go.' She clutched Buel's arm. 'I mean it . . . I'll . . . sign a deed to the ranch — if that's what you want.'

His thin-lipped smile drew a shiver from her. 'Get back into your room.' The finality in his words, his gesture, told her it was useless to protest. She threw Ross a pitiful look, went with heavy feet toward the side-porch door. Two of the cowboys were lifting Tenn's body as she passed. She kept her eyes from them, disappeared into the house.

Dater spoke. 'Where do you want we should put him?' He jerked a thumb at Ross. 'The grain shed would hold him,' he added. A wide grin split the man's face. 'No chance of him breaking out of the grain shed. It's rat-proof.'

Buel nodded. 'It will do,' he said. 'Keep a man on watch at the door, Dater, and put somebody at the girl's window.'

'I savvy,' Dater replied. 'All right, fellers, shove Chaine into the grain shed.' His head swung in a quick look in the direction of the yard. 'Somebody comin',' he added.

They heard the rattle of wheels, the sharp rhythmic thud of a buggy team. Buel showed sudden excitement. 'Rick DeSalt,' he muttered. 'Wonder what brings *him* so late?' He hurried down the flagstones. The others followed with the prisoner, leaving one man to guard Jean's window. The girl, already back in her room, saw him stoop over Breezy's body. She sensed his purpose, put her head out of the window.

'Leave him alone, you miserable thief.' Concealed in her lowered hand was the thirty-two Tenn had wrung from her grasp and left lying on the floor. She resisted the impulse to threaten the man with it. The gun was an asset she could not afford to lose. 'Leave Breezy alone,' she repeated.

The man, a swarthy-faced half-breed, grinned up at her. 'You shut yore damn mouth,' he said. He went on with his search of the dead man's pockets.

Men were coming in through the gate. Jean drew back, watched them. Rick DeSalt and her step-uncle. Behind them followed two heavily armed men. Rick was using a bodyguard since the night of his encounter with Ross Chaine.

She heard Rick's exclamation as he caught sight of the dead cowboy.

'Murder,' she heard Buel smoothly tell him. 'Chaine killed him, and killed Tenn. The girl's mixed up in it, Rick. Chaine was trying to get her away. Tenn and Breezy mixed with him and he killed 'em both. I'm holding him and the girl for murder.'

'Your story will do as good as any, Buel.' The saloon man's tone was sardonic. 'It will clean up a mess for you if you make it stick.' He laughed softly. 'Clears the girl out of Flying A, and when Chaine is dead, that deed you got from his aunt for Bar Chain will be good as gold.'

'I don't like the way you say it,' complained Buel.

'I'll say what I please,' sneered Rick DeSalt. 'It's a damn smart scheme, Buel. Only one flaw. You'll be a fool if you go pretending any law-abiding stuff. Take my advice and finish Chaine off with a dose of hot lead. As for the girl ——' He broke off with a suggestive lift of the shoulder.

The two men passed beyond reach of Jean's aghast ears. She turned from the window, went slowly to the bed and sat down. Buel Patchen would take DeSalt's advice. She was sure of it. The look on Buel's face had been enough for her. Ross would be a dead man before the light of day. She heard a gentle tap on the bedroom door and sprang to her feet, stood staring, breathless, her heart beating quickly. Somebody was cautiously turning the key in the lock outside.

Instinct prompted her to move swiftly to the window and noiselessly draw the curtain. It was dark in the room, but there was a chance the swarthy-faced guard's eyes were sharp.

The door opened quietly. Sing Gee slipped into the room, cautioning finger on lips. She ran to him. The old Chinese took her hand, patted it comfortingly. 'Heap bad,' he said compassionately.

'Sing!' She spoke in a low whisper. 'Sing — they're going to kill him.'

'Heap bad,' he said again.

'I can't bear it. I — I love him.' She began to tremble.

'Me plenty savvy.' Sing Gee nodded, shrewd eyes like glinting pieces of brown glass in the dark of the room. 'Me go catchee him befoh can kill. You be leady foh heap quick lide. I savvy, you bet.'

She gave him an incredulous look. 'How?' Her whisper was a disbelieving wail. 'How, Sing?'

'Plitty soon you savvy,' replied the cook. He turned back to the door. 'I go now. Boss maybe want whiskey.'

Jean stopped him. 'Try and get this gun to Ross.' She pressed the thirty-two against his hand.

The Chinese shook his head. 'You keep,' was all he said and he softly closed the door behind him. He left the key lying on the floor. Jean snatched it up and locked the door on the inside. She had a gun they didn't know about, and a door locked on her side. The thought gave her a feeling of temporary security. Window or door, she would shoot to kill, if Buel Patchen tried to force his way in.

Voices reached her through the window. 'We'll let him lay in his bunk till mornin',' a man said.

Jean stood rigid, hands clenched, her face pale. They were taking Breezy away. Faithful old Breezy, shot down in cold blood. She could have wept. But it was no time for tears, Jean told herself fiercely. Breezy would not want her to cry for him. He would want her to keep on fighting until Buel Patchen was destroyed.

Her step-uncle was in his big office chair, listening with frowning attention and growing worry to Rick DeSalt's explanation for his near midnight visit.

'I've been warning you this Olveras might be Ross Chaine,' Rick said. Angry memories gave the saloon man's face a grayish look. 'Chaine held me up the night I was here, on the way back to town. Put me afoot and scattered buggy and harness to hell and gone in the brush. I tried to ride one of the horses and got bucked off into a clump of cat's-claw.' Rick showed a bandaged hand. 'Buel — we're going to have a little hanging party on this ranch tonight, and I'm pulling on the rope that sets Ross Chaine to dancing on air.'

Buel looked at him silently, but it was a silence that seemed to satisfy the other man. His lips twisted in a smile. 'It's got to be done, Buel. Chaine is too close to the truth. It's him — or us.'

'It won't be us,' Buel Patchen said. His glance went to a bottle on a small side table. It was empty. He got out of his chair, went to the door. 'Sing!' he called into the hall. 'Bring a bottle of whiskey — quick!' He returned to the chair, smiled at DeSalt. 'We'll have a drink on it,' he said in his smooth rich voice. 'Luck rides with us, Rick.'

'Listen!' DeSalt frowned. 'We've got Chaine, but we'll have to get Kinners and Lally and do it fast. Those two longhorns are in with Chaine. They know all he knows, and there's that Mexican devil, Torres. He helped Chaine frame up this Olveras scheme so Chaine could spy on you. They've played you for a sucker with this cow deal you thought you had on with Torres.'

Sing Gee came in with whiskey bottle and glasses which he placed on the desk between the two men. He shuffled out. Buel Patchen picked up the bottle and splashed the liquor into the glasses. His hand was shaky.

'Those are man-size drinks,' Rick DeSalt said with a short laugh.

'I'm not much of a drinker,' Buel told him. 'Right now I'm needing a stiff one — a lot of 'em.' He tipped the glass to his lips, emptied it with a long gulp. He put the glass down, sighed, wiped his lips, gave the other man a wild look. 'Tenn is dead,' he groaned. 'My boy — dead — *murdered!*' He refilled the glass, emptied it again.

'Here's to hell with Chaine,' DeSalt said. He tossed down his drink, shuddered, eyed the bottle doubtfully. 'Got a wallop, that stuff.' He went back to the cattle deal. 'You're going to feel a lot more sick, Buel. Torres and a bunch of Mex vaqueros have got Harve Welder and his outfit corralled at Oxbow. What do you make of *that?*' He reached for the bottle and helped himself liberally. 'Sure has a wallop,' he muttered again as he put down the empty glass. He spoke with an effort, his voice thick. 'You heard me, Buel. Chaine is rustlin' those cows.'

'Huh?' Buel's head rolled from side to side. He made an effort to straighten up in the chair, stared at

DeSalt with glassy eyes. 'Huh — Chaine ... hell ... we'll — we'll hang — Chaine ... fix the girl, too ——' His head suddenly lolled sideways, his eyelids drooped, closed.

Rick DeSalt stared at him vacantly. He tried to get out of his chair, muttered irritably, 'Need another shot.' He tipped the bottle over his glass, splashed in the liquor and downed the drink in a single gulp. 'Damn queer-tastin' hootch .... Looks like Buel's passed out on me. ... Can't take his liquor like a man should.'

He made another effort to get out of his chair, stood up on unsteady legs, frowning gaze on the whiskey bottle. 'Guess I'll get a fresh bottle from the Chink ... this stuff's no good, not fit to drink.' He staggered into the hall, made his way to the kitchen where his two body-guards occupied chairs drawn up to the table. A whiskey bottle stood between them, but the two hard-faced men were not drinking. They were slumped low in their chairs, snoring heavily.

DeSalt looked at them from the doorway. His head dropped lower and lower, his glassy eyes uncomprehending. Suddenly he collapsed, slid down against the side of the door and lay sprawled on the floor.

Sing Gee's face peered at him from the darkness of the open outer door. The hint of a malicious smile flickered across the inscrutable wrinkled face. He slipped softly into the room, picked up a long-bladed meat knife from a chopping block near the stove and was gone without another glance at the three unconscious men.

Chapter

16

FOR ALWAYS

ONE SMALL WINDOW framed a square of moonlight in the blackness of the granary. Ross leaned against a pile of barley-filled sacks and studied its possibilities with speculative eyes. A tight squeeze, but it could be done if a man had the use of his two hands.

He wriggled his bound wrists experimentally. The bite of the rawhide was not reassuring. It was a problem, and one that must be solved without too much time lost. He knew with grim certainty that Rick DeSalt's arrival would add fuel to the disaster that had so suddenly exploded in his face. DeSalt would demand immediate action. He had reason to fear Ross Chaine. He would not pass up such a chance to put an end to the cause of his fear.

Ross shifted his look to the heavy door. A man was on guard outside. No chance that way. In fact there seemed no chance at all.

He straightened up from the pile of sacked grain, the muscles of his face hard and grim. Bound wrists or thick adobe walls were not going to hold him. More than his own life was at stake. Buel Patchen had gone too far to stop at half-way measures. Old Breezy's discovery of the damaged latigo was proof of his murderous intentions toward the girl who stood between him and the unchallenged possession of the ranch he coveted.

The thought of Jean steadied Ross. Jean's life depended on his escape from the granary.

His eyes gradually adjusted to the darkness. Objects began to take vague shape. He moved closer to the window. It was held in place by large nails. Even if he could free his hands it would be necessary to find a tool with which to draw the nails. It would be impossible to break out the glass and the frame without arousing the guard's suspicions.

Ross again strained tentatively at his bound wrists. No use. The knots were tied by cowboys, and cowboys tied knots that stayed tied.

He moved on around the wall, careful to avoid stumbling over objects that littered the hard mud floor. It became apparent that the grain room was used for more purposes than storing grain. Discarded bits of harness lay in a pile under the window. He made out the outline of a broken wagon-tongue, a plow, an iron bar that he knew was a barbed-wire stretcher, various odds and ends that collect on a ranch.

Something caught his eyes, a vague outline against the adobe wall, something that glinted in the faint flicker of moonlight that struck across from the window opposite.

One brief look was enough for Ross. A scythe, leaning against the wall, its long curved blade pointing up from the floor.

He moved quickly, silently, stood for a moment, studying the lie of the broad blade. Its head rested on the floor, supported by the long handle, its tip swept up waist-high. Conscious of a hammering heart, Ross turned, pressed his back cautiously against the blade, fumbled gingerly at the edged tip with his fingers and carefully got it placed against the rawhide thongs.

The scythe was sharper than he had dared hope. The keen edge sliced easily under his careful pressure. The thongs loosened, fell from his wrists.

He wasted a minute, rubbing out the numbness, then fumbled in the littered corner until his hands closed over the iron bar. He ran his fingers over the claw that curved from the end. One of the flanges was broken, which explained why the bar had been discarded. Ross was satisfied it would serve to pry out the nails that held the window in place.

He set to work. There was enough of the claw left to grip under the nail-heads. The powerful leverage of the long bar brought them out easily. He drew them cautiously, fearing a rusty squeak that would betray him to the guard. He had found and was using his one chance. There would be no more chances if he failed this one.

It required another minute to lift the window from its frame and lower it quietly against the wall. The upper nails had been too high for his reach and he had carried sacks of barley and placed them under the window. Piled one on the other they made a firm platform.

He paused now for a cautious look at what lay beyond the window. The feel of the soft night wind on his face made his pulse quicken. He filled his lungs, ears alert for any sound from the man watching outside the door on the other side of the building.

The problem of the guard was next on the list. Ross reached for the long claw-bar, noiselessly lowered it out of the window and leaned it against the wall. Reassured by the continued quiet he squirmed through and in a moment was on the ground outside. The faint sound of footsteps approaching from the house suddenly reached him. He seized the long iron bar, crouched close to the wall. The thought of discovery sent cold prickles down his spine.

The footsteps drew closer, curious shuffling steps. Certainly not the crisp quick crunch of a cowman's high-heeled boots.

Ross chanced a cautious look around the corner of the building, stifled an astonished grunt. The newcomer was Sing Gee. A whiskey bottle was in his hand, an affable grin on his face.

Ross heard the guard's surprised voice. "Lo, Sing! What the hell!'

'Boss say me catchee dlink foh you,' Sing Gee replied. 'Boss say you catchee him Loss Chaine in glain house, Boss say him bad man . . . he say you catchee big dlink . . . not get heap tired . . . let him Loss Chaine make foh lun away flom you.'

The man guffawed. 'Hell! Ain't no chance a-tall for Chaine to make a break . . . not with me on the job.' Ross, cautiously watching, saw the guard reach for the bottle. 'A good drink'll hit the spot at that. I was never one to turn down a free drink.' He tilted the bottle to his lips.

It was at that moment that Ross moved, so swiftly, so without sound, that not even the old Chinese heard his approach. Ross caught the glitter of a long-bladed knife as it dropped into Sing Gee's hand from the sleeve of his blouse. The next instant Ross swung the heavy iron bar against the unsuspecting cowboy's head. The man dropped, lay twitching. The contents of the whiskey bottle gurgled softly under an outstretched arm.

Sing Gee bent quickly over him, straightened up and looked at Ross. 'Him not dead.' The knife in his hand lifted. Ross shook his head, stooped and jerked the gun from the senseless man's holster.

'Keep watch, Sing,' he muttered. He lifted the bar from the catch, pushed the door open and dragged the cowboy inside. When he came out the man's wide-brimmed stetson had replaced his Mexican hat and he had discarded the short braided jacket. He saw the knife in the cook's hand, snatched it and sliced the silver conchas from his trousers. The change would satisfy the casual glance. Ross looked like any other puncher in that uncertain moonlight. He said curtly, 'Where is she, Sing?'

'Allee same her room,' Sing Gee replied. He replaced the heavy bar and started across the yard. 'I tell her catchee you soon. You velly good man,' he added with an admiring glance at his tall companion. 'You got plenty blains, you bet.'

The pair halted near the garden gate. Sing Gee told Ross about the half-breed guard under the girl's window. 'We catchee him big s'plise,' chuckled the cook. 'Me go walkee up path, say, "hello . . . likee dlink, mistah?" He likee dlink, you bet . . . he talkee 'bout dlink . . . not get flightened you walkee up loud, make sclatch noise with spurs. He no savvy you Loss Chaine. . . . You glab quick . . . get Missie Jean out window . . . we all lun plenty quick to gully where Bleezy put horses.'

'The horses are still there, Sing?'

The Chinese nodded. 'Me go lide allee same you,' he said. 'Me no go 'long you, me die damn quick. Savvy?'

Ross looked searchingly at the inscrutable face. He guessed that Sing Gee had not been idle. No time now for surmises. He nodded. 'Get moving. I'll follow about fifteen feet behind. The man won't suspect. I'll have him before he gets a good look at me.'

Sing Gee pushed through the gate, went up the flag-stoned walk, slippered feet beating softly. Ross followed, boot heels clicking, spurs rasping. The guard would have no reason to suspect the old Chinese cook — the tall, nonchalantly striding shape following him.

The man stepped into view from the deep shadows of a bush as the Chinese turned into the walk that ran under the girl's window. 'Hi there, Sing.' His glance went to the second newcomer clattering up the walk, wide hat-brim pulled low over his face. It was apparent he thought Ross was one of Rick DeSalt's bodyguards. He had no reason to suspect the man approaching him with such complete self-assurance was Ross Chaine. He had seen his companions drag Chaine away to the grain shed.

Sing Gee halted, looked back at the guard. 'You likee dlink, huh?'

'Sure,' grunted the half-breed. He faced around to the cook. 'Sure I ——' Too late, he sensed the danger behind him. He whirled. Ross struck hard with the steel barrel of the forty-five commandeered from his first victim. He hated striking even an enemy from be-hind, but life and death were in the balance — the life of Jean Austen. Her safety allowed for no scruples. These men were killers and time was too short to treat them with mercy.

The half-breed's hand never reached the gun in his holster. Ross caught him as he collapsed, dragged the senseless man behind the bush. He stripped off the gunbelt and thrust it at Sing Gee who buckled it around his lean hips.

Jean, waiting and watching behind the curtains of her window, had seen the swift and merciless disposal of the guard. She was already climbing over the sill when Ross reached her.

Soundless as ghosts the three sped to the yard that lay between them and the pasture they must cross to reach the horses hidden down in the gully.

A voice broke the stillness. 'Somethin' wrong, Dater! Cain't find Shorty round no place!'

They heard Dater's excited reply, the sound of

crunching boots as he ran from the bunkhouse toward the grain shed.

Jean stifled a dismayed little cry, saw Ross leap to Rick DeSalt's buckboard less than twenty feet away. A single rope tied the team to the hitching post. Jean and Sing Gee sped after him. The cook's sharp meat knife slid down from his loose sleeve. He sliced the tie rope with a single slash while Ross and Jean scrambled into the driver's seat. Angry shouts came from the grain shed. Ross swung the team sharply around to the avenue gate. Sing Gee grabbed hold and scrambled into the back seat of the careening vehicle.

More shouts, the stamp of running feet as the Flying A men tumbled from the bunkhouse. A gun roared and a bullet spatted into the back seat. Sing Gee screeched something in Chinese, jerked out the gun Ross had taken from the half-breed and sent a screaming fusillade of lead at the dark shapes of the pursuing men.

Ross laid on the whip, the horses sprang forward. The buckboard rocked and careened down the avenue. Jean clung desperately to the seat. She was appalled. A few more minutes would have seen them safely beyond dangerous pursuit. Those few saving moments had been denied and now the wolf-pack was in full cry at their heels.

Ross swung the team into the Dos Cruces road. Jean gave him a despairing look. Escape was hopeless *that* way. The men behind them would soon have their horses out — be in full chase.

They rocked along for perhaps a quarter of a mile and suddenly the road made a sharp turn around a low brush-covered ridge. Ross leaned back on the reins and drew the horses to a quick halt. His swift gesture was plain. Jean and the cook scrambled down from the buckboard. Sing Gee gave the bewildered girl one of his inscrutable smiles. She sensed he knew what Ross was up to.

Ross made the reins fast to the whip-socket, giving the lines enough play to keep any drag from the bits. He jumped out, slashed at the horses with the whip. The surprised team tore away at top speed, the buckboard rattling at their flying heels.

'Let's get out of here,' Ross said. He seized Jean's hand, plunged into the brush with her. Sing Gee followed closely. Soon they were on the far side of the hogback and pushing down a steep slope to a boulder-strewn gully. The sound of the stampeded buckboard team faded into the distance.

'Listen!' Jean halted. 'They're chasing the buckboard!'

From beyond the hogback rolled the swiftly passing thunder of horses' hoofs as the Flying A men tore past.

The girl flashed Ross an admiring look. 'That was clever,' she said. 'They'll be miles away before they overtake the buckboard . . . find out we're not in it.'

'You bet,' chuckled Sing Gee. 'He catchee plenty savvy in blain.'

They found the three horses where Ross and Breezy had left them. The old Chinese eyed Breezy's buckskin apprehensively. He could cook better than he could ride. He got into the saddle gingerly and followed his companions. For the moment at least, the buckskin seemed in an amiable mood. Sing Gee muttered a Chinese prayer of gratitude.

'Mendoza?' Ross looked inquiringly at the girl riding by his side. 'Breezy said you planned to catch the morning stage for Santa Fe.'

Jean shook her head. 'I've changed my mind.' The hard quality of her voice drew a sharp look from him. 'I can't run away . . . not after what they've done to

Breezy. I'm staying — and I'm fighting them. It's my fight now, as much as yours.'

'I don't know, Jean.' His tone was troubled. 'Haven't you friends — somebody you'll be safe with?'

'I'd rather be with you, Ross,' she said simply.

They rode on in silence. Moonlight spread a lacework of silver and black across the desert landscape. A coyote yipped at them from a distant knoll. Ross halted his horse. They listened for the space of a minute. No sound of pursuit reached them. Only the bark of the coyote touched the stillness.

Ross broke the silence. 'It will be best for you to catch the Mendoza stage,' he said to the girl.

She shook her head. 'I'm staying,' she repeated.

Their eyes met, and something passed from one to the other in that fleeting instant. The half frown left his face, and he leaned toward her, put his hand over the small, strong hand on the pommel of her saddle. 'Always?' He spoke the word softly.

Her eyes did not waver. 'Always,' she said. '*For always*, Ross.'

They rode on, into the lifting hills, toward the dawn that slowly flowed over the high peaks.

Chapter
17

CHUCHO RIDES AGAIN

I T HAD BEEN a slack evening in the White Buffalo. Less than a half score customers, and most of them more interested in the poker game going on in the back room than in calling for drinks.

The paunchy bartender's gaze roved gloomily around the long room, came to rest on a lone Mexican sitting at a table near the street door. He was slumped low in his chair, apparently asleep.

The bartender scowled, spoke in an aggrieved voice, 'Wake up there, feller! Go do your snorin' some other place.'

The Mexican opened an eye. '*No quiero*,' he muttered. His eye closed again.

'I wasn't askin' did you want a drink,' yelped the barman. 'I was tellin' you to go do your snorin' some place else. We sell likker here, Miguel.'

The Mexican's head lifted from his cradled arms. He blinked sleepily at the man behind the bar, then looked at the empty glass in front of him. '*No quiero*,' he repeated. 'No wan' dreenk.'

'Then git to hell out of here,' shouted the barman. The chip on his shoulder was getting him down. 'You've been settin' there long enough.'

The swing doors slammed open and his attention

switched to the newcomer. He stared, open-mouthed,
eyes wide with astonishment. 'Looks like you tangled
with some bob wire, Harve,' he said in a shocked voice.
'Or did your bronc pitch you into a bunch o' cat's-claw
like what happened to Rick the other night?'

The Flying A foreman sagged heavily against the bar.
His face was bruised and scratched, his shirt ripped open
and he was minus his gun-belt. He chose to ignore the
bartender's curiosity. 'Give me a drink,' he rasped.
'Make it fast, Spike.'

The bartender slid bottle and glass in front of his
customer. 'Wasn't lookin' for you to come in so close
to midnight,' he observed. 'What's up, Harve? You
sure look like hell!'

Harve Welder filled and drained his glass. He
belched, rocked on his heels, stared critically at his re-
flection in the mirror behind the bar, large bony hand
still grasping the neck of the whiskey bottle. He tilted
the bottle and refilled the glass. 'No, Spike ——' The
fury behind his thin smile brought an involuntary flinch
from the bartender. 'It wasn't bob wire and it wasn't
cat's-claw and to hell with your guesses.' He drained
the glass, slammed it with a splintering crash on the
floor and ground the pieces under his heel. 'Where's
Rick? I've got to see him. Hell's broke loose!'

'Rick ain't here,' Spike answered. The deadly rage
of the man frightened him. He reached for his mop,
made nervous passes at imaginary wet spots. 'You could
ask Stack Jimson,' he added. Out of the tail of his eye
he saw the Mexican push through the swing doors into
the street. Miguel was scared, too. He knew when the
going was good. Harve Welder was sure on the prod.
'You could ask Stack,' he repeated.

The Mexican halted outside the saloon door. His lean
body was suddenly straight, trigger-taut, his eyes, no

longer heavy with sleep, roved sharply up and down the street. With a satisfied grunt he slipped into the alley between the saloon and the store.

The swing doors were still vibrating when Harve Welder pushed out to the sidewalk and headed uptown toward the flare of the big kerosene lamp that hung in front of the livery stable. The Mexican, crouched like a stalking cat in the dark alley, watched him for a moment, then stealthily followed.

Stack Jimson was sitting in his tiny office, playing solitaire and drinking whiskey straight from a bottle that stood on the littered table. His hairy and mottled arms bulged from the upturned sleeves of a red undershirt. His big potbelly flowed over the leather belt and a grayish red stubble covered his flabby round face. He looked like a huge repulsive spider as his head lifted in a wordless stare at his visitor.

Welder glowered down at him. 'Where's Rick?' He spat the question.

Stack deliberately laid his handful of cards on the table. 'You look some banged up, Harve,' he said. 'Git tangled with a grizzly b'ar, or have you met up with Ross Chaine?'

Welder cursed him, repeated his question. 'I've got news that'll make Rick feel a damn sight worse than I look,' he added.

'Rick has went to see Buel,' Stack said. 'Took Roscoe an' Downs with him.' His loose lips widened in a wheezy chuckle. 'Rick ain't takin' no more chances sence the night he run into Chaine.'

'Hell's broke loose,' Harve Welder told him. 'Chaine's got a gang of Mex rustlers in with him. They jumped us over at the Oxbow camp, took our guns and shoved us into a ten-foot bob-wire corral they made us string up at the point of their guns.'

'The hell you say,' commented the liveryman.   He took a long swig from the bottle, handed it up to Welder's outstretched hand.   The foreman drank, slammed the bottle back on the table.

'We worked a couple of wires loose and all of us would have got away.   A Mex come along just as I crawled into the open.   I grabbed him, stuck his own knife into his heart, but the yell he let out spoiled the play for the boys.'   Welder reached for the bottle again, wiped his mustache with shirt sleeve.   'I lay low in the brush.   It was dark and the coyotes couldn't make out who was gone.   Worked over to the remuda back of the corral and got me a horse.   No chance to get a saddle on him . . . had to ride bareback into Dos Cruces.'

Stack Jimson got out of his chair, reached for his flannel shirt and struggled into it.   His big mottled face emerged, he jerked a thumb at a small closet door. 'Git yourself a gun, Harve.'   He buttoned the shirt, pulled on a coat and a greasy-brimmed hat from the peg behind him.   Welder reappeared from the closet, buckling a gun-belt around lean hips.

Stack Jimson spoke again, the wheeze gone from his voice, his tone cold and sharp.   'It's worser than just a raid, Harve.   We ain't fools.   It's Chaine or it's our necks — if we don't act quick.'   He grabbed his gun-belt down from another peg and started into the stable. Welder stopped him with a question.

'How many fellers in town?'

Stack considered for a moment.   'Most a dozen, I reckon.   Some of 'em is over at Rick's place in a poker game right now.   Mart an' Stinger will be over to Mamie's joint.   We'll pick 'em up.'   His voice lifted in a shout that brought a stable-hand running from one of the stalls, a pitchfork in his hand.   'Start throwin' saddles on quick as you can make it, Slivers,' barked the liveryman. 'We're needin' mebbe fourteen broncs. Jump to it, feller!'

The roustabout nodded, dropped the fork, snatched a lantern from a peg and hurried down the dark runway behind the stalls.

A sleepy-eyed, unshaven face peered down at them from the hay-loft. 'What's the ruckus, Stack?'

'Hell, Denver, didn't know you was up thar! Come on down an' hightail it over to the White Buffalo. Tell the boys to come on the jump. We're goin' for a ride.'

The man scrambled down the ladder, stood brushing bits of straw from hair and clothes. 'Where to shall I tell 'em we're ridin', Stack?'

'Buel Patchen's,' Stack Jimson answered. 'Git movin', Denver. An' take a look over to Mamie's place for Mart and Stinger.'

Denver disappeared into the moonlight. They heard the clatter of his booted feet as he ran.

'Let's go help Slivers throw on them saddles,' Jimson said. He snatched another lantern from a peg and started down the runway. He was amazingly light on his feet for so heavy a man.

Neither of them saw the shape crouching near the wide-open doors of the big barn. The Mexican waited for a few moments, long enough to see the bobbing lantern disappear through the door that led to the horse corral at the far end, then soundless as a ghost he sped away. In less than five minutes he was in a deep gully back of the town. Another five minutes brought him to a horse concealed in the piñon scrub.

Soft lamplight still glowed from the windows of the *cantina* of Lico Estrada when Miguel rode into the plaza and flung out of the saddle. He ran to the door with a noisy jingling of spurs that brought Lico himself. The innkeeper gave him a sharp look. Miguel nodded to the unspoken question. 'It is bad news,' he said curtly.

Lico closed the door, drew the heavy bar in place and with a gesture for the man to follow, went past the deserted bar into a small, low-ceilinged room. Two narrow windows were set high in the massive adobe walls, and under the windows were pallets. On one of the small beds was stretched the giant frame of Pete Lally, fully dressed. Gentle snores came from his slightly open mouth. On the second pallet sat Buckshot Kinners, lively interest in his eyes as he looked at Lico's companion.

'What's up, Lico?' Buckshot's gaze went to his partner. 'Pete! Wake up, feller!'

Pete Lally sat up with a start, hand grabbing at the gun in his holster.

Buckshot grinned at him, jerked a nod at Miguel. 'Looks like we've got news.'

Pete swung his legs from the cot, felt in his pockets for tobacco and papers. 'All right, Miguel,' he drawled. 'We're listening.'

The Mexican told his story in curt words. The partners listened attentively, growing concern on their faces. They had feared trouble would break, which was why they were staying overnight with Estrada. Their own ranch was too far away for quick action, and Lico had ways of getting valuable information. It was Lico who had told them of Ross Chaine's return to Flying A that night — his determination to get Jean Austen away from the murderous clutches of her step-uncle. The word had reached Lico from Don Vicente Torres, also the startling news of the strange affair at Oxbow. The daring coup that had made prisoners of Harve Welder and a good half of Flying A's tough outfit seemed too good to be true. Buckshot and Pete were uneasy from the moment Lico beamingly gave them his version of the swiftly moving events. They were going to stick around, they told Lico. They wanted to be close if anything happened. At their insistence, Lico sent Miguel to keep watch on things at the White Buffalo.

'It's sure a mess,' Buckshot said, when the Mexican finished his story. 'More than a dozen of 'em headin' for the ranch, and Ross back there ag'in, passin' himself off for Señor Olveras. Like as not he's asleep in bed by now, not knowin' Harve Welder is loose. He's trapped for sure. Harve and his bunch will bust in on him, fill him with lead, or dangle him from the nearest tree.' Buckshot groaned, muttered profane words.

'There's a chance Ross wouldn't lose no time at the ranch,' Pete argued in his deliberate voice. 'He'd likely get the girl away quick as he could.' He looked at Lico Estrada. 'We've got to get word to Don Vicente. From what Miguel says, Vicente don't know that Welder got away. Not unless he counted his prisoners over one by one after the dead vaquero was found.'

Buckshot nodded agreement to the advisability of warning the Mexicans at Oxbow. 'Buel Patchen won't waste time,' he declared. 'Welder will scrape up all the men he can get together and head pronto for Oxbow. Torres and his vaqueros are due to be slaughtered if we don't get him away from there.'

'We've got to figger this thing out careful,' Pete Lally rumbled.

'And damn fast,' grunted his partner. He looked at Estrada. 'We'll be wantin' our horses in a hurry, Lico.'

The innkeeper spoke briefly to Miguel who went jingling away. 'The horses will be at the door in five minutes,' Lico told them.

'We've got to get word to Ross and we've got to warn Torres,' Buckshot went on. 'Won't be hard to reach Torres.' He shook his head gloomily. 'I'm up a tree

when it comes to Ross. We'd be killed on sight, Pete.
No chance for us to get within gunshot of Flying A.'

There was a grim silence as they considered the problem. Lico was the first to speak. 'Listen, my friends!
An idea!'

The partners stared at him, waited for him to continue. 'I think of Chucho ——'

Buckshot interrupted him. 'The kid?' He shook his
head. 'We can't send a kid, Lico.'

Lico gestured impatiently. 'Who will suspect a small
boy? No, no, my friends, it is Chucho who will warn
young Chaine. Chucho is smart. If he is caught and
questioned he can tell them he has run away to be a
vaquero on the big ranch.' Lico smiled at their suddenly thoughtful faces. 'He need not be caught. He is
a young fox for cunning. All he need do is lie in watch
for Breezy, who is our friend. Breezy can carry the
word to the girl and she will warn Chaine.'

'He's got to get there before Harve and his gang hit
the ranch,' reminded Buckshot, only half convinced.
'It's a long shot, Lico.'

'A long shot is better than no shot,' countered the
innkeeper. He went swiftly from the little room.

Buckshot and Pete exchanged worried looks. 'I've a
notion the kid can do it,' Pete said slowly. 'There's one
angle to it, Buckshot. Chucho may find that Ross has
lit out with the girl. He won't have a chance to let
Ross know that Harve has got away and that hell is due
to bust loose at Oxbow.'

'There's only one place Ross will head for,' Buckshot
told him. 'He'll head for the Bar Chain, hole up some
place. He knows we'll be on the watch for him there
most every day.'

'The kid will have to pick up his trail,' Pete decided.
He broke off, smiled at the boy who suddenly appeared

in the doorway with his grandfather. 'How about it, Chucho?'

'Sure thing I go,' answered the boy. He finished tucking his shirt inside his overalls and grinned at them. 'You pay one dollar cash for my bank?'

Buckshot and Pete reached into their pockets like one man. Each of them produced a shining gold piece. Chucho's eyes glistened. 'Ten dollars!' His English deserted him. '*Madre de Dios!*'

He deftly caught the coins, thrust them into his pocket. 'I ride like hell,' he said.

A slim, dark-haired girl paused hesitantly in the doorway, hands tightly clutching a hastily flung-on *mantilla*. 'What is it?' Her soft voice was breathless with apprehension. 'Is it Vicente? *Ay Dios mio!* He is hurt — dead!'

Lico Estrada looked at her sternly. 'Go back to your bed, Chaquita, or at least put on some clothes.'

She stamped an impatient little foot. 'But answer me!' Her big dark eyes implored the LK partners. 'I want the truth!'

Pete Lally smiled reassuringly. 'There is trouble, Chaquita, but Vicente ain't hurt so far as we know. Buckshot and me is headin' over to Oxbow quick as Miguel gets our saddles throwed on.'

'*Ay que alegría!*' Her tone was relieved. 'He is so brave and reckless, my Vicente. He laughs at death — but he is so reckless my heart beats with fear for him.'

Chucho grinned at her impudently. 'He makes songs about you,' he said. 'I heard him singing about your eyes.'

'Enough!' Lico told him sharply.

'I do not mind,' Chaquita threw her young brother a delighted smile as she vanished.

'Get started, Chucho,' urged Buckshot. 'You've got

to make the ranch before Harve Welder gets there. Savvy?'

'You bet.' Chucho spoke confidently. 'I know the short cuts and will ride like hell.' He listened attentively to their instructions as he followed them out to the moonlit night. 'It is a big job,' he said. 'But I am American like you. I will ride the same as that Paul Revere I read about in my book at the school.' He was off like a rabbit across the yard.

'He will yet be governor, that one,' said his grandfather proudly.

'Shouldn't be s'prised none,' chuckled Pete Lally. He swung into his saddle.

Before the two friends were half-way across the plaza they heard the sharp rataplan of hoofs, saw a swiftly moving shape disappear down the brush-covered slope beyond Estrada's small corral.

Pete shook his head doubtfully. 'Seems like a tough job we've lined up for the kid. Ain't so sure we're doin' right.'

'He'll make it,' reassured Buckshot. 'Chucho is awful smart, and he's tickled to pieces. No call to worry about *him*. Chucho's got what it takes.'

They pushed their horses to a distance-eating running walk, and for several minutes neither man spoke a word.

Buckshot broke the silence. 'Wonder what that smoke talk was we seen up on the Chuckwallas this morning? Do you figger it was The Prophet wantin' to get some word to Ross?'

'I reckon that's the answer, Buckshot. If Ross seen that smoke talk it'll likely make sense to him.'

'The thing has got to break,' Buckshot said. 'This Oxbow bus'ness has spilled the beans. That moon yonder is drippin' blood, Pete.'

'I sure hope Ross gets away with the girl.' Pete's voice

was heavy with gloom. 'I ain't so sure, Buckshot . . . I ain't awful hopeful he can make it.'

Buckshot Kinners was silent. His face was suddenly a grim mask as he rode along by the side of his giant partner.

Chapter

18

MAD WOLF

JEAN ALMOST REGRETTED the daylight that pressed down from the sunlit peaks. She wanted to be a long way from the ranch before her step-uncle picked up the trail. Daylight meant a more swift pursuit. Ross Chaine was a brave man, but he would be only one against many. There would be no mercy in Buel Patchen. She thought of the cut latigo and shivered. Buel Patchen wanted her dead. He wanted to possess her ranch — had planned to kill her if she refused to marry his dreadful son. The cut latigo was proof he had made up his mind she was not going to marry Tenn.

She heard Ross speaking to her, and something in his low voice sent a thrill of apprehension through her.

'Pull in behind that mesquite,' he said.

She obeyed, spurred the mare into a quick plunge toward the sprawling mesquite. Ross and Sing Gee followed.

'What is it?' She spoke breathlessly.

'Something was moving back on the ridge.' Ross got down from his saddle, crawled around the mesquite. The other two watched him nervously as he lay there prone on his belly, eyes fixed on the ridge. To their surprise he was suddenly on his feet and waving his hat, and then, shrill and clear in the early morning stillness, came a voice.

'Señor! It is Chucho! Señor — please to wait for me!'

Ross stepped back to his horse and swung up to his saddle. He wore a broad smile as he looked at Jean. 'Chucho,' he said. 'A good friend.' He rode from the concealment of the mesquite. They followed him and Jean saw a small boy riding furiously up the sandy wash on a red and white pinto pony.

Grinning from ear to ear, Chucho slid from his saddle. '*Por Dios!* Almost I not find you at all. It would have been bad for me not to find you. I would have to give back the gold money to the old *señores*.' Chucho patted his pocket. 'Now it is mine for the bank — ten dollars. *Dios* — I am more rich every day.'

'Buckshot and Pete send you, Chucho?' Ross held his impatience in check. 'Lucky I spotted you back there on the ridge.'

'You bet!' Chucho lost his smile. '*Los señores* say for me to tell you hell she has broke loose at the Oxbow. Harve Welder have bust out and *los señores* plenty scared he catch you at ranch.'

Jean's aghast look went to Ross. The grim mask of his face told her nothing, but she could guess his thoughts. The margin of time had been so perilously thin. A miracle had got them away before Harve Welder could reach the ranch. Or was it the sheer courage, the indomitable will of this Ross Chaine? Jean's heart went out to him. She knew from his stony look that the news of the foreman's escape had inexpressibly shocked him. She listened in miserable silence to the Mexican boy's shrill voice. It seemed that Chuco had narrowly missed running into Dater and his men in pursuit of the runaway buckboard team. He had seen Welder and a lot of riders come up from Dos Cruces and join the puzzled Flying A men gathered around the empty vehicle. The entire group had started back for the ranch, taking the buckboard and team with them.

'I was like the coyote in the brush, so still they not see me,' Chucho said proudly. 'I hear what they say and I know you have gone from rancho. I wait, and when the men ride away in big dust I go back to my horse . . . ride quick to look for you like *los señores* tell me.'

'I'm mighty obliged to you, Chucho. You've done me a favor I won't forget.' Ross fumbled in his pocket, drew out a gold piece. 'Here's something for that bank of yours.'

The boy hesitated, longing eyes on the ten-dollar gold piece. 'No!' He shook his head. '*Los señores* paid me. I must not be the pig.'

'Come here, Chucho.' Jean's eyes were misty. She bent low from her saddle and kissed him.

'*Por Dios!*' Chucho's eyes sparkled. 'That is more fine than ten dollars, you bet.'

The shimmering disk of the sun pushed clear of the mountain rim, splashed the sandy wash with dazzling sunbeams and long shadows from clumps of mesquite. Ross knew that every moment was precious. Harve Welder was back at the ranch. With the reinforcements from Dos Cruces he could muster more than thirty men.

He studied the problem swiftly, coolly. Welder would head for the Oxbow camp. Nearly half of the men on Flying A's payroll were prisoners. Harve would want to extricate them from the clutches of Vicente's vaqueros. His force would outnumber the Mexicans by at least two to one. Vicente's outfit stood in danger of being massacred unless Pete and Buckshot persuaded Vicente to make a run for it. Ross was not sure of Vicente. The

Mexican ranchero was a proud and reckless man.
He had promised to hold the prisoners for his friend.
Pete and Buckshot would have trouble persuading him
to run for it. And there was Tony Birl. No matter
what happened to the rest of the prisoners, Tony Birl
must be held at all costs. Tony could name the murderers of Bill Austen and Jim Chaine. He could be made
to talk, and Harve Welder knew it. Harve would want
to make sure that Tony would never have the chance to
talk.

An exclamation from Jean drew his attention. 'Ross
— those puffs of smoke again!'

His glance went quickly to the lofty pinnacle of
Chuckwalla Peak.

'No!' Jean gestured at the saw-toothed hills in the
east. 'Over there — up in Red Creek Flats!'

Ross seemed to freeze in his saddle as he looked. He
said nothing, just stared until the puffs of smoke vanished.

'What does it mean, Ross?' The girl looked at him
with puzzled eyes.

'It means I've got to get up there in a hurry,' he
answered a bit grimly. 'I should send an answer, but I
can't risk making smoke talk so close to the ranch.'
His mind was racing. He was sure Harve would head
for the Oxbow. He was also sure that Buel Patchen
would send men to hunt down and destroy Jean and
himself.

He came to a swift decision, fumbled in his pockets
and drew out an old envelope and a pencil. 'I've got a
new job for you, Chucho,' he said. He scrawled a few
brief lines on the back of the envelope. 'Can you make
it to the Oxbow on that pony? He looks done up.'

Chucho eyed his pinto doubtfully. 'Maybe not so
quick,' he said. 'I have ride him like hell already to
find you.'

'You'll have to ride like hell to make the Oxbow ahead of Flying A,' Ross told him grimly. His look went to the rawboned buckskin under the monkeylike huddle of Sing Gee. Old Breezy's horse. He had seen the speed of that buckskin only the morning before when Breezy had so easily outdistanced Tenn Patchen and overtaken the girl's red mare. The buckskin was fast and tough, still fairly fresh.

'All right, Chucho,' he said. 'We'll fix up a horse trade with Sing Gee.'

The saddles were quickly switched. Chucho scrambled on the buckskin. His eyes were sparkling as he held out his hand for the pencil-scrawled envelope. 'I *will* ride like hell,' he promised.

'You're on *my* payroll this trip.' Ross smiled. 'Ten bucks, Chucho.' The gold piece was suddenly in the boy's hand, along with the note.

'*Por Dios!*' Chucho gulped. 'I get so rich I will go to the American college.' His quirt swung with a double crack. The buckskin sprang forward with a startled snort.

Five miles away, Harve Welder was in the ranch-house kitchen, staring with startled eyes at three heavily snoring men. He hastily bent over the man lying on the floor near the hall door. Stack Jimson, followed by Dater and some half dozen men, pushed into the room from the yard. The fat liveryman uttered an astonished oath.

'Drunk, huh?'

'I ain't so sure, Stack.' The foreman spoke in a puzzled voice. 'Rick ain't one to get hisself hawg-drunk.' He jerked upright and ran into the hall. The others clattered noisily at his heels, followed him into the ranch office, and for a moment there was a hush as they gazed at the limp form in the office chair.

Dater said softly, '*By damn!*' and looked stupidly at the foreman. 'Never seed the boss drunk no time, but he's sure sleepin' off a bender.'

Harve's look fastened on the whiskey bottle. He picked it up, sniffed suspiciously. 'Don't smell natcheral,' he announced.

Stack Jimson took the bottle, sniffed, poured some of the whiskey into a glass and tasted it. He grimaced. 'Somethin' wrong with this hootch.' He spat, wiped his lips. 'Been doped,' he said.

'*By damn*,' repeated Dater. 'The Chink done it . . . the Chink doped 'em. It was him setting in the back seat of the buckboard an' pourin' lead at us.' The Flying A man swore softly. 'Couldn't see good in the dark, but it was the Chink all right.'

'Go git some cold water,' rasped Harve. 'We got to snap Buel out of this, an' Rick too. My Gawd, there's hell bustin' loose all over the place an' Buel an' Rick layin' here sick as poisoned pups.'

'Not forgettin' Downs an' Roscoe,' added Stack Jimson grimly. 'A hell of a pair them two are, lettin' Rick get hisself doped. A good sousin' in the horse trough is what them jaspers git right now.'

Despite various heroic remedies it was almost two hours before Sing Gee's victims were able to sit up and take an intelligent interest in affairs. Harve Welder fretted and cursed. The resourcefulness of Ross Chaine appalled him. He was afraid to leave the ranch for fear of what Chaine would do next. The man was a devil, he told Stack Jimson. No matter what he did Ross Chaine was always one jump ahead of him.

'He's got me goin' loco,' Harve complained. 'Dater says they had him throwed in the grain shed, his hands tied behind his back. Inside of fifteen minutes he busts out and knocks Shorty cold . . . throws him inside the grain shed and walks bold as brass over to the house where Piute is keepin' lookout on the gal's window. Chaine smacks Piute with the gun he's grabbed from Shorty and hightails it away in Rick's buckboard with the gal and that Chinaman. The feller ain't human, Stack. He just ain't human!'

'They wasn't in the buckboard when Dater caught the team,' reminded Jimson. 'They got to be some place close, Harve.'

Dater came into the office with the news that three horses were missing from the corral. 'The gal's bay mare, Breezy's buckskin and that new black horse the boss traded for last week.'

'Must have had 'em staked out before the getaway,' surmised Harve. 'You should have checked up on the horses right after you grabbed Chaine,' he added with an oath. 'Seems like I've got to do all the thinkin' on this ranch.'

Dater gave him a sulky look. 'I ain't shakin' down no foreman's pay,' he muttered.

'None of your damn lip!' Harve glared at the man. His nerves were frayed raw and he was in a dangerous mood. 'Get busy, Dater. Take a couple of the boys and comb the chaparral. You'll maybe pick up Chaine's trail. It's my guess he'll head for Mendoza with the gal . . . get her away on the stage.'

Dater hesitated. 'What'll I do if she caught the stage?'

'Hightail it back to the ranch. We'll leave what to do with her up to the boss.'

'The boss figgered to throw her in jail for framin' with Chaine to kill Tenn and Breezy,' Dater told him.

The foreman and Jimson exchanged skeptical grins. Dater's eyes narrowed as he looked at them. 'I ain't believing Chaine killed Tenn and Breezy any more than you fellers do,' he said. 'Chaine's gun was full loaded when I picked it up.' He shrugged dusty shoulders. 'Tenn killed old Breezy, and Breezy triggered Tenn before he passed out.' Dater shrugged again. 'I'll say Breezy done a good job.'

'You better go easy on that talk,' rasped the foreman. His hard eyes raked the man. 'Ain't sure I like it from you, Dater.'

The cowboy's sunburned face took on a grayish look. 'I'll get goin',' he mumbled.

Stack Jimson's sharp, restless eyes followed him as he stepped into the hall. He pursed his heavy lips, shook his head. 'Somethin' wrong with that feller,' he said softly.

The foreman stared at him; and what he read in the fat man's eyes jerked him out of his chair. He stood for a moment, breathing hard, hand on his holstered gun.

Dater had left by the front door; they could hear the quick chop of his high-heeled boots on the flagstones, the rasp of dragging spurs. Welder was suddenly running swiftly from the room. Jimson heard the slap of leather as gun left holster. The liveryman tensed in his chair, he leaned his head forward, expectant, listening. Tobacco juice dribbled from a corner of sagging pendulous lip, his eyes narrowed to slits of cold glass in folds of mottled skin.

The sound of the foreman's voice calling his name made Dater do a curious thing. His hand was reaching for the gate latch. It dropped to the gun in his holster as he whirled in a sidewise leap that took him to a big hydrangea bush close to the walk. The crash of a forty-five shattered the early morning quiet of the garden. Smoke curled from the gun in the hand of the man standing on the porch steps.

The bullet slapped into the gate post behind Dater. His own Colt spat fire and smoke. He saw Harve Welder flinch, heard the clatter of his gun as it hit the stone steps. Dater made a leap for the gate, jerked it open and ran into the yard.

Two men started toward him from the horses bunched near the water trough. One of them shouted excitedly, 'What's up, Dater?'

'I'm leavin' this damn place for keeps,' panted the cowboy. His eyes flamed a threat at them. They halted, gaped stupidly at him. Dater singled out his horse from the bunch and sprang into the saddle. 'Welder's a killin' mad wolf,' he shouted at them. 'I'm ridin' a long ways from here.' The horse jumped into a dead run under the bite of spurs.

The garden gate slammed open and Welder burst into the yard. The sight of Dater disappearing in a cloud of dust drew an enraged yell from him.

'What are you standing there for like damn fools?' he shouted at the two men.

'I ain't stoppin' him,' one of them said sullenly. 'Dater don't miss his shots. You ain't sendin' *me* after him, Harve.'

'Me nuther,' muttered his companion. His hand slid down to gun-butt, eyes challenged the foreman. 'Go chase him yourself, Harve.'

Welder cursed them and flung back through the gate. He was at a disadvantage. He could not afford to antagonize the remaining members of the outfit. He was shrewd enough to realize that Dater was not only well-liked, but also feared because of his deadly skill with a gun.

Stack Jimson grinned malevolently at him from the doorway. 'Got away from you, huh.' He wagged his big head ominously. 'Too bad, Harve — too bad.'

The foreman picked up the gun Dater's bullet had knocked from his hand. The hammer was bent. He flung the useless gun aside with a curse and rubbed his numbed hand. 'I'm needin' a drink,' he said in a hollow voice. 'My Gawd, Stack! When do you suppose Rick and Buel will get their senses back? I cain't leave for Oxbow till I've had a talk with 'em. I've got to know what they figger to do.' He pushed through the door and into the ranch office, stood glaring helplessly at the two snoring men.

Chapter

19

WAR CLOUDS

Don Vicente Torres was proving as stubborn as Ross had feared. His promise was sacred, he told Buckshot and Pete. Their advice was well-meant, but he could not leave his friend Chaine in the lurch. He had promised to hold the prisoners safe at Oxbow.

'A Torres no easy break the promeese,' he said. He smiled at his stocky, powerful half-brother. 'Torres men do not run from a fight,' he added in Spanish.

Carlos Montalvo lifted an expressive shoulder. 'Run is not a word we know, Vicente.'

'You're a pair of doggone fools,' grumbled Buckshot. 'This here thing calls for common sense. Harve Welder is loose and that means the beans is spilled clean out of the pot. He'll be back most any time and it's goin' to be a massacre. You ain't got a chance, Vicente.'

Don Vicente scowled. 'Thees Welder hombre keel my vaquero. He mus' feel Torres knife in 'eart.'

'*Sí*,' grunted Carlos Montalvo. 'I keel thees Welder.'

The LK partners exchanged exasperated looks. Pete turned to his horse. 'We done all we can, Buckshot,' he said. 'I'm thinking we'd best head for Bar Chain in a hurry. There's a chance Ross is there with the girl. We've got to figger what to do with her.'

Estevan hurried up to the group standing near the

camp shack. 'A rider comes,' he said in Spanish to Torres. 'He comes very fast.'

They could hear the furious rataplan of a running horse. 'Comin' like a bat out of hell,' muttered Buckshot. His eyes widened as the rider swung into view. 'Doggone — if it ain't Chucho!' He broke into a run. The others followed.

Chucho jerked the buckskin to a sliding halt, grinned at the wondering faces and pulled a crumpled envelope from inside his shirt. 'For *los señores!*' he shrilled. 'By damn, I come fast! This horse has legs that go and go!'

Pete Lally reached for the envelope. 'Where from, son?'

'Señor Chaine,' Chuco told him importantly. 'For bringing it to you I am on his payroll for ten bucks. *Válgame Dios!* I get so rich every day!'

Pete read the pencil-scrawl, handed it in silence to his partner.

'This fixes it, Vicente,' Buckshot said. 'Ross says for you to clear out of this camp pronto.'

'The promeese ees no more, eh?' Torres shrugged. 'I do w'at he say.'

'He says to turn all the prisoners loose, except Tony Birl,' Buckshot went on. 'He wants us to head quick as we can for Bar Chain.'

Pete Lally looked doubtful. 'Ross wasn't takin' time to think,' he argued. 'Don't seem like good sense to go turn those fellers loose.'

Diego and Estevan exchanged looks, fingered their keen-edged machetes thoughtfully. Buckshot shook his head at them. 'No chance, fellers.'

'Their throats would slit easily,' Diego murmured in Spanish.

'Silence!' Don Vicente spoke sharply. 'Torres men kill in fair fight. They do not murder.'

'They are wolves — and we kill wolves,' muttered the Yaqui.

'We'll take 'em along and turn 'em loose some place in the hills,' Pete decided. 'Be a fool trick to leave 'em here to join up with Welder when he comes.'

The idea appealed to Buckshot. He elaborated on it. 'We'll set 'em afoot without their boots. They'll be awful wore out and heartbroke by the time they get to Dos Cruces.'

'You do think up the doggondest layouts,' admired his big partner.

'They won't dast show their faces in these parts ag'in,' asserted Buckshot. 'They'll be so doggoned 'shamed they'll make dust away from Dos Cruces quick as they can get leather soles to their sore feet.'

'Let's get started,' Pete Lally said. 'We don't want to be making dust signs for Harve Welder to spot when he hits the camp.'

Carlos Montalvo sped away, voice lifted in shouts to the vaqueros. Vicente threw a cautious look at the partners and moved close to the buckskin horse. 'The little Chaquita,' he said softly in Spanish, 'she is well, my Chucho?'

'She is sad for fear you will be killed,' Chucho answered with a sly grin. 'I tell her you make songs about her and then she is happy.'

'Your words are golden music in my ears,' smiled Don Vicente. 'Take this, to jingle with the others in your pocket. You are a smart boy.'

'It is music I like,' grinned the boy as he took the coin. 'What is it I must say to Chaquita?'

'A smart boy,' repeated Vicente with an approving nod. 'Tell the beautiful Chaquita that I return soon to the *cantina* of your grandfather to beg his permission to offer her my name. She will honor and grace Rancho Torres.'

'I will remember the words,' Chucho promised. He smiled impishly. 'Chaquita will kiss me.'

'Lucky one!' The tall ranchero sighed, rolled his eyes. 'You will live with us in Sonora, Chucho.'

'Not so!' Chucho looked alarmed. 'I am American and will some day be very rich. People will lift their hats when I ride in the street and say "That is Chucho . . . he is very rich and our great governor." '

'Good!' Don Vicente chuckled. 'Chaquita and I will visit you at the governor's palace in Santa Fe.'

Buckshot looked around at them. 'Get goin', Chucho,' he said. 'You want to be a long way from here when them Flying A fellers hit the camp.'

'You bet,' grinned Chucho. '*Adios, señores.*'

'The kid has sure earned his money,' Buckshot declared as the boy splashed across the ford and was lost to view.

'He is on my payroll now,' Don Vicente said with an enigmatic smile. He turned to the horse Estevan led up, swung into the saddle and rode with Pete and Buckshot toward the lifting hills. Estevan and Diego clung like shadows to the *ranchero*, their eyes roving watchfully. Behind them followed Carlos Montalvo and his vaqueros with the closely guarded prisoners.

They topped the low ridge beyond the camp. Diego muttered an exclamation and jerked rifle from saddle-boot. 'One comes!' he said. 'A gringo!' The rifle leaped to his shoulder.

Estevan was perhaps a split second longer in getting his rifle out. The lone horseman pulled in sharply. His hand lifted in the peace sign.

Buckshot Kinners spoke sharply. 'Call those dogs of yours off, Vicente!' He said in a lower voice to Pete, 'I'm a liar if that feller ain't Ned Dater.'

At a word from Vicente, the Yaquis reluctantly lowered their guns, and reassured by Buckshot's hail, **Dater** rode over to the clustered group of horsemen.

'What's your business with us, Ned? Are you alone?' Buckshot's voice was hard, his eyes unfriendly.

'Right now I'm alone, Buckshot.' Dater's face was pale. He was hardly more than twenty, a range-toughened youth with a resolute bearing that not even their hostile looks could dent. 'I'm a few jumps ahead of Harve Welder, but my gun ain't smokin' on *his* side no more.'

'Speak your piece in plain talk,' Peter Lally rumbled. 'You mean you've quit Flying A, Ned?'

'I'm hopin' the dust I've made will choke them damn wolves to death,' Dater replied. 'Harve Welder handed me my time with hot lead. I handed same back and left there on the run.'

'You had a good job with us, Ned,' reminded Buckshot severely. 'You quit the LK for Patchen's outfit. You was old enough to know better.'

Dater hung his head. 'I been a damn fool,' he muttered. A deep red crept over his pleasant young face. 'Ain't carin' to talk in front of all these hombres.'

Pete and Buckshot swung their horses away, beckoned Dater to follow. 'Now ——' Pete halted his horse. 'Give us the truth, Ned.' His voice was kindly. 'Buckshot and me always figgered there was something queer — the way you went over to Flying A.'

'Well ——' Dater stammered. 'I seen Jean one time, in town . . . she kind of got me.'

'We savvy, boy.' Pete nodded soberly. 'So you went and hired out to Buel Patchen so you could see her a lot.'

'That's about it,' admitted Dater. His face was pale again. 'Pete, those Patchen wolves murdered old Breezy last night . . . tried to make us think Chaine done the killin' . . . accused the girl along with Chaine. I'm

knowin' different.   Chaine's gun was full loaded.   Tenn
shot Breezy, and Breezy got in a last shot that killed
Tenn.   Best thing he ever done!'

'We ain't heard about what went on at the ranch yet,'
Pete said.   'We only know that Ross and Jean got
away.   We're headin' for them now.'

'I'll tell you somethin',' Dater went on.   'Breezy
accused Buel of cuttin' the girl's saddle latigo, claimed
Buel was plannin' to get her killed.   That's why Tenn
shot Breezy.'

The partners exchanged grim looks.   It was Buckshot
who spoke.   'We savvy, Ned.   You got to thinkin', huh?'

'I'll say!' Dater swore softly.   'And then Harve showed
up.   He's a ravin' mad wolf.   Guess he was treated awful
rough, face all bleedin', a black eye, his shirt about tore
off his back.   He found things in a mess at the ranch.
Seems like the Chink doped the whiskey and old Buel
and Rick DeSalt were still snorin' their heads off when
I lit away from there.   That's what's held Harve back
from gettin' here with the bunch.   He's all set to shoot
the guts out of these Mex hombres.'   Dater glanced
apprehensively over his shoulder.   'I wouldn't hang
round here too long, Buckshot.   No tellin' how quick
Harve will come poppin' over the ridge.'

Buckshot and Pete looked at each other thoughtfully.
'I reckon we've got the picture,' Pete said.   'How about
it, Buckshot?   You think the way I do about him?'

Buckshot nodded.   'You want your job back, Ned?'

Dater gave them a dazed look.   'You mean ——'

'Sure.   You're hired right now.'   Buckshot glanced at
his partner, who nodded.   'Make dust over to the LK,
Ned.   Tell Joe you're on the payroll ag'in.'

'Joe won't take my word for it,' worried Dater.

Pete fished a piece of paper from a pocket and scribbled a few lines.   'This will fix it with Joe,' he said.

Dater read the note. He gave the partners a startled look, grinned, pushed the paper into shirt pocket. 'I'll be ridin' with the bunch,' he told them exultantly. 'I sure crave to line my gun on Harve Welder.'

'You'll maybe have the chance,' Buckshot said grimly. 'Get goin', Ned, and tell Joe when Pete and me say for him to come on the jump we mean, *come on the jump*.'

'I'll tell him plenty,' promised Dater. He spurred away, hand lifted in a parting salute to the curious-eyed vaqueros.

Pete and Buckshot rejoined Torres. 'All right, *amigo*,' Buckshot said. 'Let's go.'

They rode on toward the hills. 'There's that smoke talk ag'in,' Buckshot said suddenly. 'Looks like it's up in Red Creek Flats this time.'

'Sure is mysterious,' Pete commented.

They watched with puzzled interest until the puffs of smoke vanished.

'A sign,' Don Vicente said solemnly. 'Mooch smoke will come from our guns . . . a 'appy sign for good fight, no?'

'You're a bloodthirsty devil,' jeered Buckshot.

'Me?' Vicente laughed loudly. 'No, no, my frien'. I am in mooch loafe. I weel now make nize song to my Chaquita.' He began to hum a gay little tune, beating time with his hand.

Diego and Estevan exchanged disgusted looks.

Chapter
20

THE CAVE AT BAR CHAIN

IT SEEMED INCREDIBLE to Jean that hardly thirty-six hours had passed since her secret ride with Ross to Bar Chain. So much had happened in those peril-packed hours — the veil torn from her eyes and the man she had trusted revealed as a sinister arch-killer. Ross Chaine's coming had only hastened the inevitable moment when Buel Patchen would have struck. She knew now that only her marriage to his son would have saved her from some cunningly contrived fatal accident. Her step-uncle would have made a public exhibition of sorrow and grief. None would have known of the crime that made him owner of the Austen ranch. Jean was sure Buel was in some way connected with the supposed fatal accident that had taken her father's life. He had not appeared at the ranch until after Bill Austen's death, but according to Pete and Buckshot there was a story that Buel and Harve Welder were once members of a border-rustling gang. Harve Welder was an experienced cowman and her father had been glad to put him on the Flying A payroll. It was significant that within three months of the hiring of Welder her father was dead.

She was not so clear in her mind about the conspiracy that had ravaged Red Creek Valley and made a ghost town of Alamos. She had been too young when the thing happened. There were vague stories of a bitter feud between her step-uncle and Jim Chaine . . . something to do with water-rights. Jim Chaine was a violent and disagreeable man. At least, Jean had learned to believe so from the things Buel Patchen said about him. A little too smart with a running-iron, and too friendly with rustlers. Buel always claimed that quarrelsome, unscrupulous Jim Chaine had been killed by rustlers. A case of thieves falling out. It had not seemed very important to her at the time. She only knew that after Jim Chaine's death there had followed quiet years on the range. Buel's new big dam at the headwaters of Red Creek turned thousands of desert acres into lush alfalfa fields. Flying A prospered and money was plentiful. Buel sent Jean to the best school in El Paso. He would say in his bell-toned voice that he wanted her to be the smartest and best-dressed girl in the county. 'You'll likely be Mrs. Tenn Patchen some day,' he would add with a chuckle.

Jean had been home from school less than six months when the conversation she overheard between her step-uncle and Harve Welder sent her on that early morning ride to Alamos. She had heard stories of Ross Chaine from time to time. Nothing good of him either. A bad chip off the old block, her step-uncle would say. One of the most ruthless killers in Oklahoma's notorious No Man's Land.

But she had ridden to Alamos to warn him of the death-trap. A senseless thing to do, but the impulse had flowered from childish memories of the red-headed boy whose fists had once pounded the bigger, already brutal Tenn Patchen for pinching and slapping her.

So much had happened in the few days since that morning in Alamos. Her world turned topsy-turvy, herself a hunted thing, hiding in a big cave on the Bar Chain ranch.

Sing Gee looked up at her from the fire he was carefully nourishing with bits of dry cat's-claw. The wood burned with a clear hot flame that gave out hardly any smoke. 'Plitty quick have coffee,' the old cook said with an encouraging smile.

She nodded, went carefully through the thorny tangle of brush and entered the cave. Ross was saddling the palomino. An Indian was giving the other horses a feed of grain from a sack that leaned against the wall. He was an old man with white hair and surprisingly bright eyes in a wrinkled brown face. His name was Injun John and Ross had known him for years, ever since he was a small boy. Pete Lally had sent him to take care of the palomino.

He gave the girl a friendly grin, picked up a carbine that leaned against the wall near the sack of grain.

'Me watch,' he said to Ross. He disappeared into the thicket. For all his years there was no stiffness in his joints. He seemed to drift from the cave with the soundless stealth of a coyote.

'The coffee is ready — almost,' Jean said. She watched while Ross drew the cinch tight. 'You're going up there — to the Flats?'

'Yes.' Something in her voice drew his keen look.

'Is it something to do with that smoke talk?'

He nodded. 'Let's get to that coffee. You've had a tough night of it. Try and get some rest after you've had some food.'

She stood staring at him, the beginnings of a frown on her brow. Ross smiled across the saddle at her. 'It's lucky for us Pete and Buckshot packed those supplies in from their place. Sing Gee says there's bacon, salt pork. beans, flour, sugar, coffee, and a lot of stuff

including a bottle of whiskey for snakebite.' He chuckled. 'Still luckier to have a top-hand cook like old Sing
on the job.'

'I'm going up there with you,' Jean said.

Ross shook his head. 'You're safer here. Nobody
knows about this cave. Injun John will stick close on
lookout — keep you warned.'

'I'm going with you,' she repeated in a determined
voice.

'It's too risky,' Ross said firmly. 'Don't make it more
difficult for me, Jean. I've got to get up there in a
hurry — before it's too late.'

'I'd rather be with you — than stay here alone.'

'Pete and Buckshot are sure to turn up during the day.
You'll be safe with them . . . a lot safer than with me —
for a while.'

'What do you mean by — *too late?*' Jean put a hand
on his arm, held him back. 'Ross — I must know *every-
thing*. I am beginning to suspect so much, and really
know so little. I want to know about Rick DeSalt.
He is mixed up in it, too, isn't he?'

'I can't prove anything for a fact, yet,' Ross told her
gloomily. 'If Welder doesn't get Tony Birl away from
Vicente, or kill him, I'll have proof enough to hang
Rick DeSalt.'

'He killed your father? Is that what you suspect?'
She faltered. 'I've been wondering if Buel killed him.'
Again she faltered. 'You see — I've been thinking about
that — that dam. Buel didn't build the dam until after
your father was murdered.'

'The thing started when Buel Patchen sent Welder to
get on your father's Flying A payroll,' Ross said. 'Buel
wanted to get his hands on the ranch. He dared not
show up until your father was dead. Your father knew
he was no good.'

'You mean — Harve — killed Dad?' Horror, fierce anger tightened her voice.

'We haven't the proof it was Harve — yet,' Ross said. 'Harve claims your father accidentally shot himself while crawling through a barbed-wire fence. His story is a lie and shows that Harve either is the murderer, or planned the murder.'

'Where does Rick DeSalt come in?' puzzled the girl.

'Rick knew Buel and Harve when they were rustling cattle down on the border,' Ross explained. 'In fact, he was one of the gang, a sort of border broker . . . handled the stolen cattle. When the gang was broken up he hid out in Dos Cruces, went into the saloon business. That was sixteen or seventeen years ago.'

'I still don't understand about him,' Jean said. 'Unless you mean he planned things.'

'That is just what Rick did. He learned that Buel was your mother's brother-in-law. Buel was her only living relative. She was almost sure to want Buel to manage the ranch in case of your father's death. Rick saw a chance for a big cleanup.'

'I see.' Jean's face was a white mask in the dim light that filtered into the cave. 'He told Buel Patchen — and then Harve came along — got a job with Flying A.'

'Rick played safe,' Ross went on. 'He let Harve and Buel do the dirty work, but from the moment of your father's death he had his grip on them, made them dance to any tune he called.'

'He was always so nice to me.' Jean shivered. 'He used to tease me about Tenn . . . pretend he thought I was in love with Tenn.' She gave Ross a hard, bright look. 'Rick DeSalt must have known I was to die — too, if I didn't marry Tenn.'

Ross nodded grimly. 'Nothing was going to stop DeSalt once he had a foothold. His next move was to eliminate my father. He was jealous of Jim Chaine's influence and of the growing prosperity of Alamos. He was the big man in Dos Cruces and didn't like losing trade to Alamos. He set Buel onto Jim Chaine. You know what happened. My father was killed on his own doorstep. Buel built the big dam that left Red Creek a dry wash. The hundred or so small ranchers down in the lower valley were forced to abandon their farms. Alamos just naturally died.'

'He murdered the valley, too,' Jean said with a little catch in her voice.

'Just as certain as he murdered my father, DeSalt murdered Red Creek Valley — murdered Alamos.' The look in his eyes drew another shiver from the girl. 'You know now why Buel sent a killer to waylay me on the trail. My return to Red Creek meant only one thing to DeSalt and Patchen. They had to get me. They're still trying to get me.'

'It's been so long since — since it happened,' Jean said. 'When did you first suspect the truth?'

'Several months ago when I learned about an option my aunt had given Buel to sell him Bar Chain. She was still my guardian at the time, and she'd heard I'd been killed in Socorro. The thing smelled bad. I wrote to Pete Lally and did some nosing around on my own account.'

'I think they suspected something.' Jean told him. 'I used to hear them talking about Ross Chaine. I thought Ross Chaine must be a very bad man. They were clever about it.'

Ross grinned. 'They knew I was bad medicine for them all right. Anyway, when I learned of the close tie-up between Rick and Buel I began to get the whole picture.'

'It isn't finished yet — the picture,' Jean said simply.

'It's going to be finished my way.' His tone was hard.

'Yes,' Jean agreed soberly. 'Your way.' She hesitated. 'You haven't told me why you are going up to the Flats.' She paused. 'Is it something to do with the dam?'

'Yes.' Ross spoke reluctantly. 'The Prophet says the dam must be destroyed.'

'Oh!' She gave him an aghast look.

'That smoke talk you saw yesterday morning was to tell me he was on the way with the dynamite.' Ross paused, shook his head doubtfully. 'It seemed a good idea when we first talked it over. I'm not so sure. You see I didn't know as much about you as I do now.'

Her look told him to continue. 'The smoke talk we saw this morning means he is already up in the Flats. He is worried because he has not heard from me.'

'You haven't had a chance to signal back to him,' Jean surmised.

'Not a chance. The Prophet thinks something has happened — that perhaps I've been killed. His last message said he would blow up the dam himself at noon today.'

'And you don't want him to blow up the dam?' Her tone was curious.

'I don't want to ruin your ranch,' he answered almost roughly.

'It would mean new life for Red Creek — for Bar Chain,' Jean said softly.

'Yes,' Ross said in a low voice. 'Flesh and sinews for dry bones — the breath of life again in the valley.'

Jean was silent for a long moment. Ross turned to the golden horse. She held him with a quick gesture. 'No!' She spoke fiercely. 'Don't stop him! Let him blow up the dam. It is the work of wicked men and its stolen waters have cursed my father's ranch.'

His jaw set in hard lines. 'I'm going to stop him,' he insisted. 'I told you from the first I would do nothing to harm you. It was a promise I won't break.'

She saw it was useless to protest. His hand went out, clasped hers. 'We'll work out some other plan. There's water enough for all of us with a dam in the right place. It's *time* we need, time to think and plan and build for better things.'

'I'd rather you didn't stop him,' was all she said in reply.

She followed him outside to the little campfire. Sing Gee grinned at them over the coffee pot he was nursing on the red coals. 'Plenty good now.' He filled two tin cups.

Ross drank quickly, wolfed down a bacon sandwich and got into his saddle. '*Adios.*' His warm smile rested briefly on the girl as he rode away.

Forebodings seized the girl as she watched him go. She wanted to call him back. She knew it would be useless. Sing Gee spoke irritably. 'Me fix plenty good bleakfas' ——'

'I'm not hungry,' Jean told him. She wondered at herself. She had been ravenously hungry before her talk with Ross — before he had ridden away.

Sing Gee looked at her with keen, understanding eyes. 'You allee same plenty flighten,' he diagnosed.

'I don't know,' Jean answered. 'Perhaps I am, Sing. I — I wish I had gone with him.' She left him, went back to the cave. Redbird flung up her head, nickered softly. The mare was nervous, too . . . wanted to be gone from the gloomy place.

Jean stood looking at her, fingernails biting into the palms of her clenched hands. Try as she could she was unable to dispel those sickening waves of apprehension. Cold prickles chased up and down her spine.

She had to do something. Almost mechanically she reached for her saddle and threw it over the mare's back. Redbird tossed her head, pawed an eager, expectant forefoot.

A faint sound behind her swung the girl's head in a startled look. The old Indian stood watching her, his carbine in lowered hand. His hand went up in a warning gesture.

'Me see men come,' he said in his guttural voice. 'You stay still like rabbit. No make noise. Bad men hear — come quick . . . kill you.'

She stared at him, eyes wide with growing alarm. She saw Sing Gee slip in from the cat's-claw that screened the cave's mouth. The old Chinese was carrying his coffee pot and frying pan. He put the utensils down against the wall, began calmly examining the six-gun Ross had taken from the half-breed they had left lying senseless in the bushes near Jean's bedroom window.

Jean's heart stood still. Ross would be seen. He would be followed by the killers who had so quickly picked up the trail. She must warn Ross. She could not cower like a coward in the cave and let the man she loved ride into the ambushed guns of Buel Patchen's assassins. She pulled feverishly on the cinch, pulled so hard that the red mare laid back indignant ears.

Perhaps the old Chinese, the older Indian, understood, or perhaps it was the fierce, hard resolve in her eyes that held them wordless. They made no attempt to stop her as she led the mare from the cave.

Chapter
21

THE DAM

FROM SOMEWHERE in the deeps of the canyon came the vicious whine of a bullet — the reverberating report of a rifle. A second shot screamed overhead.

Ross jumped his horse from the trail and pulled in behind a thick clump of scraggly junipers. He was angry, tinglingly aware of the first bullet that had torn through his hat. He reviled himself bitterly for underestimating the men who sought to remove him from life.

He dismounted, took his rifle from saddle-boot and crawled back to the trail for a look into the canyon. It was almost a sheer drop of five hundred feet to the wide dry wash of the creek.

Patiently he scrutinized the fringe of stunted alders and willows. Nothing moved down there. The canyon seemed empty of life. Only a crow in raucous flight toward the opposite cliffs.

From where he crouched he could see a loop of the trail below him. Somebody was rounding the steep hairpin turn. Cold horror seized Ross as he recognized Jean Austen and her red mare. Almost at the same instant he glimpsed a faint curl of smoke in the fringe of willows down in the wash. As the gunshot blasted the stillness he snatched his own rifle to shoulder and fired at the hidden sharpshooter. He heard a flurry of scrambling hoofs, saw Jean swing into the upper turn and head for the same clump of scrub that hid the palomino. He ran to her, his heart in his mouth.

She gave him a tight, almost defiant little smile, shook her head at the question in his eyes. 'I'm not hurt. Don't look so — so ghastly.'

'I can't help it.' He spoke hoarsely. 'They — they tried to kill you — *a girl!*'

'Of course they tried.' She gestured expressively. 'We know they want us both dead, Ross.'

'You shouldn't have come,' he groaned.

'I *had* to come. I couldn't let them kill you without a chance to fight back.' She suddenly drooped miserably in her saddle. 'Oh, Ross! Those first shots! I thought I was too late to warn you. I wasn't caring any more — what happened.' Her voice broke.

'It's all right.' There was no heart in him to reproach her. His arm reached up, drew tight around her waist. 'It's all right.' She bent down to him. It was the first time he had kissed her. He found it sweet, reluctantly tore himself away. 'Wait here,' he said, and went swiftly back to the trail.

The fringe of willows down in the wash was vomiting horsemen. Ross took deliberate aim. His hand was steady again as he squeezed on the trigger.

One of the riders let out a yell of pain, swung his horse back into the willows. His companions followed him. Ross waited a moment. Apparently they were daunted by his marksmanship. He slid down the bank and ran to the waiting girl.

'I can hold them back for a time,' he told her. 'I can hold them long enough for you to get up to the flats.'

She read his thoughts, shook her head. 'No! I won't go! I don't care if The Prophet *does* blow up the dam. I want him to blow it to pieces. I hate the dam for what it has done to you — to your valley — to Alamos.'

'Wait!' he said again.   He hurried back to the trail.
The horsemen were still in the cover of the willows.   He
sent two more shots, saw answering gunsmoke curl from
the bushes.   He was at Jean's side again before the re-
verberations died away.

'How close did they get to you?' he asked.

'Close enough for me to know that Buel Patchen and
DeSalt are with them.'

Ross nodded.   'It's a good guess that Harve headed
for Oxbow with most of the outfit,' he said.   'I counted
six of them down in the wash.   Is that about right?'

Jean said, 'Yes.   Buel and Rick and four or five others.
I'm not sure just how many.'   She was staring with dilated eyes at his stetson.   'Ross — you — you were
almost hit!'

'That first bullet was a bit close,' he admitted with a
rueful grin.   He gestured for attention.   'Listen . . .
and don't argue!   I want you to get up to the flats and
stop The Prophet.   We don't want that dam blown up.
With a second dam at the west fork there's water enough
for all of us.'

'I hate anything that is Buel Patchen's,' Jean said
stubbornly.

Ross gave her a worried look, ran back to the trail.
She heard the crash of his rifle echoing between the
cliffs, heard answering gunshots from the deeps of the
canyon.

He was at her side again, smoking rifle in lowered
hand, his eyes hard, unsmiling.   It was necessary to get
her away from the spot.   He could hold the Flying A
men back only as long as his ammunition lasted.   The
trail was narrow and steep.   They were too smart to face
his gunfire.   But there would be no stopping them once
his rifle was useless.

'I don't want you here,' he said quietly.   'Go on up
to the flats.   I'll give you half an hour.'

'I won't leave you,' Jean told him in a low voice.

He ignored the interruption. 'There is an old Indian trail that runs west and then south into Los Gatos Canyon. We can make it that way back to Bar Chain.'

'You mean you'll come with me?' Her face brightened.

'I'll follow in half an hour.'

Jean looked at him doubtfully. He hurried on, 'I'm giving Pete and Buckshot another hour to get to Bar Chain with Vicente and the vaqueros. We'll have a chance to fight it out down at the ranch, Jean.' He gestured impatiently. 'I can't stop to argue ... not with that bunch watching for a chance to get up the trail.'

She gave in, reluctantly started her mare. 'I won't tell The Prophet not to blow up the dam,' she called back over her shoulder.

Ross was not listening. He was already on the run back to the trail's edge. Jean heard the sharp crack of his rifle as another hairpin turn hid him from view.

The mare was a good climber and in something less than twenty minutes they reached the flats, an irregular-shaped meadow cradled between low pine-covered hills. Jean glimpsed the silver sheen of a lake against a background of snow-veined crags. She pushed the mare into a fast lope.

The Prophet was not visible when she reached the dam Buel Patchen had thrown across the narrow gorge at the lower end of the lake. She halted the mare and stared with troubled eyes at her step-uncle's handiwork. He had shown real engineering skill in diverting the waters of the lake down the west fork. Jean could find no room in her heart for admiration. The dam was an evil thing, conceived in wickedness. She saw in it the likeness of Buel Patchen. She hated it.

She slid from her saddle and ran close to the huge

·nass of earth and rock. The Prophet was down on the runway that ran along the lower side of the dam. He was stooped over, hands busy with something Jean could not see at that distance.

He straightened up and looked at her.

She could only stare at him. He seemed to read her troubled thoughts, climbed wearily up the steep bank to her side. 'You are Jean Austen.' It was a statement rather than a question. 'You do not want it destroyed.'

She clasped her hands in an agony of indecision. 'Ross says you mustn't. But it is an evil thing . . . I hate it!'

'Where is Ross Chaine? He promised he would come.' The Prophet seemed to lean more heavily on the great staff he held with both hands. 'All is ready — but he is not here.' The words came from him feebly.

The grayness settling over the bearded face frightened her. 'He's coming — soon.' She told him of the fight down the trail.

'You love him? You love Ross Chaine?' His keen eyes probed her.

'Yes,' faltered the girl. 'Oh, *yes!*'

'*You* must do what he is not here to do,' The Prophet said. His long gaunt frame stooped lower over the big staff.

'You are ill?' She would have supported him. He shook his head impatiently.

'Waste no time with me. There are matches in my pocket. Take them quickly and light the fuses. There are twelve in all. Begin at the far side where the fuses are longer. You will have time to light them and get back to a safe distance.'

'Yes — yes!' Jean fumbled in his pocket, found a block of long sulphur matches.

He stood there, swaying on his tall staff like a tree

loosened by a great wind from its roots. 'Hurry,' he said in a voice that was hardly more than a whisper. 'I hear horsemen — coming. . . . You must not be stopped. It is right for you to destroy Buel Patchen's evil work.'

The force of him possessed Jean completely; she saw him as through a mist, gigantic, flaming-eyed. *Destroy Buel Patchen's evil work.* The words, no louder than the soft whispering of the wind in the pine trees, struck hammer blows at her ears. 'Yes — *yes!*' she said, breathless in her surrender to his will. She left him without another word or look and scrambled down the bluff that stood some fifteen feet above the dam. The matches clutched in her fingers, she hurried along the runway to the far side.

The Prophet stood where she had left him, head bowed against the great staff gripped between his hands. He looked neither at the girl running to the far side of the dam nor at the horseman riding furiously toward him.

Ross flung himself from his saddle and grasped the old man's arm. 'Where is she?' His frantic look went to the girl's red mare.

There was no answer from The Prophet. The staff suddenly fell away under the weight of his sagging body. Ross caught him, lowered him gently to the ground.

There was nothing he could do. The old man was dead. Over-exertion, excitement, probably both, had put too great a strain on his heart.

Ross left him without another look, went with long strides out on the bluff above the dam. Perhaps thirty seconds had passed. A man had died in those fleeting moments, and now he was staring down at the white face of a desperately frightened girl.

'*Ross!*' Her arms reached up to him, frantic, imploring.

He took one startled look, saw the sputtering fuses behind her, the slide of rock and earth that blocked her escape up the bluff. She was a good fifteen feet below him, beyond his reach. He said sharply, 'Don't move!'

Jean saw him turn swiftly and vanish. She glanced apprehensively over her shoulder at the nearest sputtering fuse. It was useless to run to the thing, stamp out those snake-tongued red sparks. There were others, all of them spluttering, hungrily feeding their way to the sticks of dynamite placed by the old prospector's expert hands. And Ross had told her not to move.

He was looking down at her again, his voice cool, encouraging. 'Catch,' he said. 'Slip the loop under your arms.'

Jean caught the rope. The feel of the braided rawhide in her hands galvanized her to a fury of action. She went up the sheer side of the bluff with the agility of a monkey as Ross pulled hand over hand on the lariat.

The last few feet brought her up with a rush that landed her breathless against his side. The impact of his hard body felt good to her. He was so strong. She wanted to cry. He gave her no time for tears or words. His arm was around her, hurrying her to the horses. She glimpsed something lying on the ground. The Prophet, bearded face upturned to the blue sky, his eyes wide and staring.

'He's dead,' she heard Ross say. He gave her no more time to look, lifted her into her saddle. 'Get away from here!' He struck the mare with the coiled lariat. Redbird snorted, sprang into a fast gallop, ears laid back in outraged protest.

Ross flung himself into his saddle and raced after the running mare. He heard a low muffled rumble that swelled into a deafening roar, an inferno of sound like nothing he had ever heard before.

The Prophet's wish was fulfilled, and Buel Patchen's

black curse swept away in the mighty deluge that was suddenly choking Red Creek from cliff to cliff. Destruction and death would be left in the wake of those thundering waters, but the curse would be gone, the valley awakened to new life. As from afar Ross heard the old man's voice, *O ye dry bones, hear the word of the Lord. . . . Behold, I will lay sinews upon you, and will bring flesh upon you, and cover you with skin, and put breath in you, and ye shall live.*

There was no room for doubt in Ross Chaine's mind. Red Creek Valley would live again and the ghosts of defeat and desolation would no longer stalk the little town of Alamos. In that stupendous roar of rushing, unleashed waters was the song of a brave new hope.

He heard Jean's voice. 'I told him you didn't want it done.' She spoke hysterically. 'I couldn't bear the way he — he looked at me. . . . I had to obey him, Ross. His — his will was in me.'

They stared at each other soberly. Events had moved with such appalling swiftness. Ross was thinking of the men he had eluded in the canyon. Small chance for them to escape that roaring turgid flood if they were still down in the wash.

'You must have followed me almost immediately,' Jean said. Her voice broke. 'Another minute would have been too late.'

'I took a chance,' he told her. 'I figured on a few minutes' start before they found out the trail was clear, and I came up awfully fast, a lot faster than they can make it.' His voice hardened. 'If they were down in the wash when the dam went out — they won't make it.'

'Ross!' The thought horrified her.

'They're murderers,' Ross reminded grimly. His voice sharpened. 'Quick — get behind those trees!'

Jean ·heard a shout, the crashing report of a rifle

Her heart in her mouth, she jumped the mare behind the clump of young pines and looked back at Ross. He was down from his horse, crouched behind the trunk of a fallen tree.

A wheezy voice broke the silence. 'No use, Chaine. We got you.'

Ross fired two quick shots, saw the speaker lurch from behind a bush. He fired again. The man dropped. Ross recognized him. Stack Jimson, the obese Dos Cruces liveryman.

Another long silence. Only the low thunder of the flood boiling down Red Creek. Ross spoke crisply. 'Come away from that tree, Rick. Or are you asking for what Stack Jimson got?'

DeSalt's nerve broke. He was suddenly running, crashing through the brush to his horse. Ross whistled sharply and as the palomino came up at a fast trot he ran alongside, grabbed the saddle horn and swung up. In an instant the big horse was on the dead run in chase of the fleeing Dos Cruces man.

As if realizing that flight was impossible, DeSalt dragged his horse to a standstill. He made no attempt to use his gun as Ross rode up. He managed a ghastly smile. 'Looks like you win, Chaine,' he said.

Ross reached out and took the gun from his limp hand. 'Who else came up the trail with you?' he asked curtly.

DeSalt hesitated, looked back at the sprawled body of the dead liveryman.

'I'm in a hurry,' Ross said bleakly.

'Nobody else,' DeSalt answered. 'Buel and the others headed down the wash to meet Harve Welder's crowd.'

Ross saw he was speaking the truth. He gave Jean a reassuring nod as she halted her mare a few yards away. 'Why didn't you go with them?' he asked the ashen-faced man. 'Why did you and Jimson come up here?'

The sly flicker in DeSalt's eyes betrayed the lie he was framing. Ross lifted his gun threateningly. 'You don't need to explain, Rick. You weren't sure I'd headed this way, but you'd seen Jean Austen on the trail. I should kill you, Rick. You and Jimson came up here to find Jean Austen . . . came to kill her.'

'You're crazy,' mumbled DeSalt. He gripped hard on the saddle horn to hide the trembling of his hands. 'You can't prove fool stuff like that on me.'

'I can prove more than that,' retorted Ross. 'You're going to hang for murder, Rick.'

DeSalt seemed to shrivel in his saddle. 'I didn't kill Jim Chaine,' he babbled. 'It — it was an accident . . . he pulled a gun on me —' DeSalt broke off abruptly, the look of a cornered wolf in his eyes.

Ross broke the tense silence. 'I hadn't said whose murder you were going to hang for.' The pent-up bitterness of more than fifteen years edged his voice. 'You didn't need any telling, did you Rick?' He got down from his saddle and reached for the coil of rawhide rope.

Chapter
22

'... AND YE SHALL LIVE'

THE BUZZARDS ROSE with a clumsy flapping of wings
that quickly leveled out and bore them skyward in
graceful, widening circles. Ross halted his horse and
stared down the soggy street. He was suspicious of
those buzzards. Their presence usually meant only one
thing. They were carrion birds and fed on the dead.

The flood had subsided, leaving pools of water in the
street, and great mounds of debris flung against gaunt
frame walls. Alamos seemed more than ever dismal and
forlorn, a town haunted by the ghosts of its lusty past.

Ross scowled. He was letting the place get him down.
Ghosts would no longer stalk the streets of Alamos. The
curse was lifted and those miserable specters of death
and disaster would vanish — like the buzzards that had
taken wing at his approach.

He rode slowly up the street, eyes searching, probing
the debris piled against the buildings by the flood-waters.
Oro's head was suddenly high, ears sharply inquisitive,
distrustful. The horse snorted, halted abruptly.

For a long moment Ross gazed at the dead man lying
in the sodden tangle of weeds and brush piled against
the front of the ramshackle building. The sight sickened
him. He broke out in a cold sweat.

He got down from his saddle and gently extricated

the body. The face was a swollen, unrecognizable pulp, but there was no mistaking those humped shoulders. The raging flood-waters had brought Buel Patchen a long way from the wide wash of Red Creek.

There was something familiar about the weather-beaten walls of the building. Ross lifted his head, looked at the partially obliterated signboard above the sagging door. The old stage office.

Memories stirred within him as he looked at the sign. He saw a small, bewildered boy climbing into the dusty stage. There were men there, watching the boy. Buel Patchen, Harve Welder, a half-score of grim, silent men. He heard the boy's shrilly defiant voice. *I'll be back some day, when I'm a man . . . I'll be back — and I'll kill the murderers of my dad.*

Ross looked down at the thing lying at his feet. It had not been for him to exact vengeance. He was conscious of an odd relief. A curious and grim finish to the tragedy of fifteen years ago.

He counted the days back to the last time he had seen Buel Patchen in that desolate, ghost-ridden street. Less than a week, hardly four days to the hour, since the morning he had watched the Patchens from the upstairs window of the Alamos Hotel. Tenn Patchen was dead, and Buel was dead. Tony Birl's confession of conspiracy and murder had doomed Rick DeSalt to the hangman's noose. Harve Welder alone still eluded the stern justice that had claimed his fellow-murderers.

The Flying A foreman had disappeared completely, fled with the survivors of the flood that had thwarted his pursuit of Don Vicente and his vaqueros. His escape troubled Ross. He desperately wanted the cold-blooded killer of Jean's father. Tony Birl's story had cleared up the mystery surrounding the death of Bill Austen.

A fleeting shadow touched the face of the dead man.

Ross looked up. The buzzards, ceaselessly soaring over-head, patiently waiting for their gruesome feast. The thought revolted him. He looked inside the stage office. The roof had fallen. No sanctuary there for the re-mains of Buel Patchen. With a wry grimace he gathered the inert mass of lifeless flesh into his arms and carried it into the lobby of the hotel several doors further up the street. Absorbed in the distasteful task he failed to see the man step stealthily from the alley behind him.

He placed his burden on the dust-grimed desk and looked around for something to use for a covering. He thought of the slicker tied to his saddle and went quickly out to the street. A voice brought him to an abrupt standstill on the porch steps. A slow, drawling voice that the softly-spoken words made all the more deadly.

'You're not gettin' away from Alamos *this* time, Chaine,' Harve Welder said. He stood in the middle of the street, a sardonic smile on his dark saturnine face, a leveled gun in lifted hand.

Ross looked at him in stony silence. There seemed nothing he could do against the threat of that steadily held gun. The Flying A foreman spoke again, wicked mirth in his quiet voice. 'I'm rememberin' what you done to Tenn Patchen that time we corralled you here in the hotel . . . hung him up like a side of beef on the stairs' post.' Harve shook with silent laughter. 'Ain't hurtin' me none, what you done to the damn fool, but it sure gives me a right smart notion, Chaine.'

Ross maintained his silence. Harve Welder was en-joying his triumph. Let him gloat. Every added mo-ment of delay meant another moment to live. No sense in hastening the man's trigger-finger.

'I'm mebbe loco, wastin' time on you, but I've got a hate for you that hurts. A dose of hot lead is too easy for you, Chaine. You come back like you promised that time when you was a kid and you sure have busted things for us.' A rasp crept into the soft, drawling voice. 'I'm leavin' you hung where you hung Tenn Patchen, and I'm cuttin' your throat.' His wicked, silent laughter again shook him. 'You'll hang there like a stuck hawg, the blood drainin' from you drop by drop till you're dead meat.' His glance went briefly to the palomino. 'I'm forkin' that yeller horse of yours, Chaine. Won't be nobody catch me this side of the border.'

'You're wrong, Harve . . . awful wrong!'

Welder's look shifted involuntarily to the man standing in a half-crouch down the street. The gun in Dater's hand spat flame and smoke. Harve Welder staggered. He was a tough and hard man and courage ran bright in his blood. The heavy forty-five in his hand crashed out three quick shots and Dater was suddenly down on his face, lean body twitching in the mud.

Welder spun around with the speed of a cat to face the man charging from the steps of the hotel porch. He was too late. Ross hit him a terrific blow. The smoking gun flipped from the foreman's hand. Ross struck again, a right and left to the jaw. Blood gushed from Welder's mouth, his knees buckled, and he went down on his face.

Horsemen suddenly crowded from the alley and raced up the street with flurries of mud swirling from pounding hoofs. The rider in the lead reined his horse to a sliding halt.

'*Por Dios!*' Vast relief was in Don Vicente's voice. 'You 'ave those nine lives of the cat, *amigo!*' He added solemnly in Spanish, 'I will burn many candles to the saints, my friend. We feared much for you this past hour.'

Ross hardly heard him. He was staring hard at Harve Welder's limp body. He bent down, rolled the man over on his back. Apparently reassured, he straightened up, smiled grimly at the circle of intent faces. 'He's going to live,' he said. 'He's going to live to feel a rope tighten over his neck.' He was suddenly running toward the cowboy sprawled in the mud across the street.

Buckshot Kinners let out a startled grunt as he recognized the dead man. 'Dater!' he exclaimed. 'It's the kid, Pete!'

The two LK men slid from their saddles. Ross gave them a curious look as they hurried up. 'I don't savvy,' he said in a puzzled voice. 'This man was one of Patchen's outfit. I'm not forgetting his face. He's the man who locked me up in that grain shed.'

'Looks like he's wiped out any harm he done you,' Pete Lally said in his slow, deep voice.

'He saved my life,' Ross admitted. 'Has me guessing, though, why he went after Welder instead of me.'

'Dater got wise to himself,' Buckshot said. 'You see, Ross, he was some sweet on Jean. . . . She never knowed it, but he kind of worshiped her.'

Ross waited for them to explain further, a bewildered look in his eyes. Pete Lally said gravely, 'The kid quit our LK payroll for Flying A on her account. . . . He got to thinkin' plenty hard that night old Breezy was shot. Dater knowed it wasn't you that shot Breezy, and when Harve told him to go chase after Jean . . . good as said for him to kill the gal, why, Dater tumbled to what was goin' on. He said as much to Harve and Harve tried to potshot him in the back.'

'That's about the story,' confirmed Buckshot. 'Dater has been on Harve's trail ever since the flood busted up the gang yesterday. We figgered he was on to somethin' when he hightailed it away from Dos Cruces in a hurry this mornin'. That's how come we got here so quick.'

Ross stared earnestly at the bronzed young face upturned to the blue sky. 'Thanks, *amigo*.' He spoke huskily. 'I'll tell Jean.'

'Where'll we take the kid?' asked Buckshot.

'Jean will want him at Flying A,' Ross decided. 'She will want him to lie close to Breezy Hessen. Dater has earned the right.' His voice hardened. 'Buel Patchen is in the hotel.'

'The hell you say!' exclaimed Buckshot.

The two partners listened attentively to his brief account of the events leading up to Harve Welder's arrival. 'I'm leaving the rest of it to you,' Ross finished. 'I want to get away from here.'

Pete Lally looked at him with shrewd eyes. 'Sure, son,' he agreed in his kindly voice. 'You've been through a lot of hell. You get out of here. Buckshot and me will take care of things.'

Ross nodded, moved toward the palomino, came to a standstill as Don Vicente swung his horse alongside. 'You leave us, my friend?' He spoke in Spanish. 'It is finished — this fight?'

'It is finished,' Ross answered. A warm smile lit his tired face. 'You have been a good friend, Vicente. I won't forget.'

Don Vicente gestured deprecatingly. 'It is nothing, my friend. A good fight is meat and drink to a Torres.' He laughed softly, looked at the two Mexicans lolling in their saddles behind him. 'Is it not so, you faithful ones?'

Estevan and Diego exchanged grim looks. Truly this master of theirs was one to try the patience. Always it was a fight, or a woman. If not one, the other. His next words drew another exchange of looks between them.

'Listen, Ross, my friend. The fighting is done, and now there is time for love.' Don Vicente blew a kiss.

'Ah, the beautiful Chaquita! You will come to the wedding?' He twirled his little black mustache, smiled happily.

'I will come,' Ross promised. 'Good luck to you, Vicente.'

'*Gracias*,' smiled the Sonoran. '*Vaya con Dios, amigo.*'

A cowboy slid from the corral fence as Ross rode into the big yard. He held a rifle in lowered hand. Ross correctly interpreted the question in his alert eyes.

'It is finished,' he said laconically.

The LK man leaned the rifle against the fence and fished in his shirt pocket for tobacco and papers. 'I'll tell the boys.' He grinned. 'Pete and Buckshot said for us to stick 'round close till they sent word. I reckon if you say it's finished, it's *finished*.'

'Harve Welder is headed for jail,' Ross told him. He looked at the cowboy thoughtfully. 'You boys had better stick around for a while. This ranch is awfully short-handed.'

'Sure,' agreed the man. 'Buckshot and Pete figgered for us to stay on a spell.' He scratched a match against scarred leather chaps and lit his cigarette. 'Looks like Patchen's outfit is sure busted to hell,' he added with a contented grin.

Ross pushed on through the patio gate. Injun John rose like a jack-in-the-box from behind a bush. He stood leaning on his carbine.

Ross answered the question in the shiny brown eyes. 'It is finished,' he said.

'Good,' grunted the old Apache. 'Me go now, huh?'

'You can go,' assented Ross. 'Thanks for helping me out, John.' His smile was warm.

'Huh!' Injun John's eyes gleamed. 'You big chief ... take plenty scalp ... we good friends.' His look went briefly to the slim girl who suddenly appeared in the doorway. 'You take young squaw.... She plenty good squaw.' He tucked the carbine under his arm and stalked through the gate.

Ross went slowly up the path, toward the waiting girl. His weariness fell away from him. His pulse quickened as he looked at her, his stride lengthened; and suddenly Jean was running to meet him, his name on her lips.

Sing Gee came to an abrupt standstill inside the small side gate. What he saw seemed to give him an enormous satisfaction. He nodded, muttered brief Chinese words and quietly withdrew, leaving them alone in the garden.

THE END

Arthur Henry Gooden recalled that "I was still a babe in arms when my parents took me from Manchester, England, to South Africa for a four-year stay in Port Elizabeth, then back to England for a brief time, and finally the journey that made me a Californian. Reaching the San Joaquin Valley in those days meant work from sunup to sundown. Always plenty for a boy to do. But there were compensations—my rifle, my shotgun, my horse. By the time I was ten I was master of all three and the hunting was good." Gooden began his career as a Western writer working in Hollywood beginning in 1919. *The Fox* (Universal, 1921) was the first feature film based on one of his screenplays and starred Harry Carey. For what remained of the decade, Gooden worked in the writing department at Universal, turning out scenarios for two-reelers and feature films as well as serials like *The Lawless Men* (Universal, 1927) based on Frank Spearman's popular character, railroad detective Whispering Smith. In the early 1930s Gooden left Hollywood to live in a stone cabin in the foothills of the San Jacinto, overlooking the sand dunes of the Colorado Desert. The life he led there was primitive: no electricity, no gasoline, no telephones, but he had his typewriter and began writing Western novels, beginning with *Cross Knife Ranch*, first published by Harrap in London in 1933. In fact, although he would eventually have various American publishers, the British editions of his novels continued to be published by Harrap until 1951. *Smoke Tree Range* (Kinsey, 1936), one of his finest stories, was brought to the screen by cowboy star Buck Jones in 1937, Gooden's only screen credit during that decade. Gooden had a distinguished prose style and was always able to evoke the Western terrain and animal life vividly as well as authentically address the psychology of many of his complex characters with the sophistication of a master storyteller.